ANN M. MARTIN

THE BABY-SITTERS CLUB®

KRISTY AND THE SNOBS

A GRAPHIC NOVEL BY

CHAN CHAU

WITH COLOR BY BRADEN LAMB

graphix

An Imprint of
■SCHOLASTIC

In memory of Neena and Grandpa
A. M. M.

For Erik Munson, Danya Adair, Alice Woods,
Bleb, and Maddi Gonzalez for being there
when I needed someone the most.

And to my incredible friends and family.
C. C.

All rights reserved. Published by Graphix, an imprint of
Scholastic Inc., *Publishers since 1920.* SCHOLASTIC, GRAPHIX,
THE BABY-SITTERS CLUB, and associated logos are trademarks
and/or registered trademarks of Scholastic Inc.

The publisher does not have any control over and does not assume any
responsibility for author or third-party websites or their content.

No part of this publication may be reproduced, stored in a retrieval system,
or transmitted in any form or by any means, electronic, mechanical, photocopying,
recording, or otherwise, without written permission of the publisher. For information
regarding permission, write to Scholastic Inc., Attention: Permissions
Department, 557 Broadway, New York, NY 10012.

This book is a work of fiction. Names, characters, places, and
incidents are either the product of the author's imagination or are used
fictitiously, and any resemblance to actual persons, living or dead, business
establishments, events, or locales is entirely coincidental.

Library of Congress Control Number: 2020946441

ISBN 978-1-338-30461-9 (hardcover)
ISBN 978-1-338-30460-2 (paperback)

10 9 8 7 6 5 4 3   21 22 23 24 25

Printed in China   62
First edition, September 2021

Edited by Cassandra Pelham Fulton and David Levithan
Book design by Phil Falco
Publisher: David Saylor

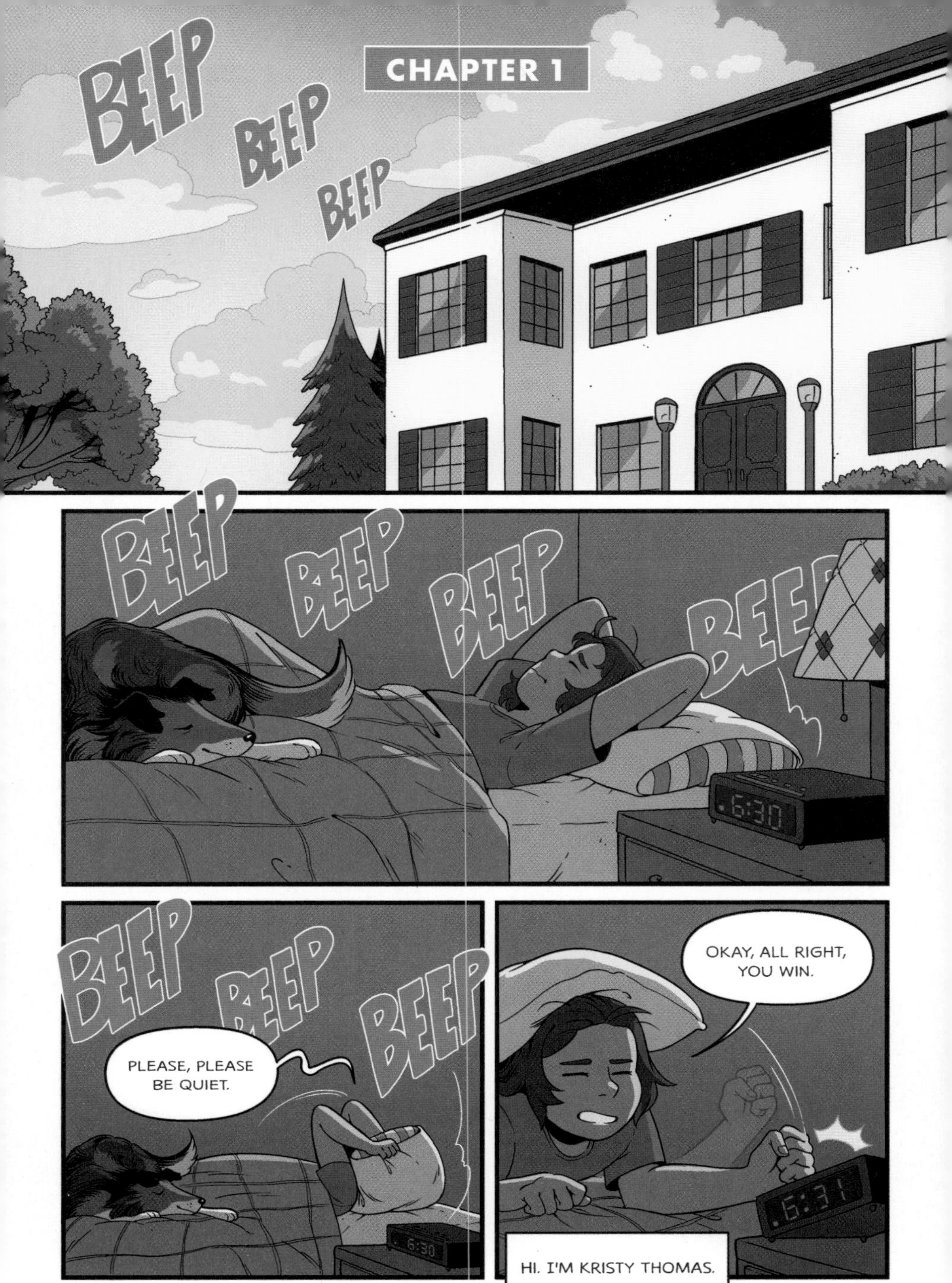
CHAPTER 1
BEEP
BEEP
BEEP
BEEP
BEEP
BEEP
BEEP
BEEP
BEEP
BEEP
PLEASE, PLEASE BE QUIET.
OKAY, ALL RIGHT, YOU WIN.
HI. I'M KRISTY THOMAS.

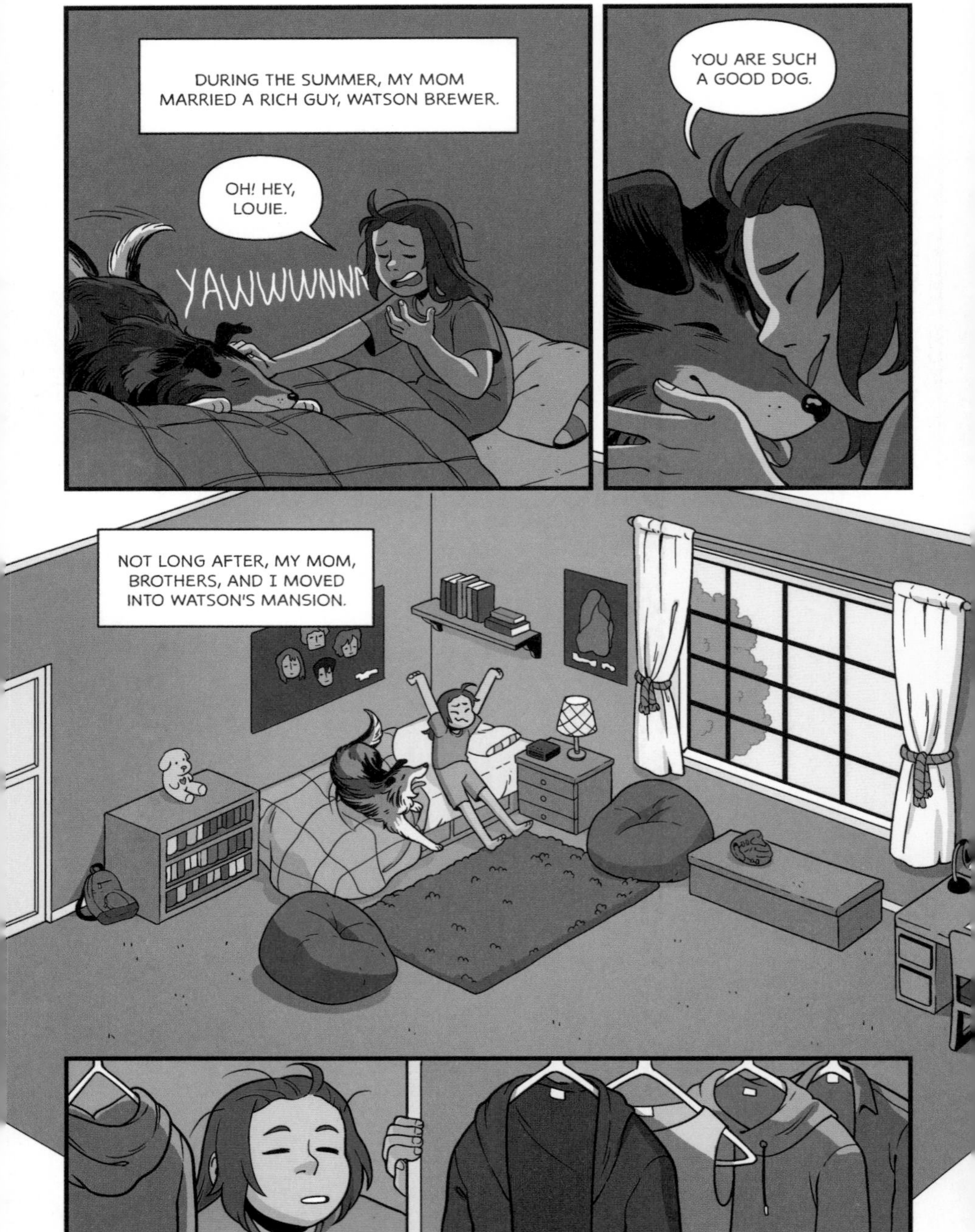
DURING THE SUMMER, MY MOM MARRIED A RICH GUY, WATSON BREWER.
OH! HEY, LOUIE.
YAWWWNNN
YOU ARE SUCH A GOOD DOG.
NOT LONG AFTER, MY MOM, BROTHERS, AND I MOVED INTO WATSON'S MANSION.

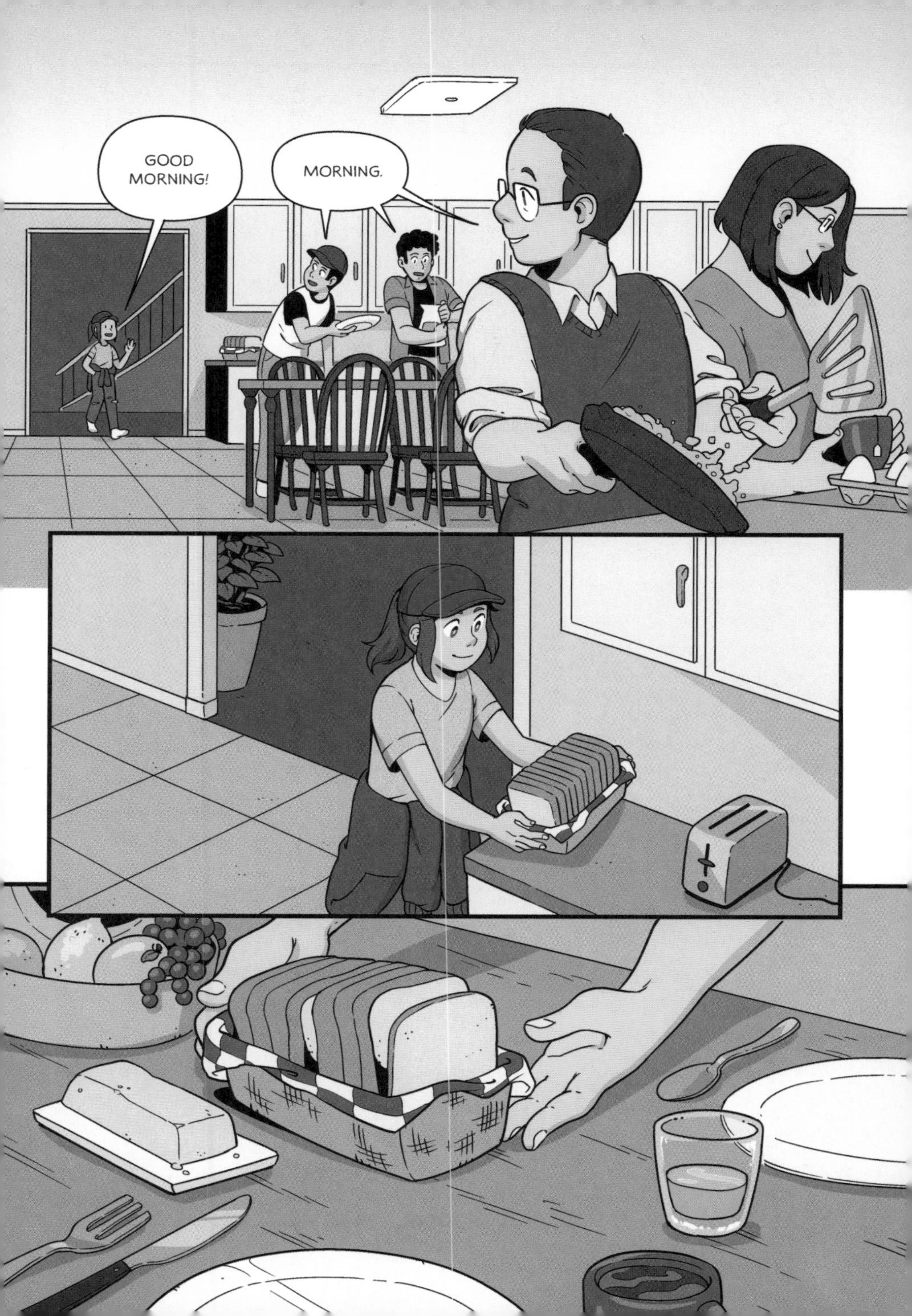

GOOD MORNING!
MORNING.

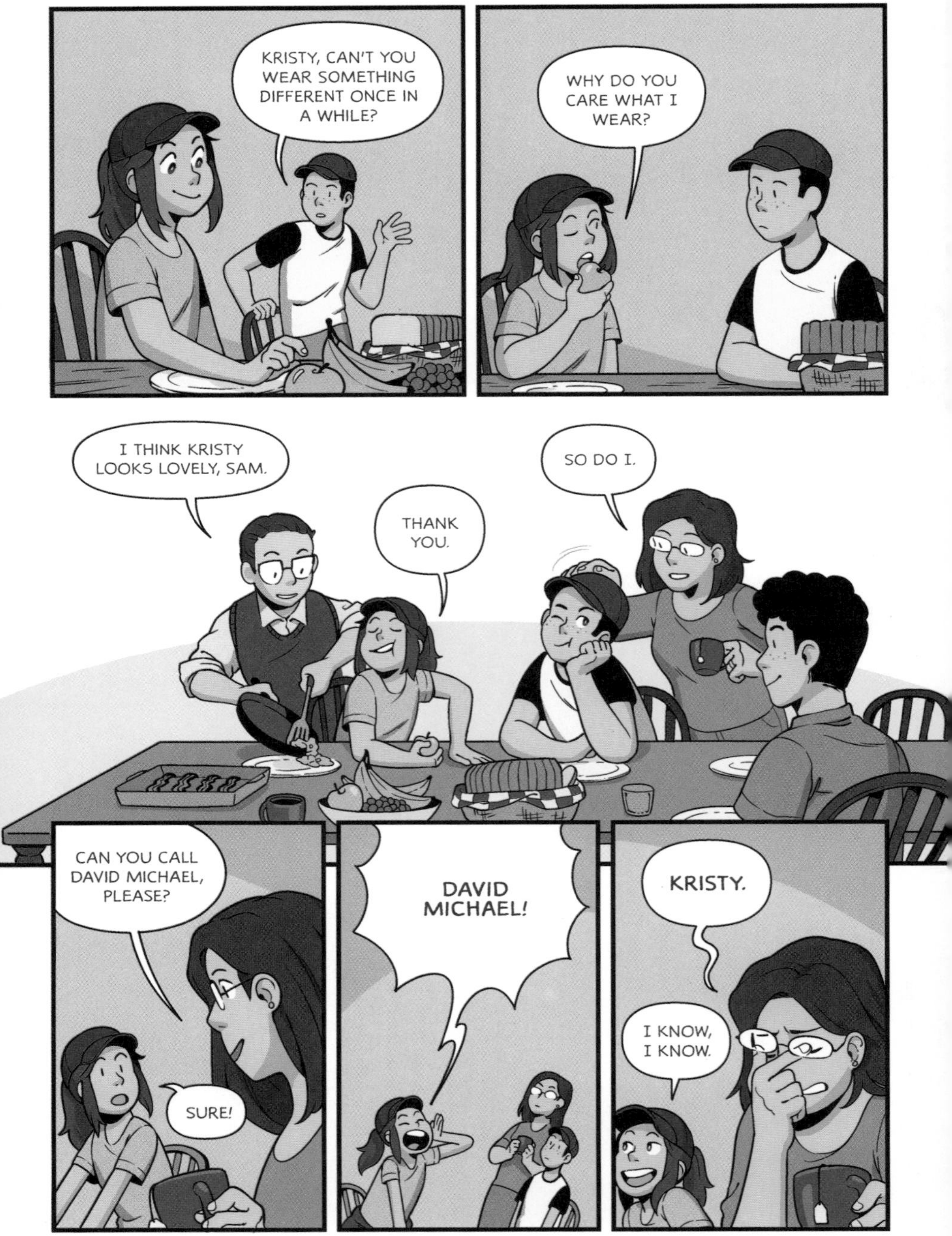
KRISTY, CAN'T YOU WEAR SOMETHING DIFFERENT ONCE IN A WHILE?
WHY DO YOU CARE WHAT I WEAR?
I THINK KRISTY LOOKS LOVELY, SAM.
THANK YOU.
SO DO I.
CAN YOU CALL DAVID MICHAEL, PLEASE?
SURE!
DAVID MICHAEL!
KRISTY.
I KNOW, I KNOW.

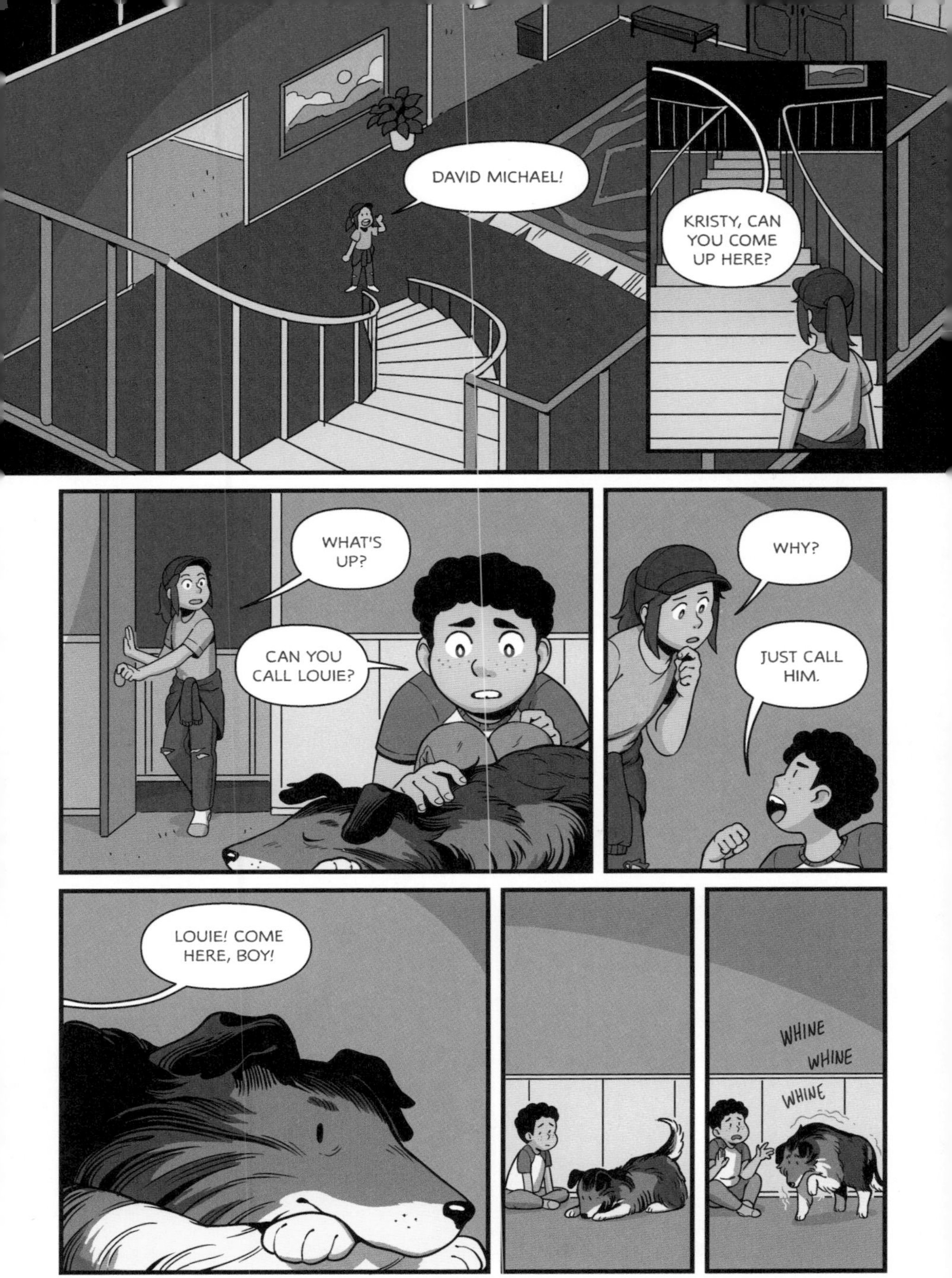
DAVID MICHAEL!
KRISTY, CAN YOU COME UP HERE?
WHAT'S UP?
CAN YOU CALL LOUIE?
WHY?
JUST CALL HIM.
LOUIE! COME HERE, BOY!
WHINE
WHINE
WHINE

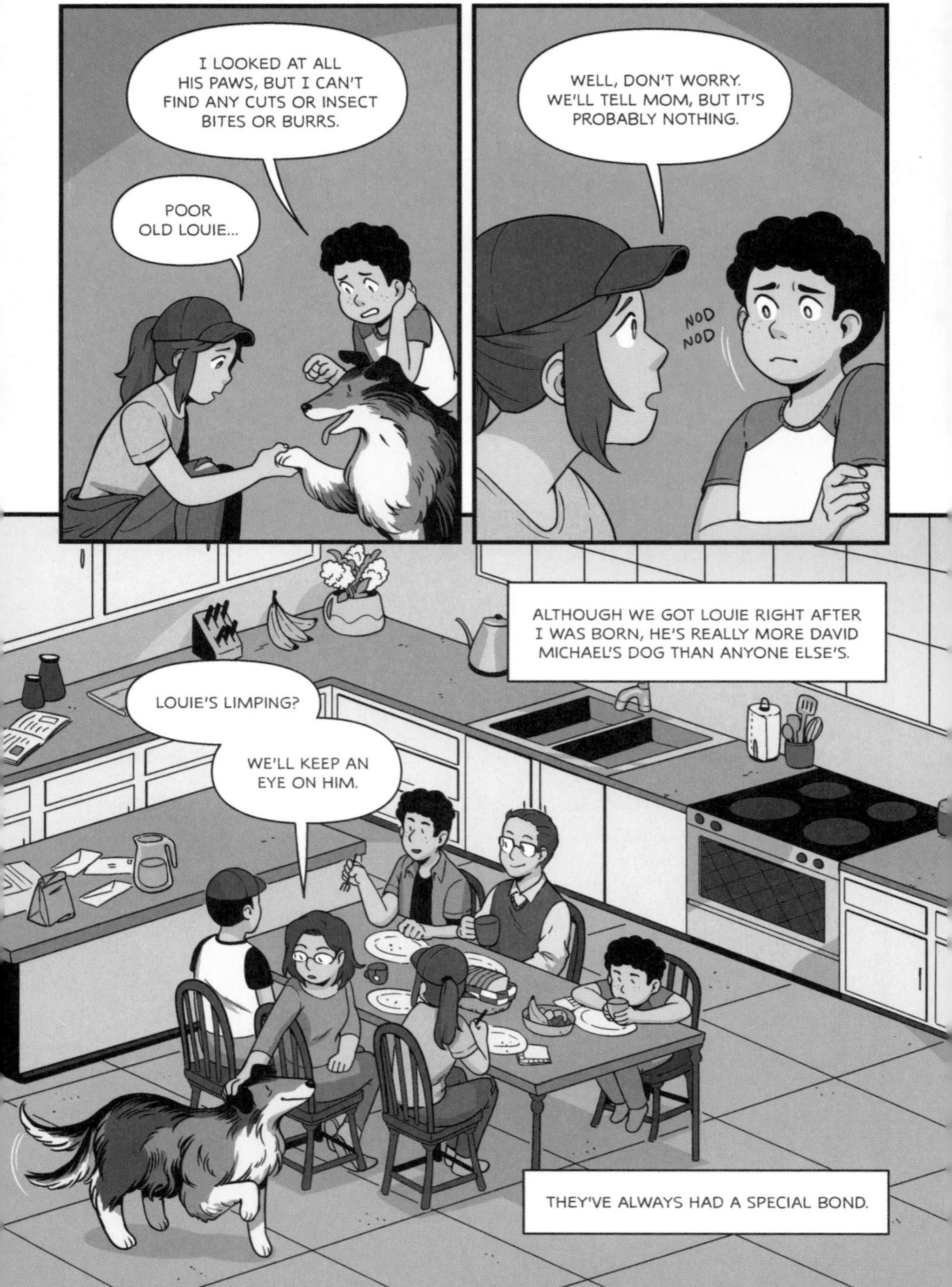
POOR OLD LOUIE...
I LOOKED AT ALL HIS PAWS, BUT I CAN'T FIND ANY CUTS OR INSECT BITES OR BURRS.
WELL, DON'T WORRY. WE'LL TELL MOM, BUT IT'S PROBABLY NOTHING.
NOD NOD
ALTHOUGH WE GOT LOUIE RIGHT AFTER I WAS BORN, HE'S REALLY MORE DAVID MICHAEL'S DOG THAN ANYONE ELSE'S.
LOUIE'S LIMPING?
WE'LL KEEP AN EYE ON HIM.
THEY'VE ALWAYS HAD A SPECIAL BOND.

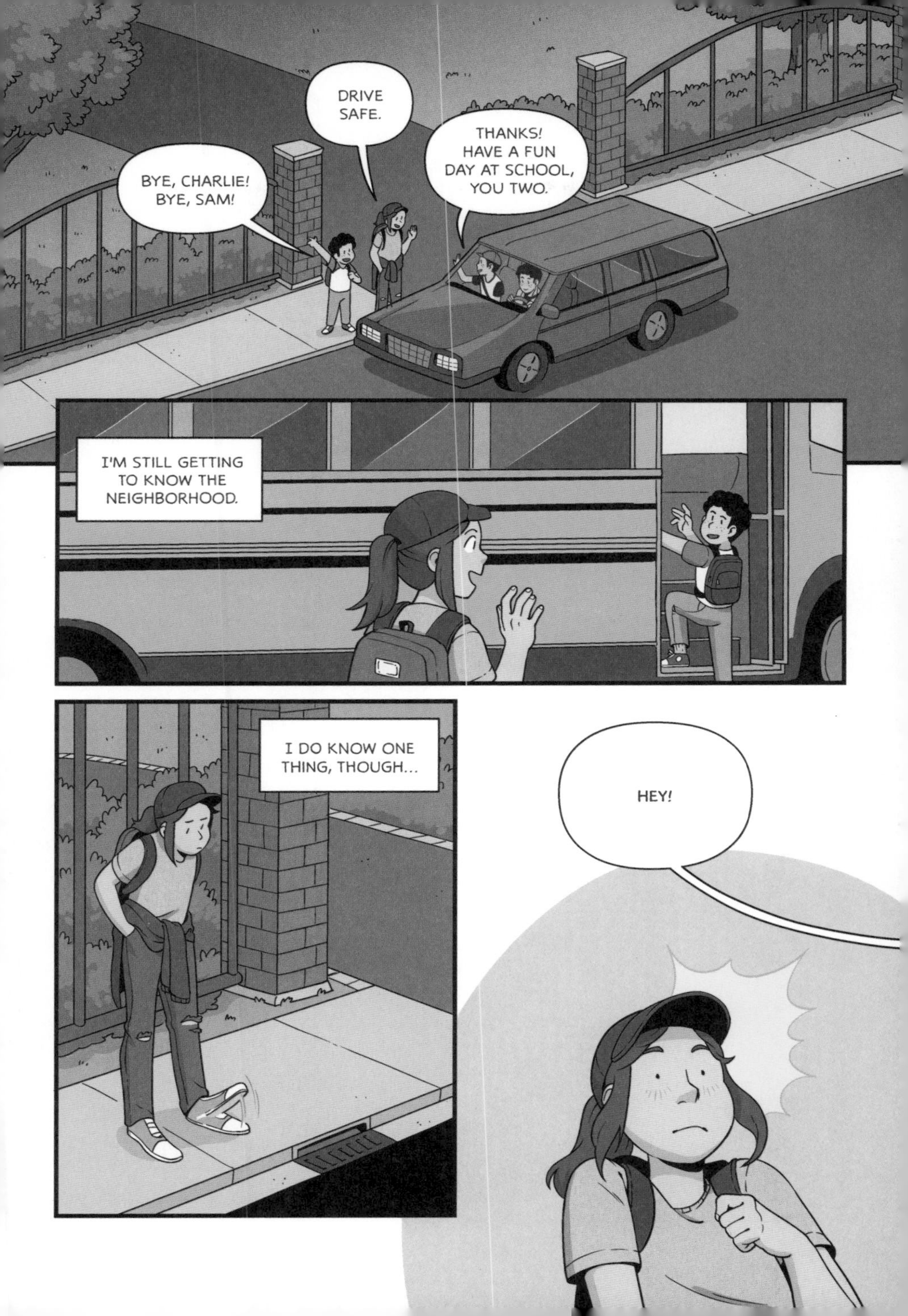
BYE, CHARLIE! BYE, SAM!
DRIVE SAFE.
THANKS! HAVE A FUN DAY AT SCHOOL, YOU TWO.
I'M STILL GETTING TO KNOW THE NEIGHBORHOOD.
I DO KNOW ONE THING, THOUGH...
HEY!

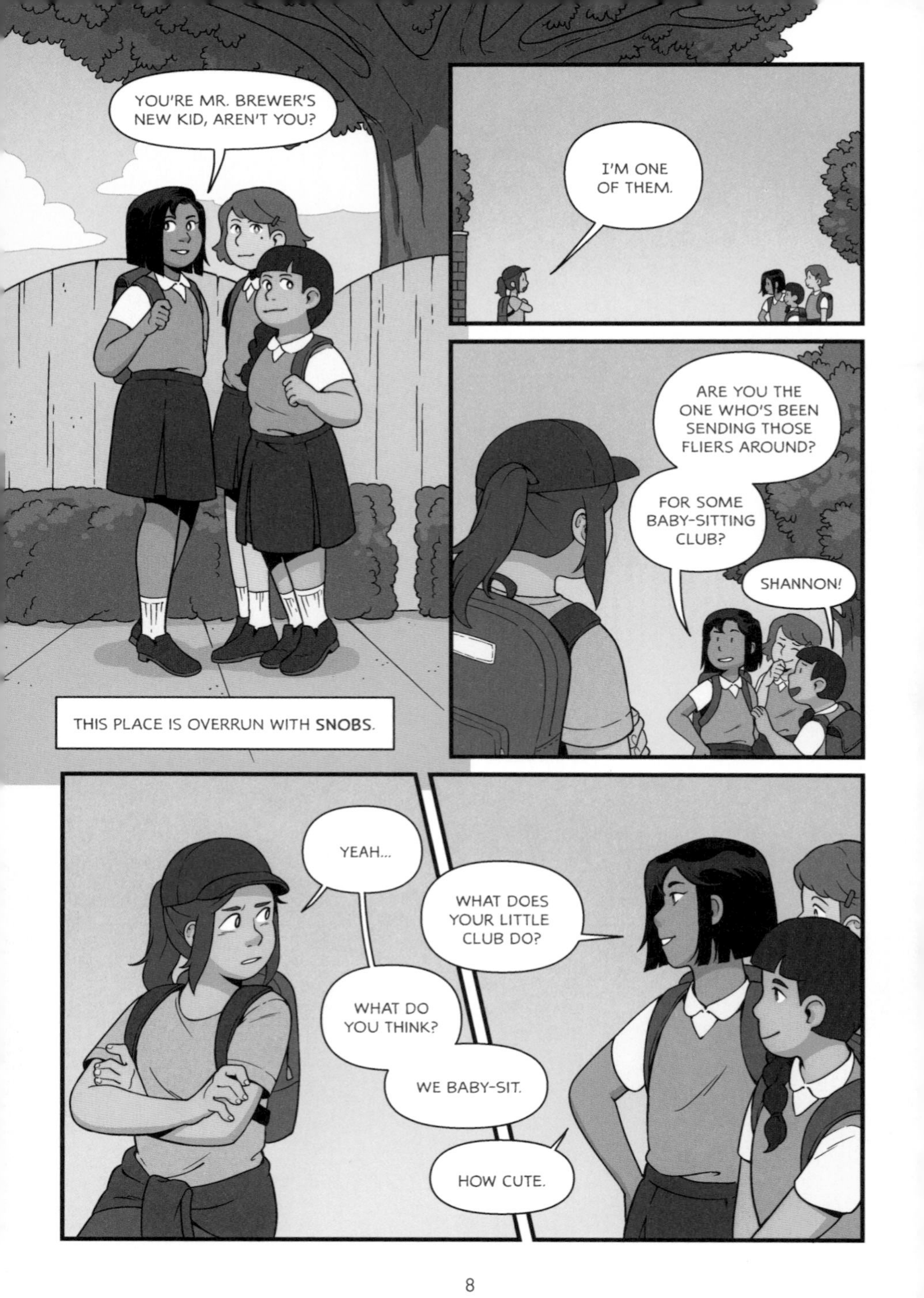
YOU'RE MR. BREWER'S NEW KID, AREN'T YOU?
THIS PLACE IS OVERRUN WITH **SNOBS**.
I'M ONE OF THEM.
ARE YOU THE ONE WHO'S BEEN SENDING THOSE FLIERS AROUND?
FOR SOME BABY-SITTING CLUB?
SHANNON!
YEAH...
WHAT DOES YOUR LITTLE CLUB DO?
WHAT DO YOU THINK?
WE BABY-SIT.
HOW CUTE.

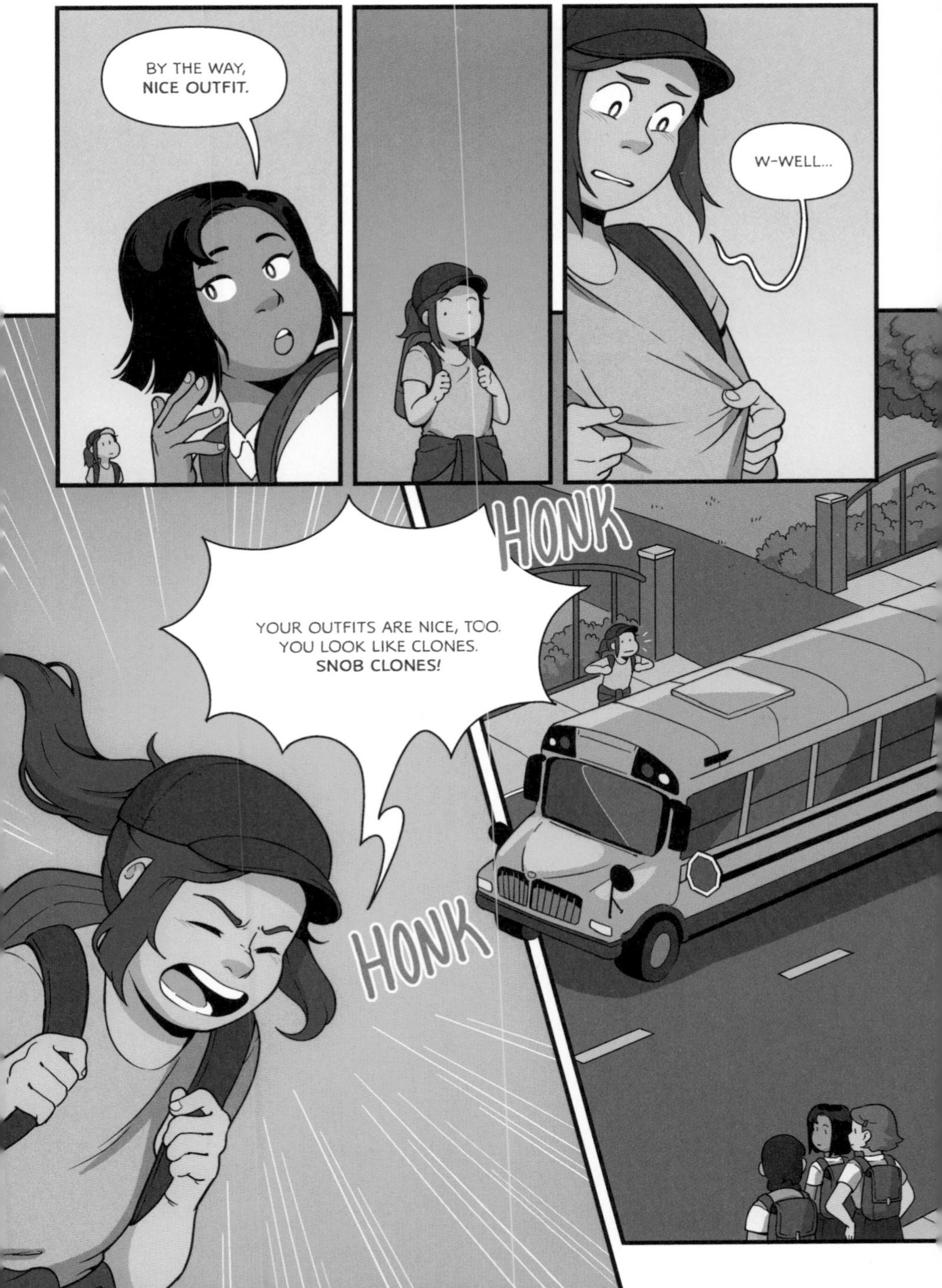
BY THE WAY, **NICE OUTFIT.**
W-WELL...
HONK
YOUR OUTFITS ARE NICE, TOO. YOU LOOK LIKE CLONES. **SNOB CLONES!**
HONK

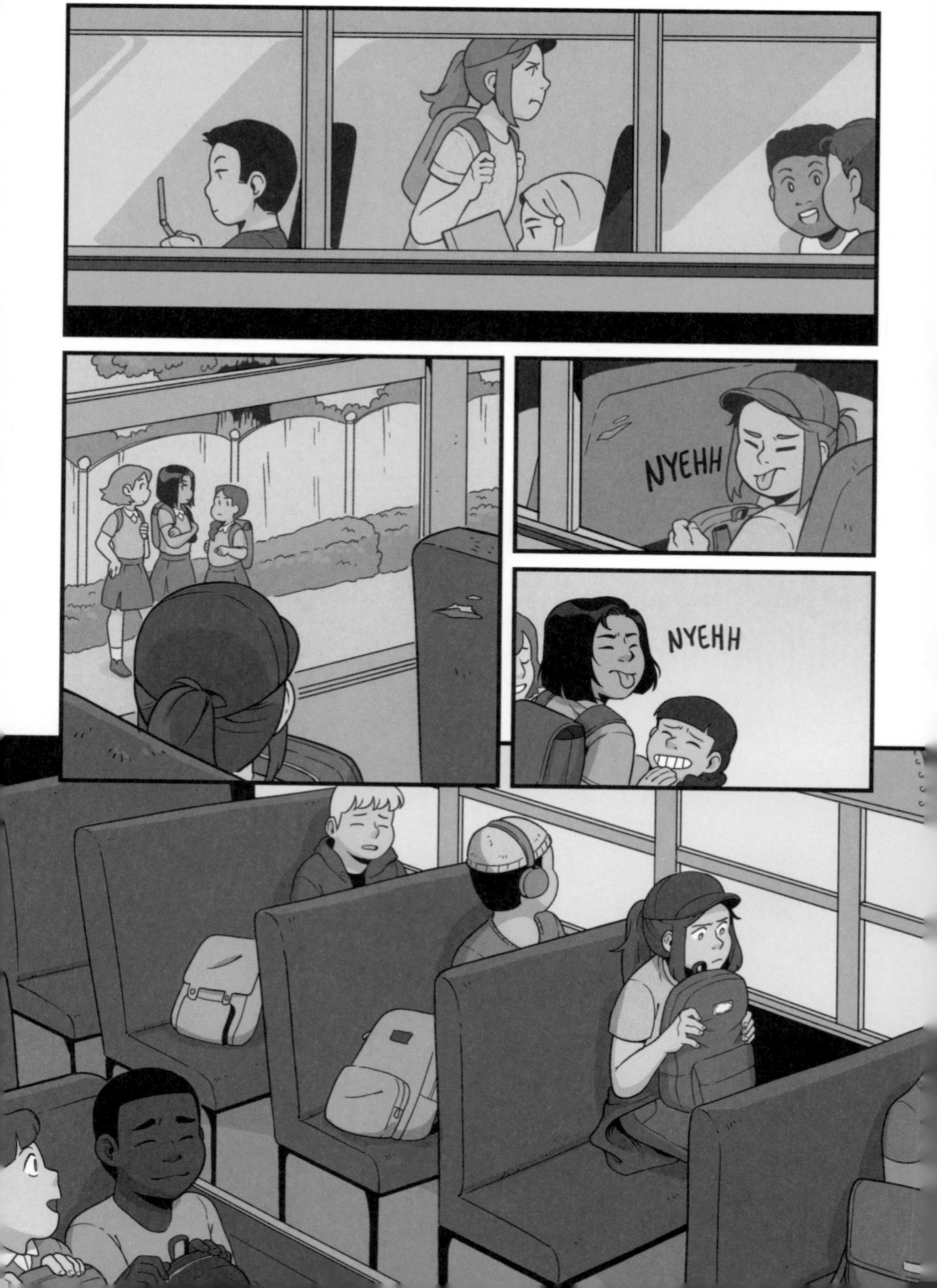
NYEHH
NYEHH

CHAPTER 2

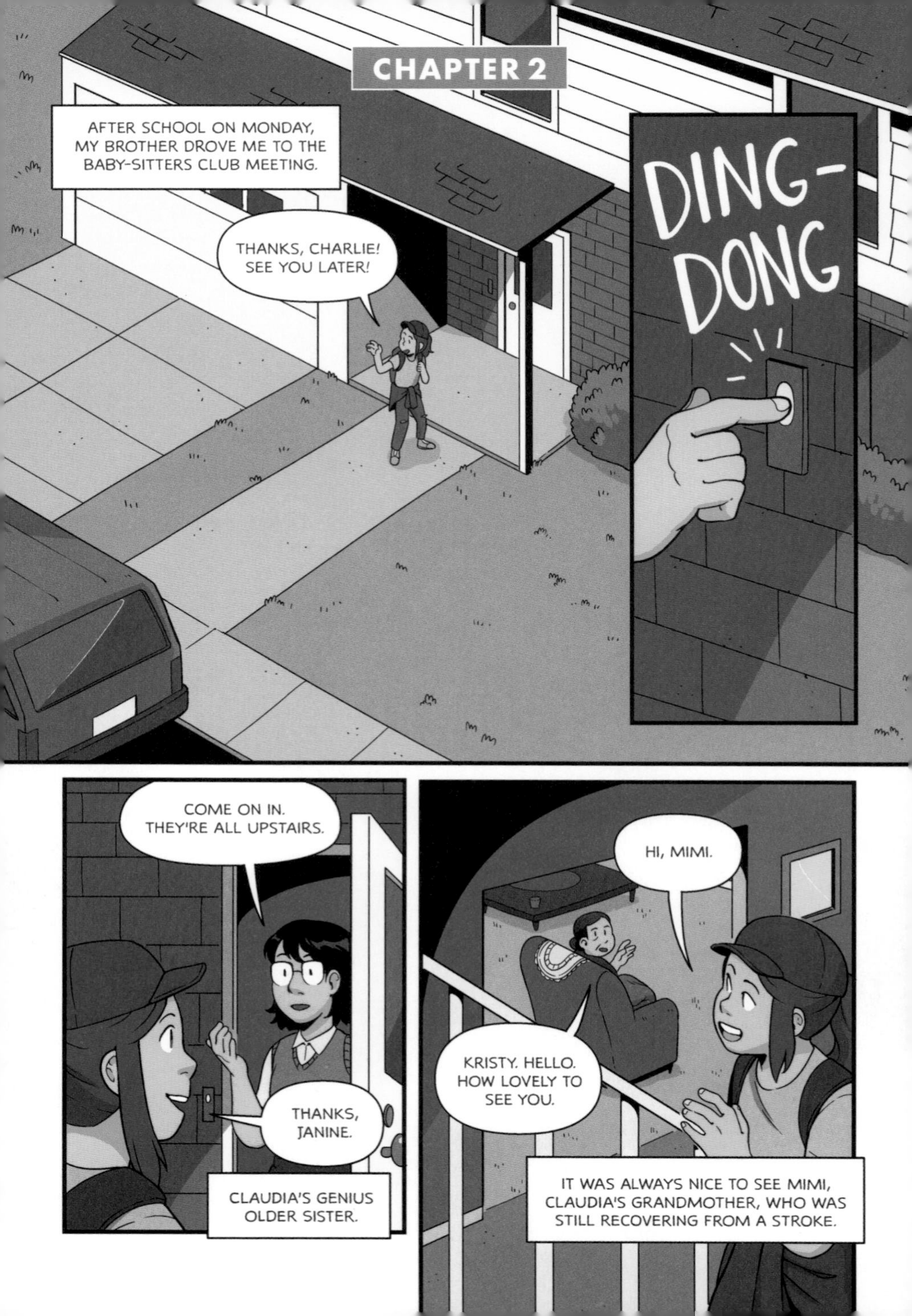
AFTER SCHOOL ON MONDAY, MY BROTHER DROVE ME TO THE BABY-SITTERS CLUB MEETING.
THANKS, CHARLIE! SEE YOU LATER!
DING-DONG
COME ON IN. THEY'RE ALL UPSTAIRS.
THANKS, JANINE.
CLAUDIA'S GENIUS OLDER SISTER.
HI, MIMI.
KRISTY. HELLO. HOW LOVELY TO SEE YOU.
IT WAS ALWAYS NICE TO SEE MIMI, CLAUDIA'S GRANDMOTHER, WHO WAS STILL RECOVERING FROM A STROKE.

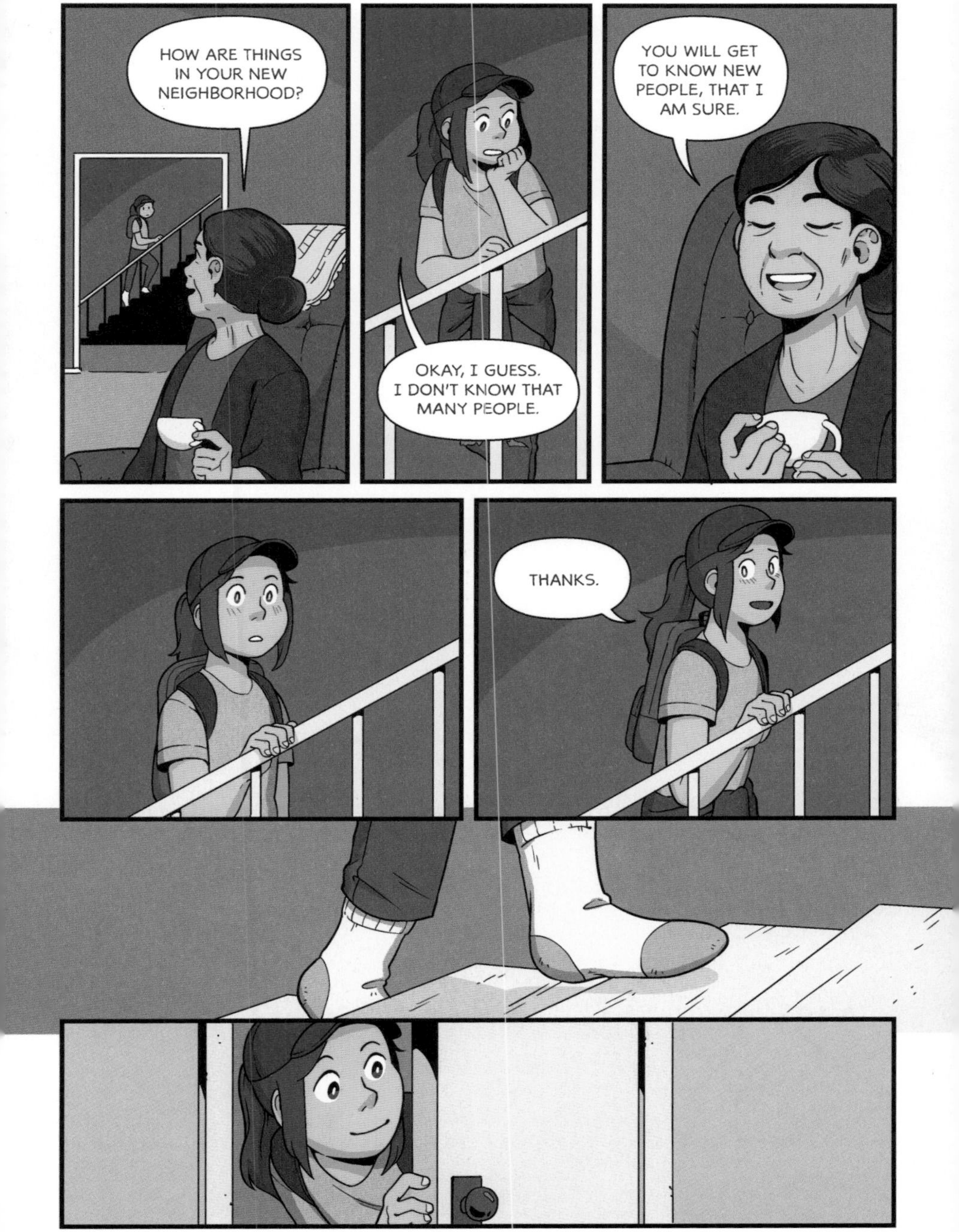
HOW ARE THINGS IN YOUR NEW NEIGHBORHOOD?
OKAY, I GUESS. I DON'T KNOW THAT MANY PEOPLE.
YOU WILL GET TO KNOW NEW PEOPLE, THAT I AM SURE.
THANKS.

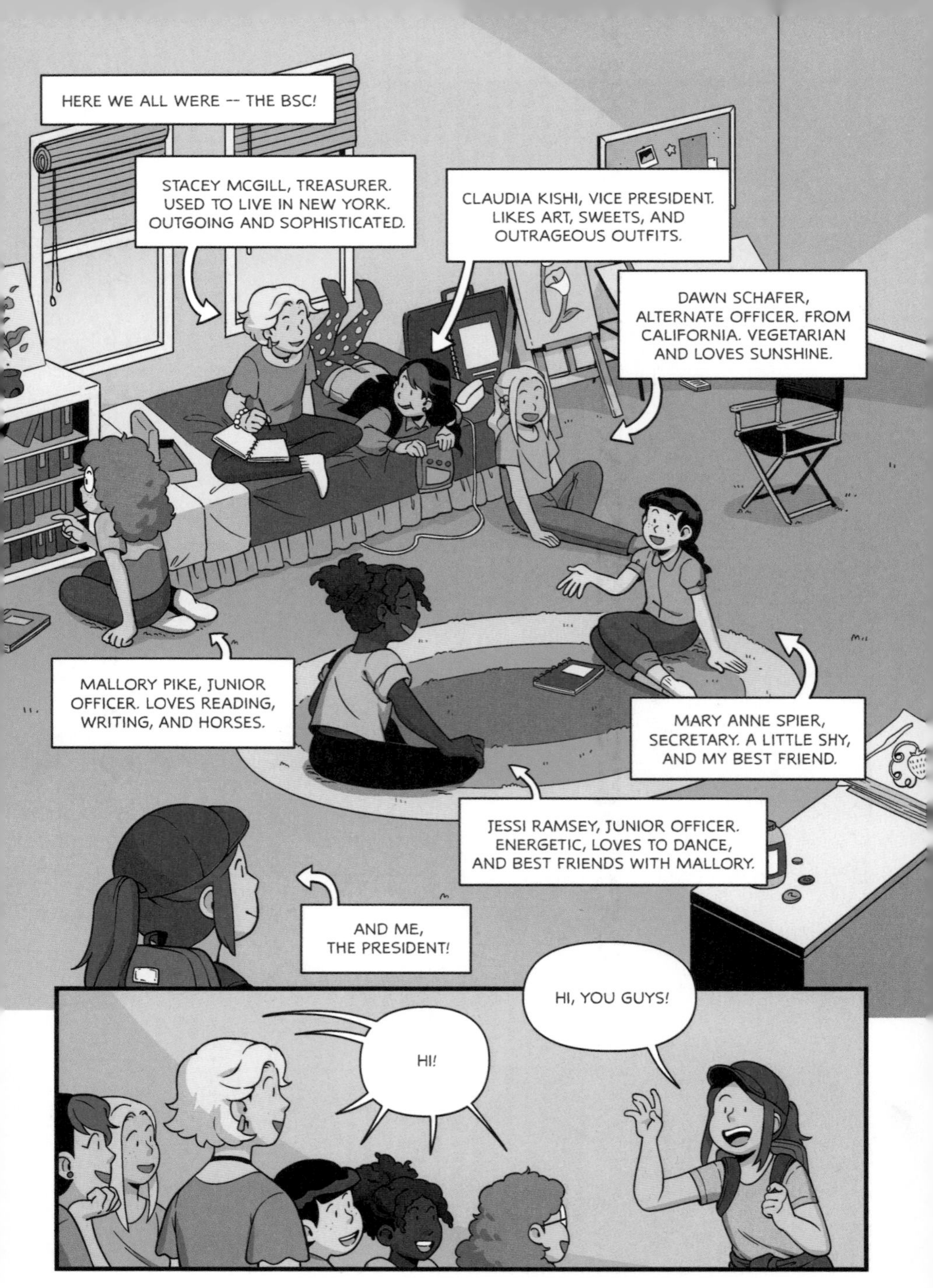
HERE WE ALL WERE -- THE BSC!
STACEY MCGILL, TREASURER. USED TO LIVE IN NEW YORK. OUTGOING AND SOPHISTICATED.
CLAUDIA KISHI, VICE PRESIDENT. LIKES ART, SWEETS, AND OUTRAGEOUS OUTFITS.
DAWN SCHAFER, ALTERNATE OFFICER. FROM CALIFORNIA. VEGETARIAN AND LOVES SUNSHINE.
MALLORY PIKE, JUNIOR OFFICER. LOVES READING, WRITING, AND HORSES.
MARY ANNE SPIER, SECRETARY. A LITTLE SHY, AND MY BEST FRIEND.
JESSI RAMSEY, JUNIOR OFFICER. ENERGETIC, LOVES TO DANCE, AND BEST FRIENDS WITH MALLORY.
AND ME, THE PRESIDENT!
HI, YOU GUYS!
HI!

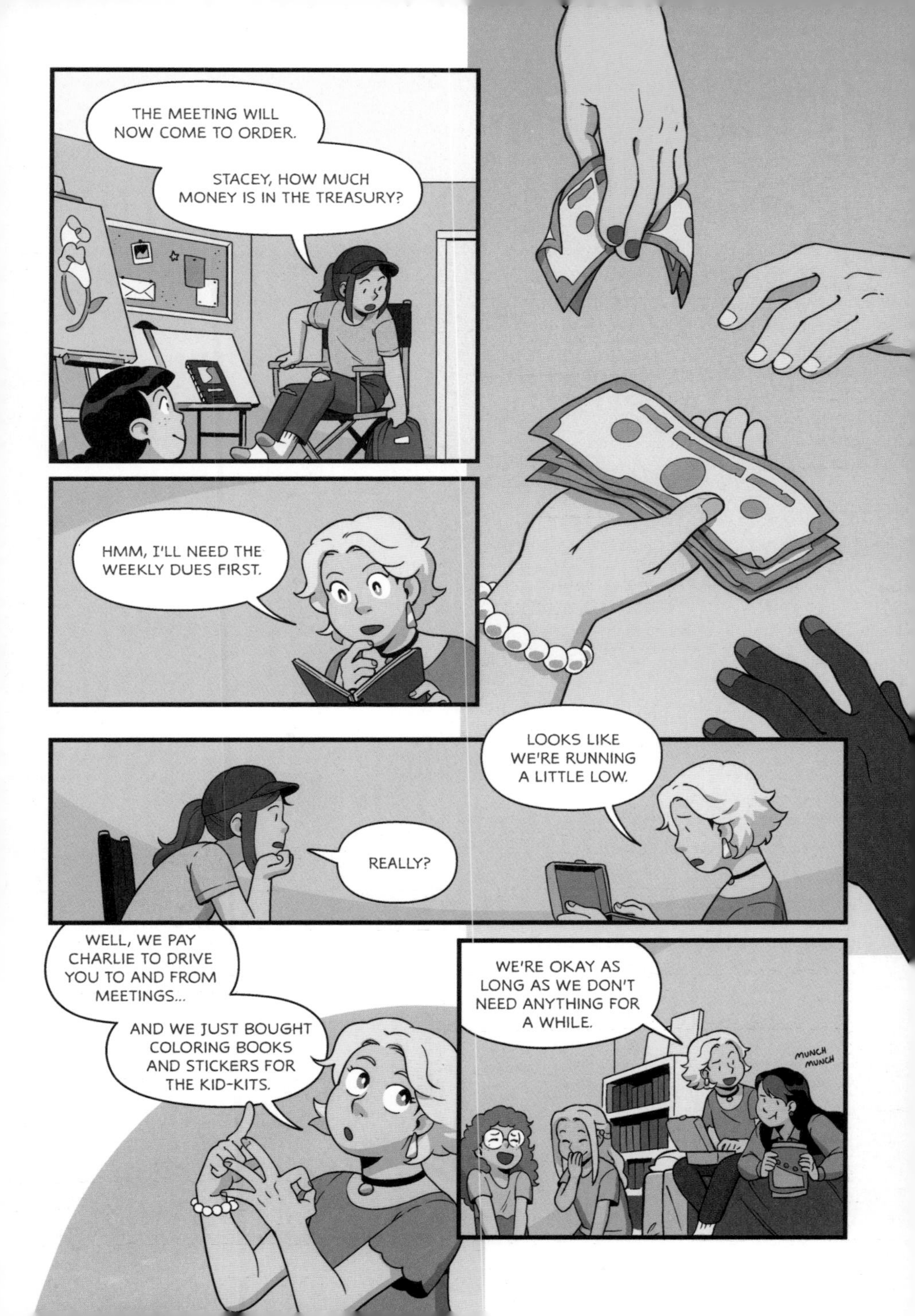
THE MEETING WILL NOW COME TO ORDER.
STACEY, HOW MUCH MONEY IS IN THE TREASURY?
HMM, I'LL NEED THE WEEKLY DUES FIRST.
LOOKS LIKE WE'RE RUNNING A LITTLE LOW.
REALLY?
WELL, WE PAY CHARLIE TO DRIVE YOU TO AND FROM MEETINGS...
AND WE JUST BOUGHT COLORING BOOKS AND STICKERS FOR THE KID-KITS.
WE'RE OKAY AS LONG AS WE DON'T NEED ANYTHING FOR A WHILE.
MUNCH MUNCH

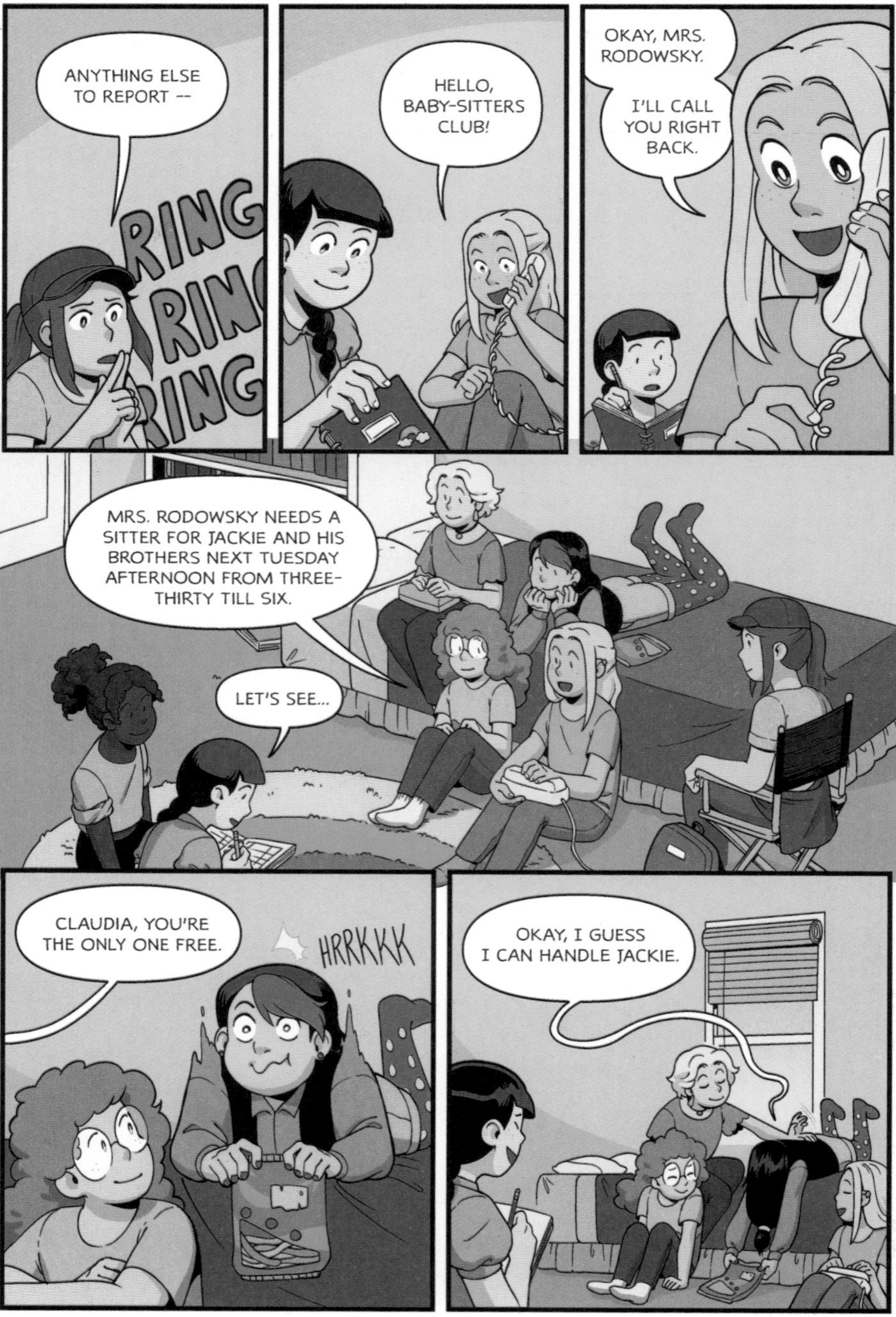
ANYTHING ELSE TO REPORT --
RING RING RING
HELLO, BABY-SITTERS CLUB!
OKAY, MRS. RODOWSKY.
I'LL CALL YOU RIGHT BACK.
MRS. RODOWSKY NEEDS A SITTER FOR JACKIE AND HIS BROTHERS NEXT TUESDAY AFTERNOON FROM THREE-THIRTY TILL SIX.
LET'S SEE...
CLAUDIA, YOU'RE THE ONLY ONE FREE.
HRRKKK
OKAY, I GUESS I CAN HANDLE JACKIE.

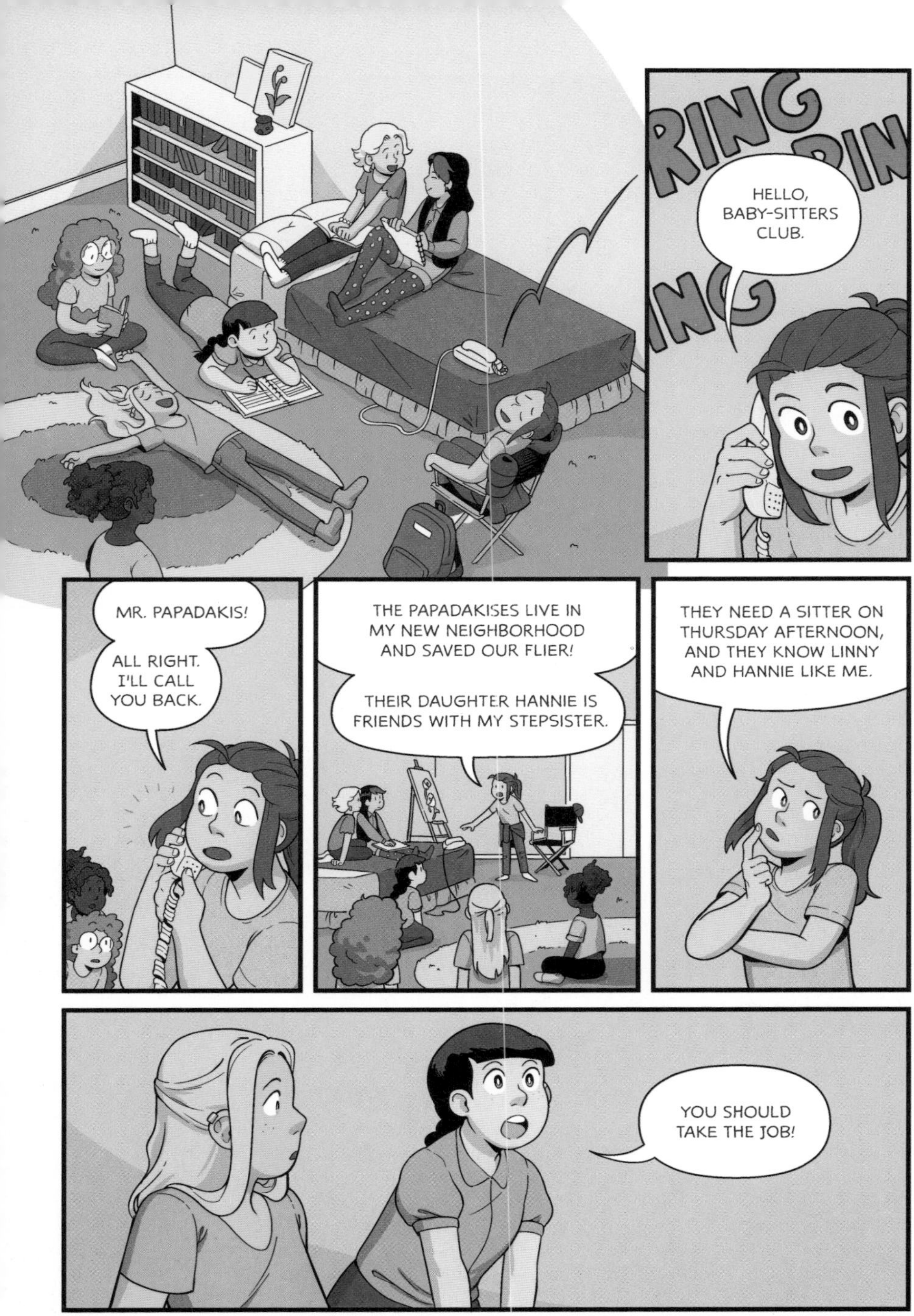
RING RIN
RING
HELLO, BABY-SITTERS CLUB.
MR. PAPADAKIS!
ALL RIGHT. I'LL CALL YOU BACK.
THE PAPADAKISES LIVE IN MY NEW NEIGHBORHOOD AND SAVED OUR FLIER!
THEIR DAUGHTER HANNIE IS FRIENDS WITH MY STEPSISTER.
THEY NEED A SITTER ON THURSDAY AFTERNOON, AND THEY KNOW LINNY AND HANNIE LIKE ME.
YOU SHOULD TAKE THE JOB!

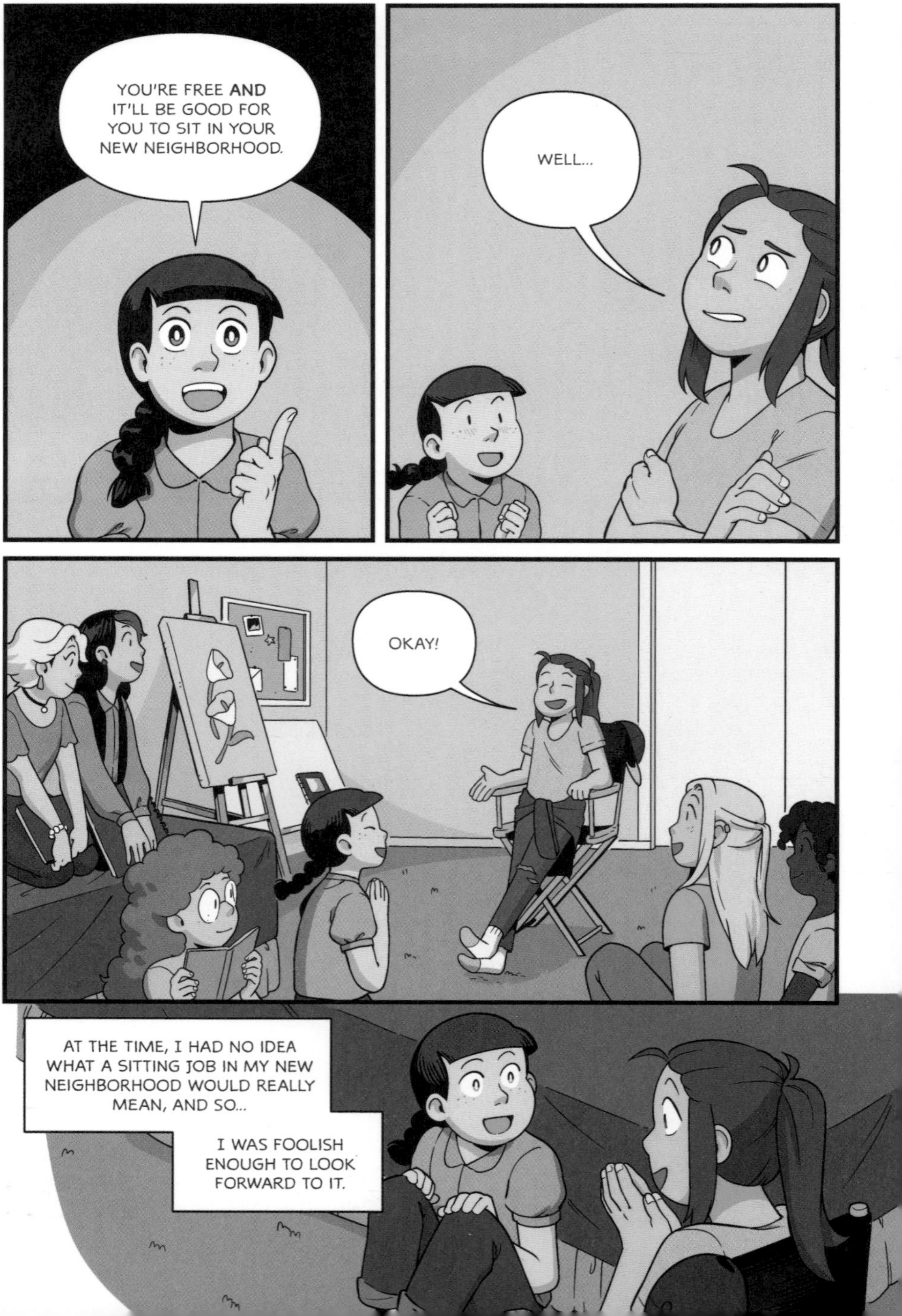
YOU'RE FREE **AND** IT'LL BE GOOD FOR YOU TO SIT IN YOUR NEW NEIGHBORHOOD.
WELL...
OKAY!
AT THE TIME, I HAD NO IDEA WHAT A SITTING JOB IN MY NEW NEIGHBORHOOD WOULD REALLY MEAN, AND SO...
I WAS FOOLISH ENOUGH TO LOOK FORWARD TO IT.

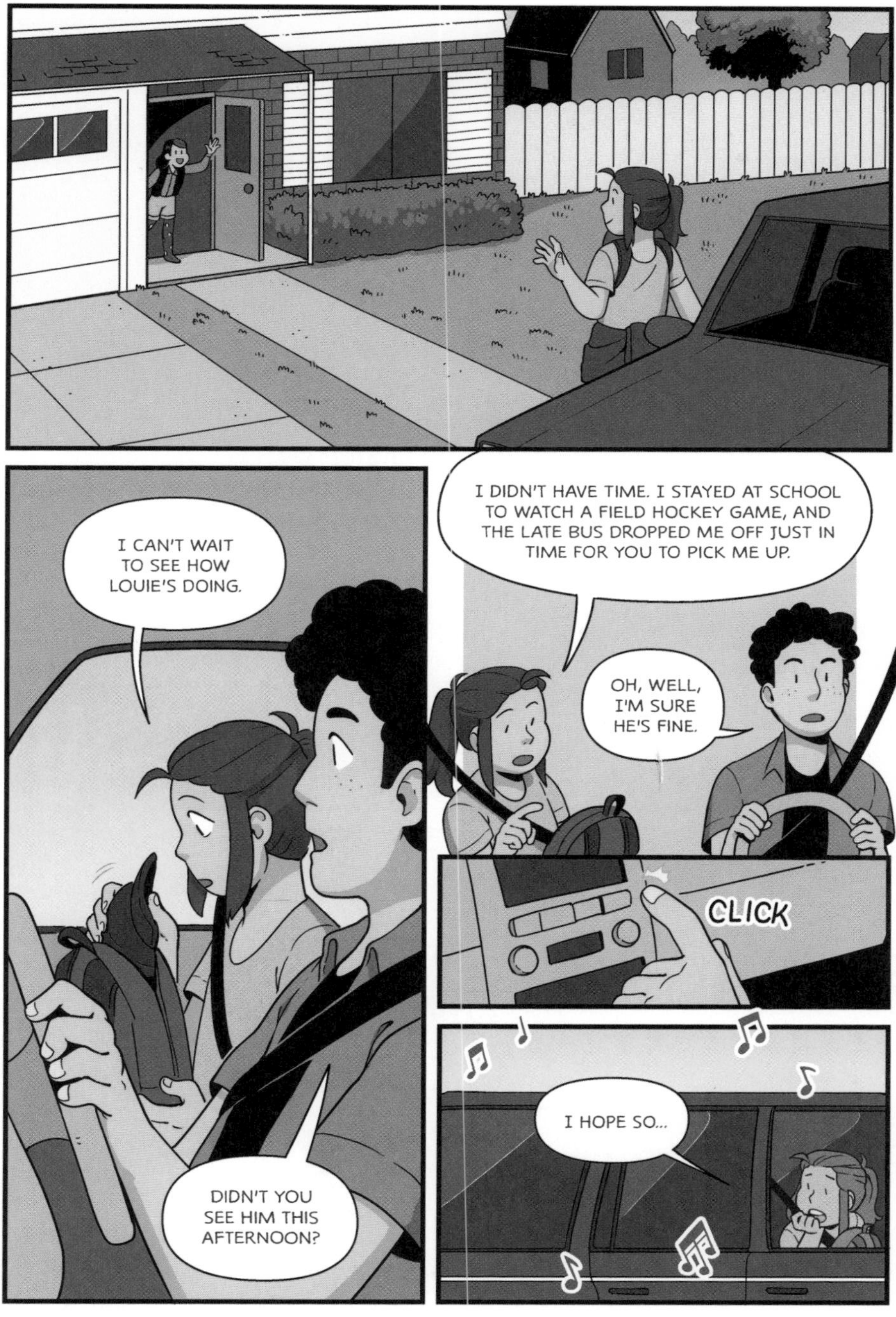
I CAN'T WAIT TO SEE HOW LOUIE'S DOING.
DIDN'T YOU SEE HIM THIS AFTERNOON?
I DIDN'T HAVE TIME. I STAYED AT SCHOOL TO WATCH A FIELD HOCKEY GAME, AND THE LATE BUS DROPPED ME OFF JUST IN TIME FOR YOU TO PICK ME UP.
OH, WELL, I'M SURE HE'S FINE.
CLICK
I HOPE SO...

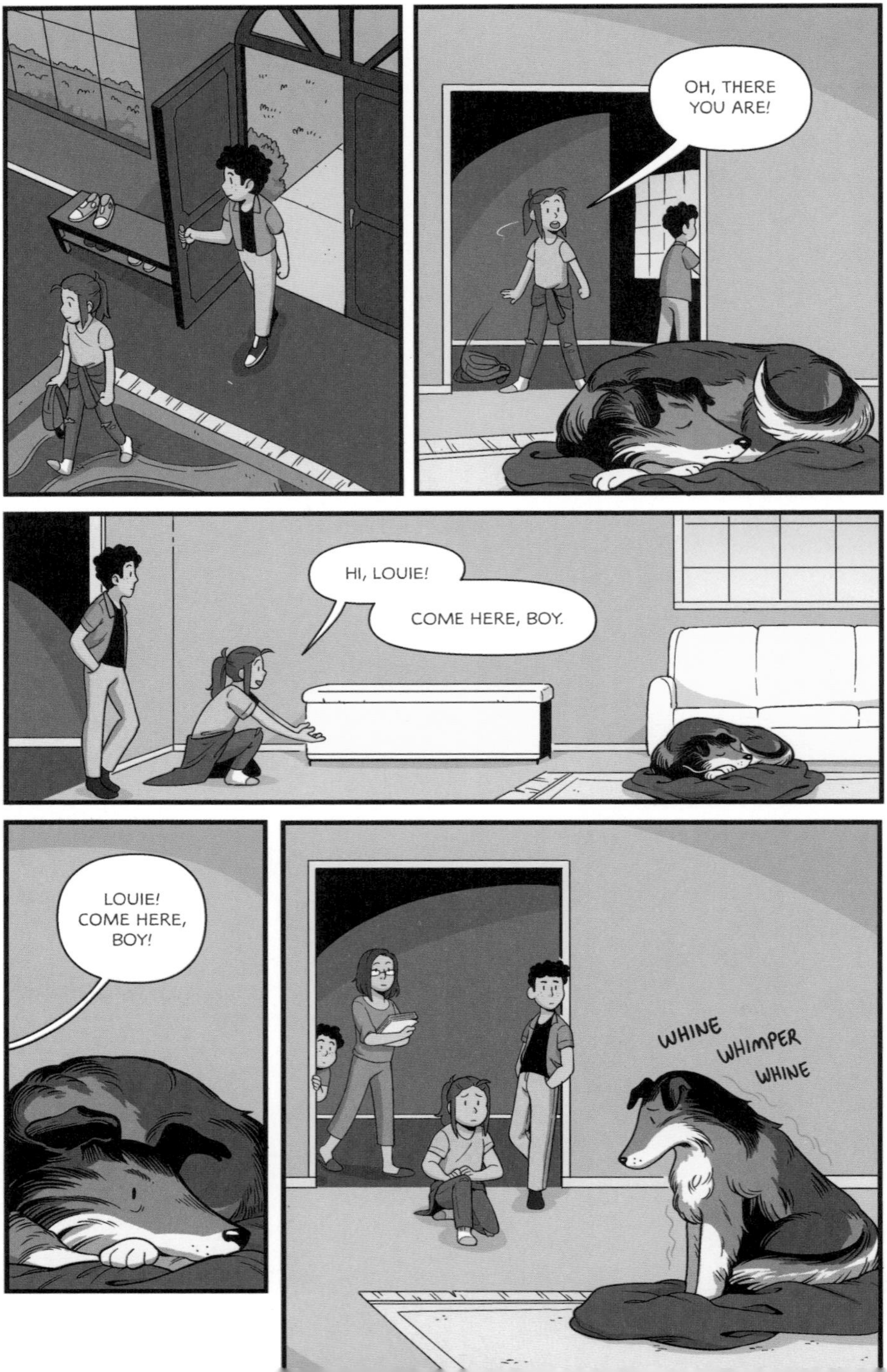
OH, THERE YOU ARE!
HI, LOUIE!
COME HERE, BOY.
LOUIE! COME HERE, BOY!
WHINE
WHIMPER
WHINE

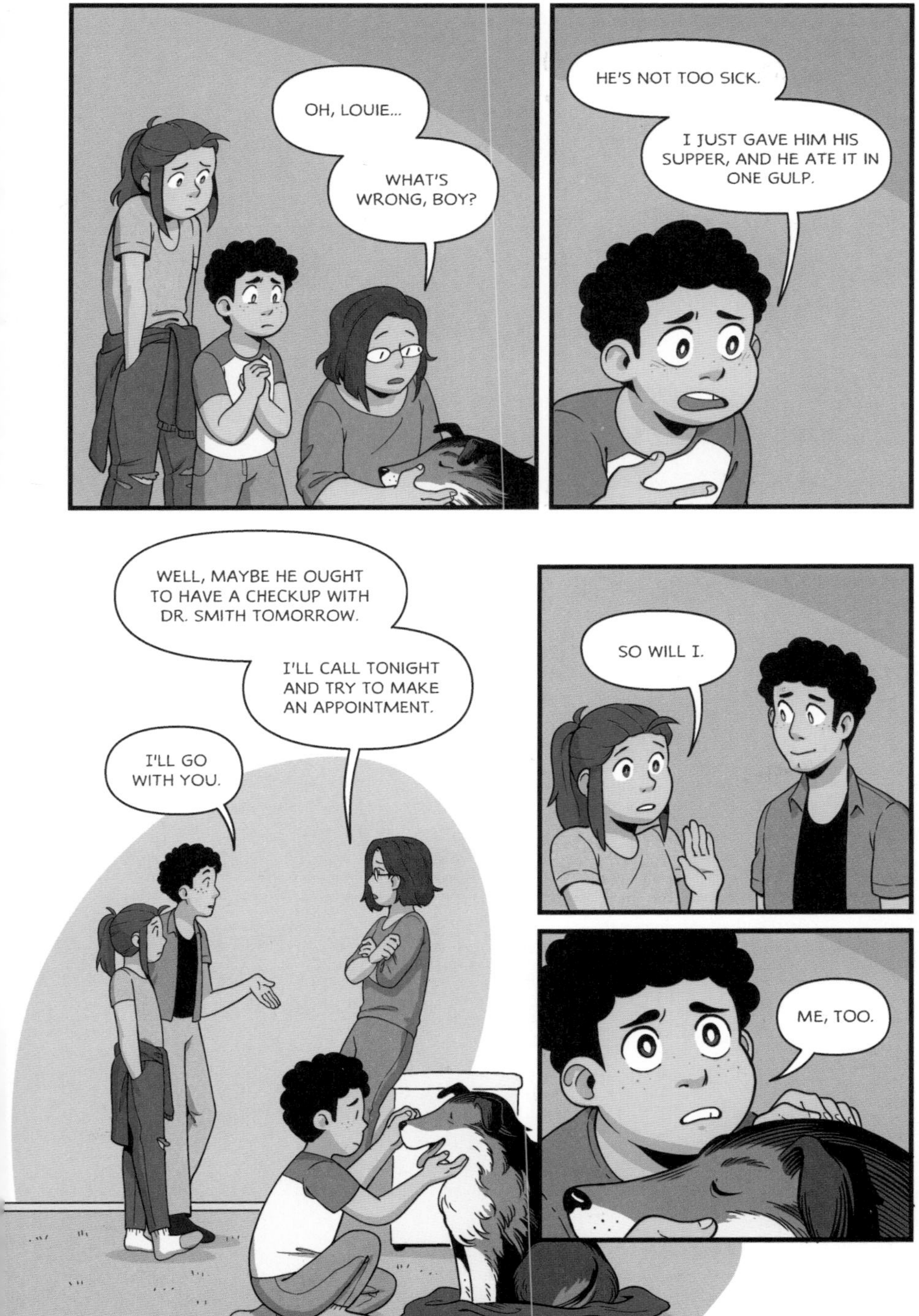
OH, LOUIE...
WHAT'S WRONG, BOY?
HE'S NOT TOO SICK.
I JUST GAVE HIM HIS SUPPER, AND HE ATE IT IN ONE GULP.
WELL, MAYBE HE OUGHT TO HAVE A CHECKUP WITH DR. SMITH TOMORROW.
I'LL CALL TONIGHT AND TRY TO MAKE AN APPOINTMENT.
I'LL GO WITH YOU.
SO WILL I.
ME, TOO.

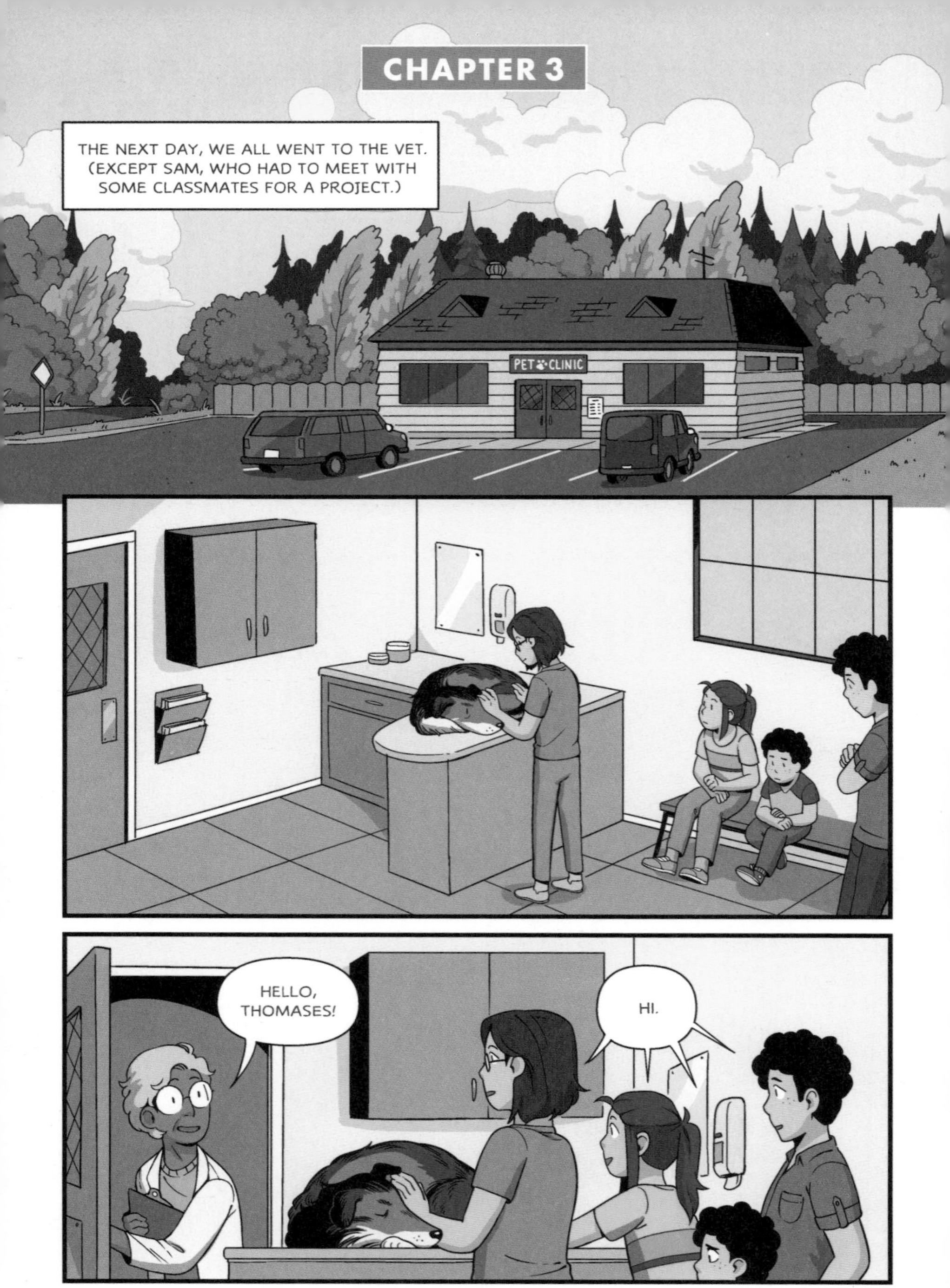
CHAPTER 3
THE NEXT DAY, WE ALL WENT TO THE VET. (EXCEPT SAM, WHO HAD TO MEET WITH SOME CLASSMATES FOR A PROJECT.)
PET CLINIC
HELLO, THOMASES!
HI.

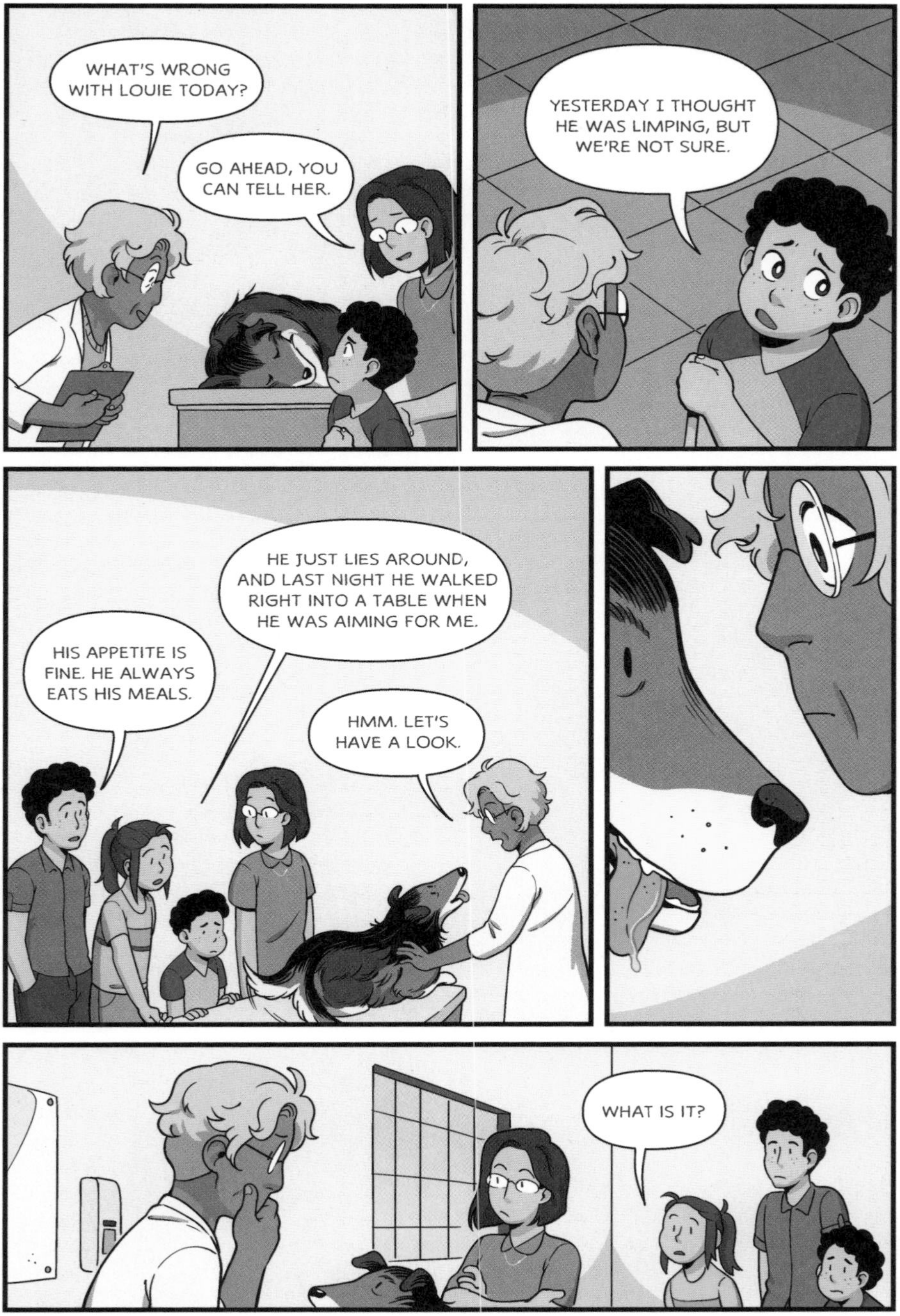
WHAT'S WRONG WITH LOUIE TODAY?
GO AHEAD, YOU CAN TELL HER.
YESTERDAY I THOUGHT HE WAS LIMPING, BUT WE'RE NOT SURE.
HIS APPETITE IS FINE. HE ALWAYS EATS HIS MEALS.
HE JUST LIES AROUND, AND LAST NIGHT HE WALKED RIGHT INTO A TABLE WHEN HE WAS AIMING FOR ME.
HMM. LET'S HAVE A LOOK.
WHAT IS IT?

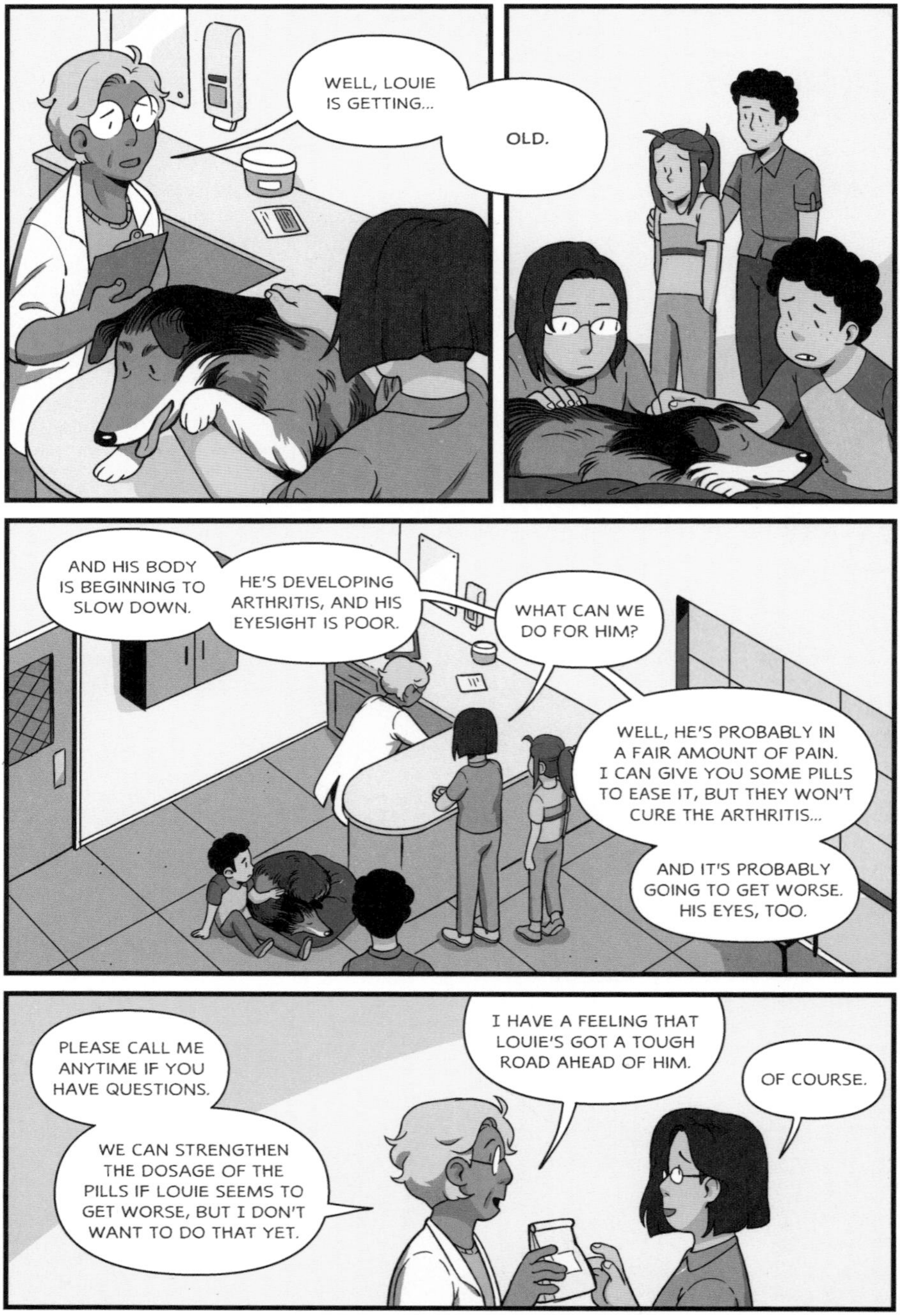

WELL, LOUIE IS GETTING...
OLD.
AND HIS BODY IS BEGINNING TO SLOW DOWN.
HE'S DEVELOPING ARTHRITIS, AND HIS EYESIGHT IS POOR.
WHAT CAN WE DO FOR HIM?
WELL, HE'S PROBABLY IN A FAIR AMOUNT OF PAIN. I CAN GIVE YOU SOME PILLS TO EASE IT, BUT THEY WON'T CURE THE ARTHRITIS...
AND IT'S PROBABLY GOING TO GET WORSE. HIS EYES, TOO.
PLEASE CALL ME ANYTIME IF YOU HAVE QUESTIONS.
WE CAN STRENGTHEN THE DOSAGE OF THE PILLS IF LOUIE SEEMS TO GET WORSE, BUT I DON'T WANT TO DO THAT YET.
I HAVE A FEELING THAT LOUIE'S GOT A TOUGH ROAD AHEAD OF HIM.
OF COURSE.

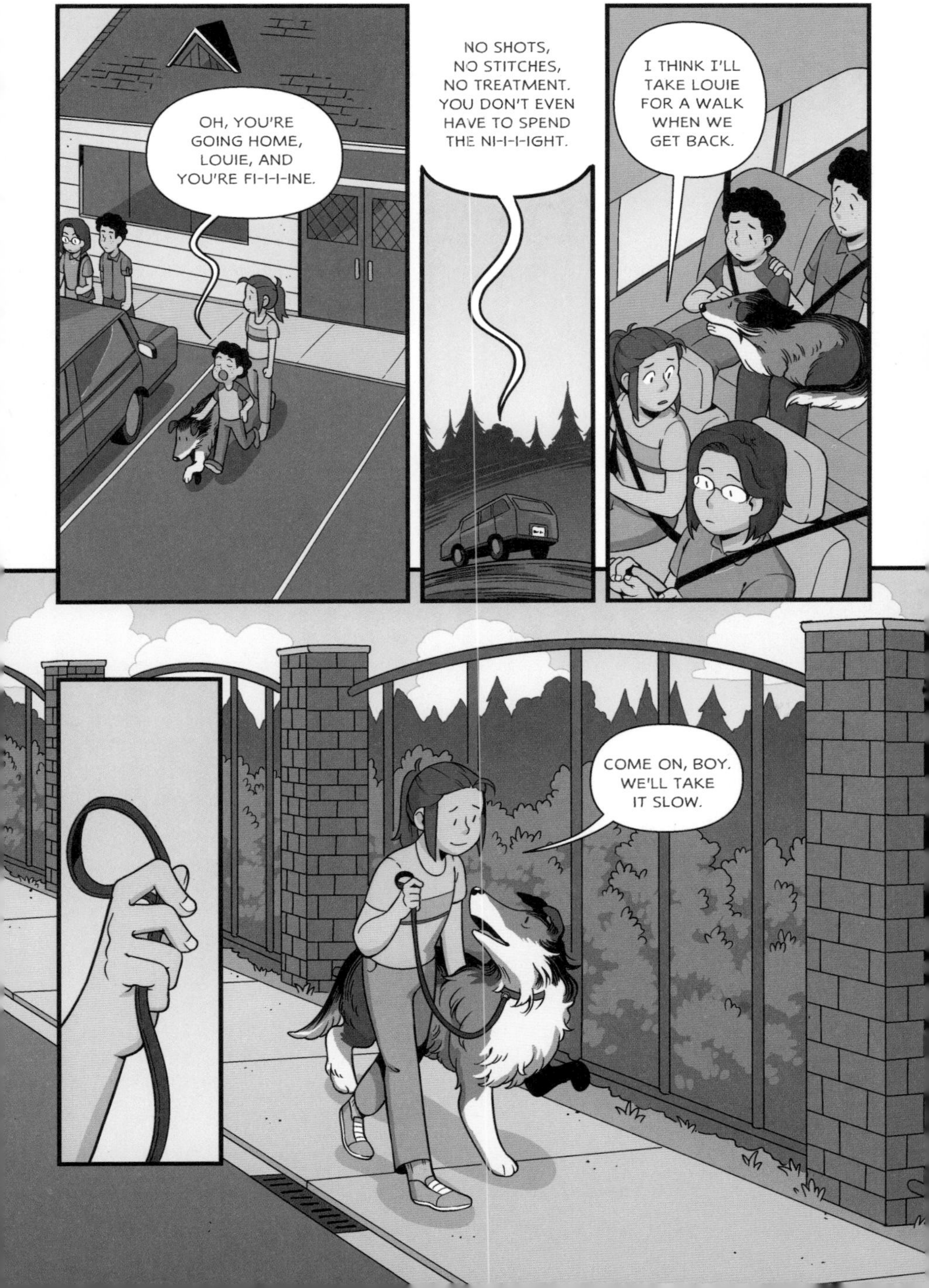
OH, YOU'RE GOING HOME, LOUIE, AND YOU'RE FI-I-I-INE.
NO SHOTS, NO STITCHES, NO TREATMENT. YOU DON'T EVEN HAVE TO SPEND THE NI-I-I-IGHT.
I THINK I'LL TAKE LOUIE FOR A WALK WHEN WE GET BACK.
COME ON, BOY. WE'LL TAKE IT SLOW.

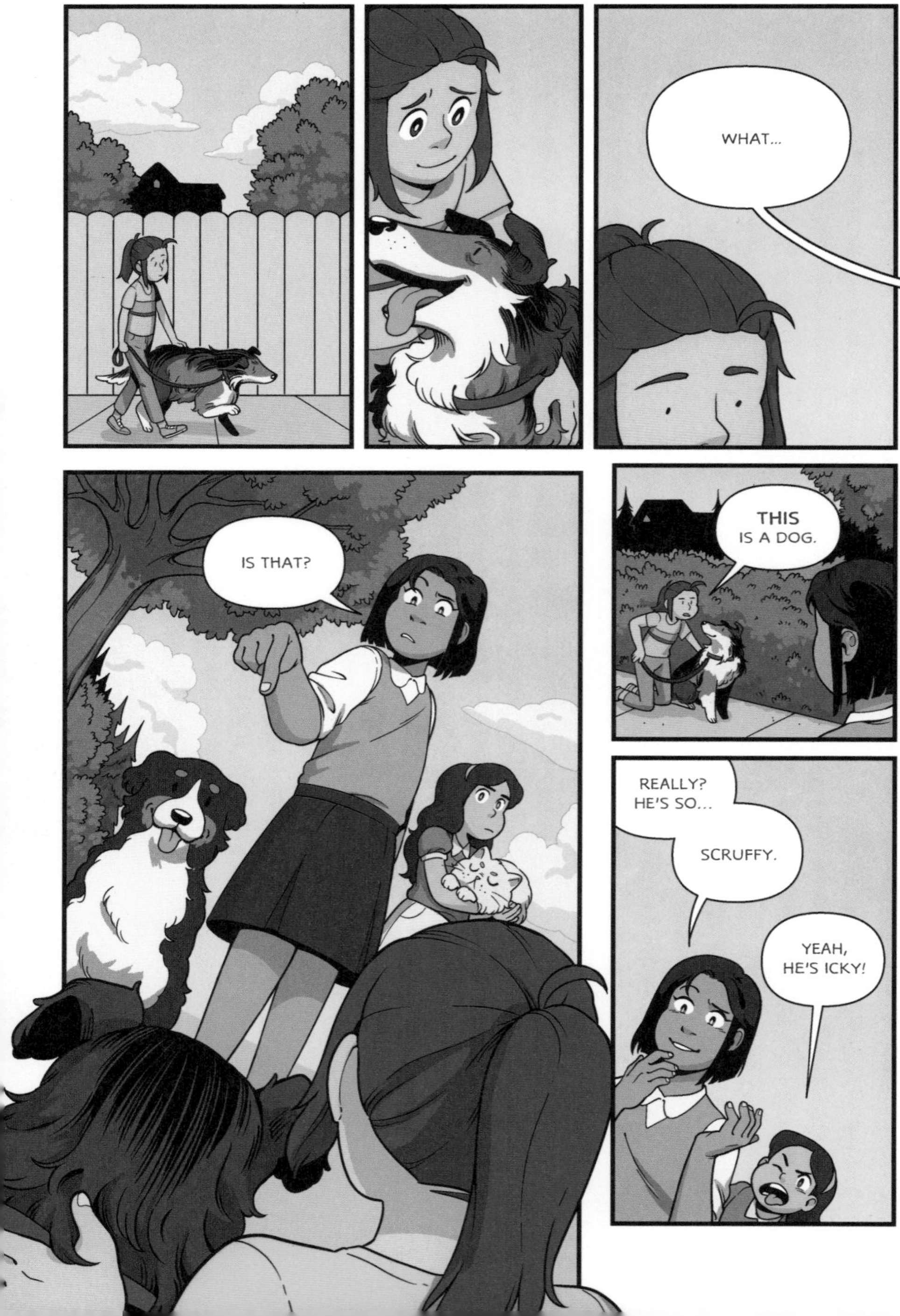
WHAT...
IS THAT?
THIS IS A DOG.
REALLY? HE'S SO...
SCRUFFY.
YEAH, HE'S ICKY!

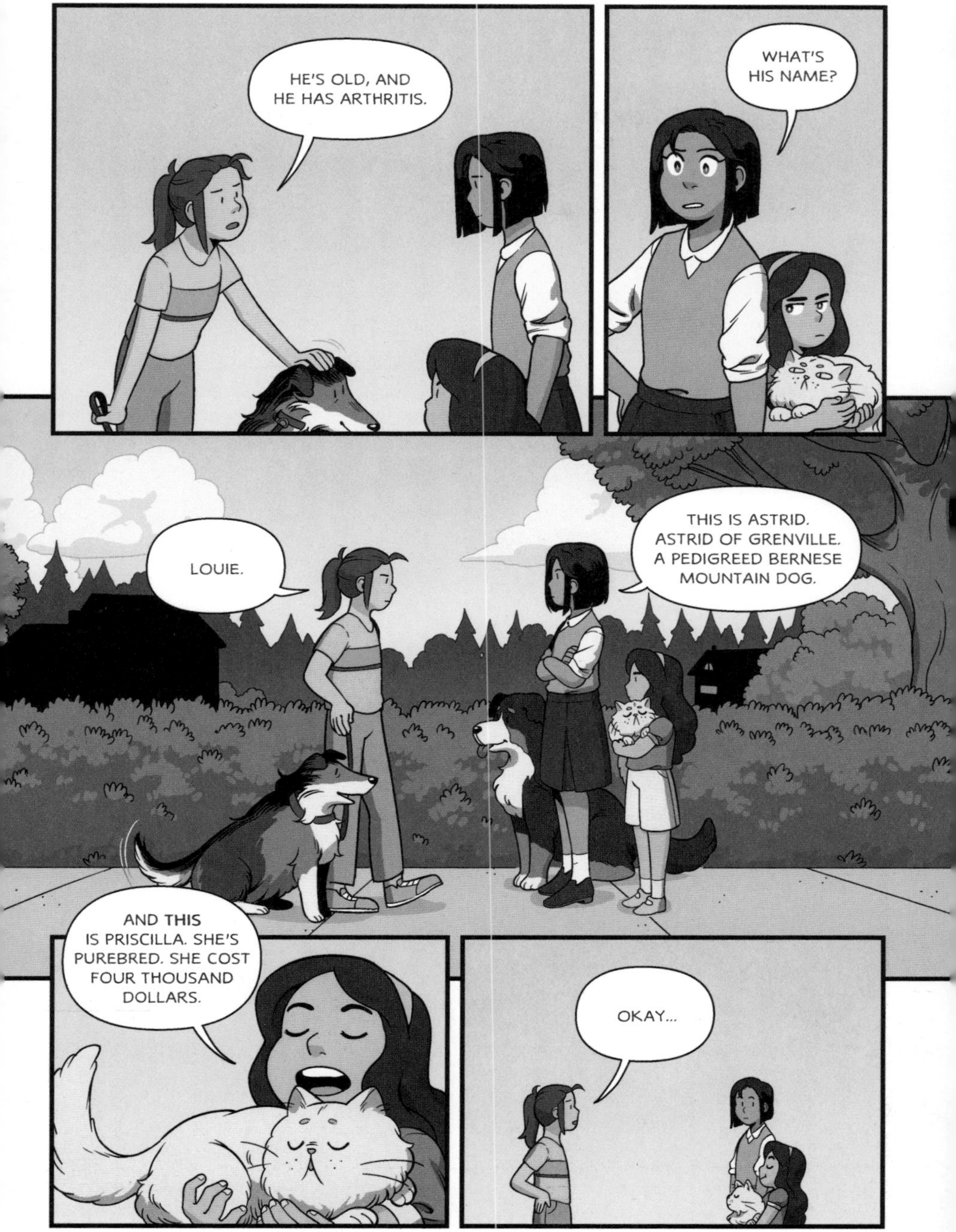
HE'S OLD, AND HE HAS ARTHRITIS.
WHAT'S HIS NAME?
LOUIE.
THIS IS ASTRID. ASTRID OF GRENVILLE. A PEDIGREED BERNESE MOUNTAIN DOG.
AND THIS IS PRISCILLA. SHE'S PUREBRED. SHE COST FOUR THOUSAND DOLLARS.
OKAY...

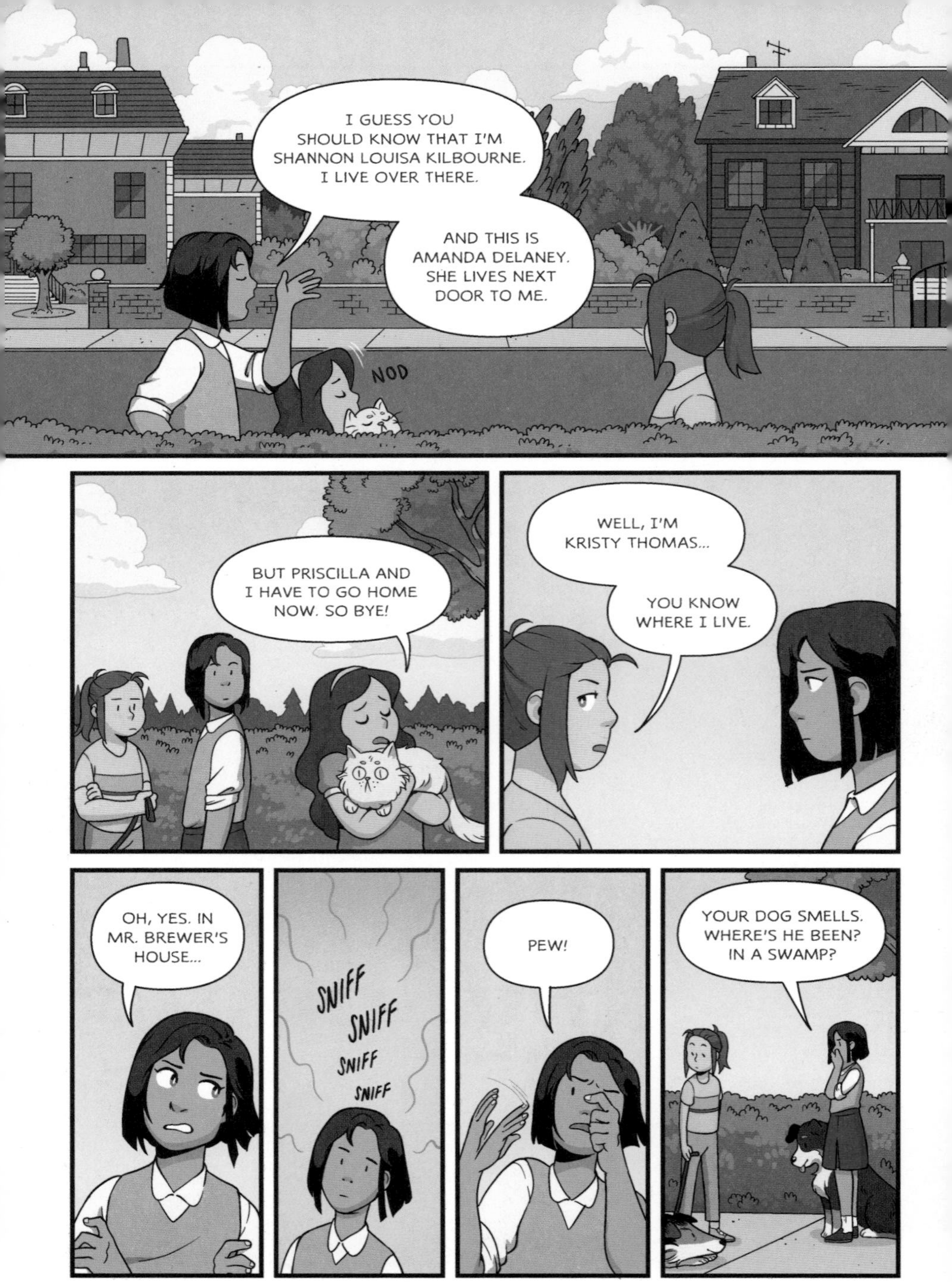
I GUESS YOU SHOULD KNOW THAT I'M SHANNON LOUISA KILBOURNE. I LIVE OVER THERE.
AND THIS IS AMANDA DELANEY. SHE LIVES NEXT DOOR TO ME.
NOD
BUT PRISCILLA AND I HAVE TO GO HOME NOW. SO BYE!
WELL, I'M KRISTY THOMAS...
YOU KNOW WHERE I LIVE.
OH, YES. IN MR. BREWER'S HOUSE...
SNIFF
SNIFF
SNIFF
SNIFF
PEW!
YOUR DOG SMELLS. WHERE'S HE BEEN? IN A SWAMP?

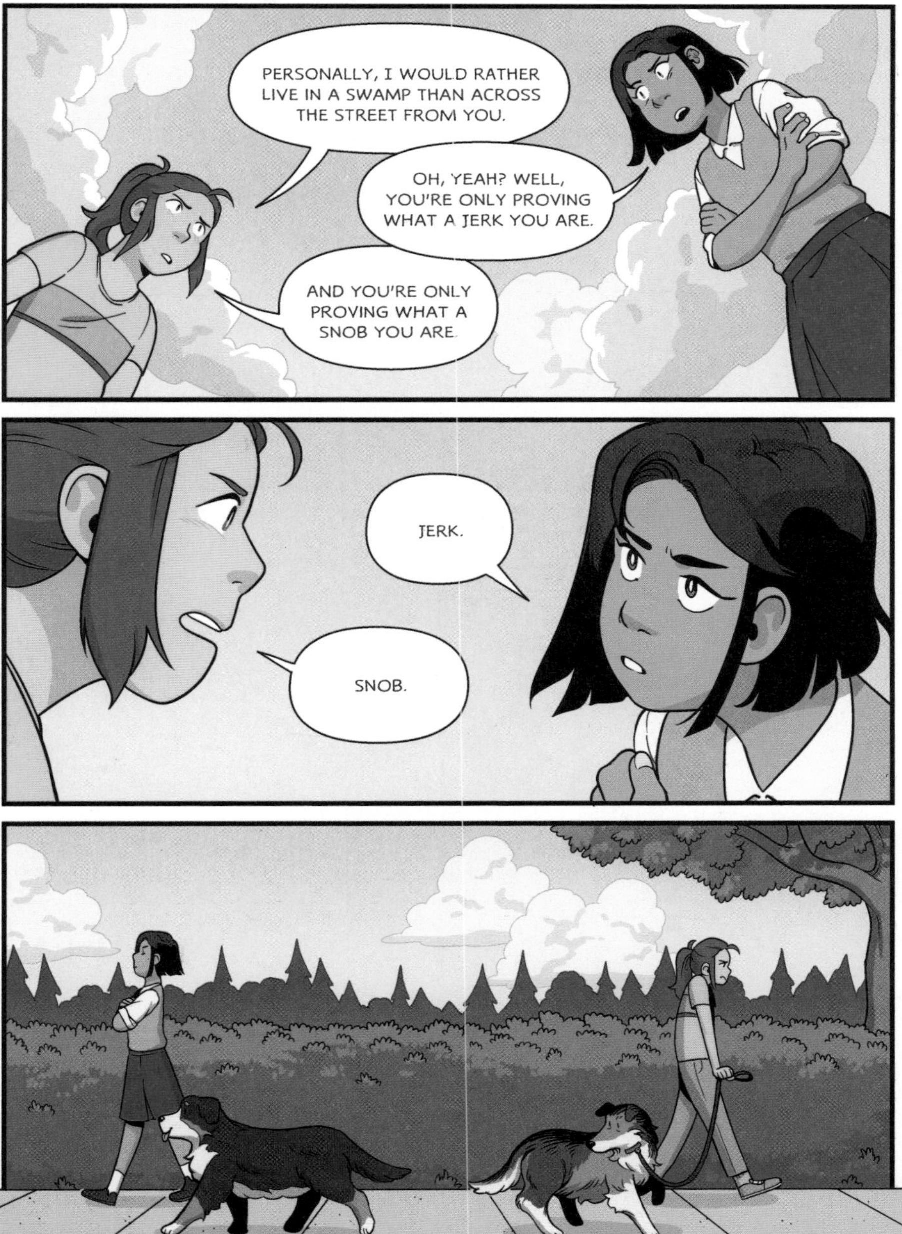
PERSONALLY, I WOULD RATHER LIVE IN A SWAMP THAN ACROSS THE STREET FROM YOU.
OH, YEAH? WELL, YOU'RE ONLY PROVING WHAT A JERK YOU ARE.
AND YOU'RE ONLY PROVING WHAT A SNOB YOU ARE.
JERK.
SNOB.

CHAPTER 4

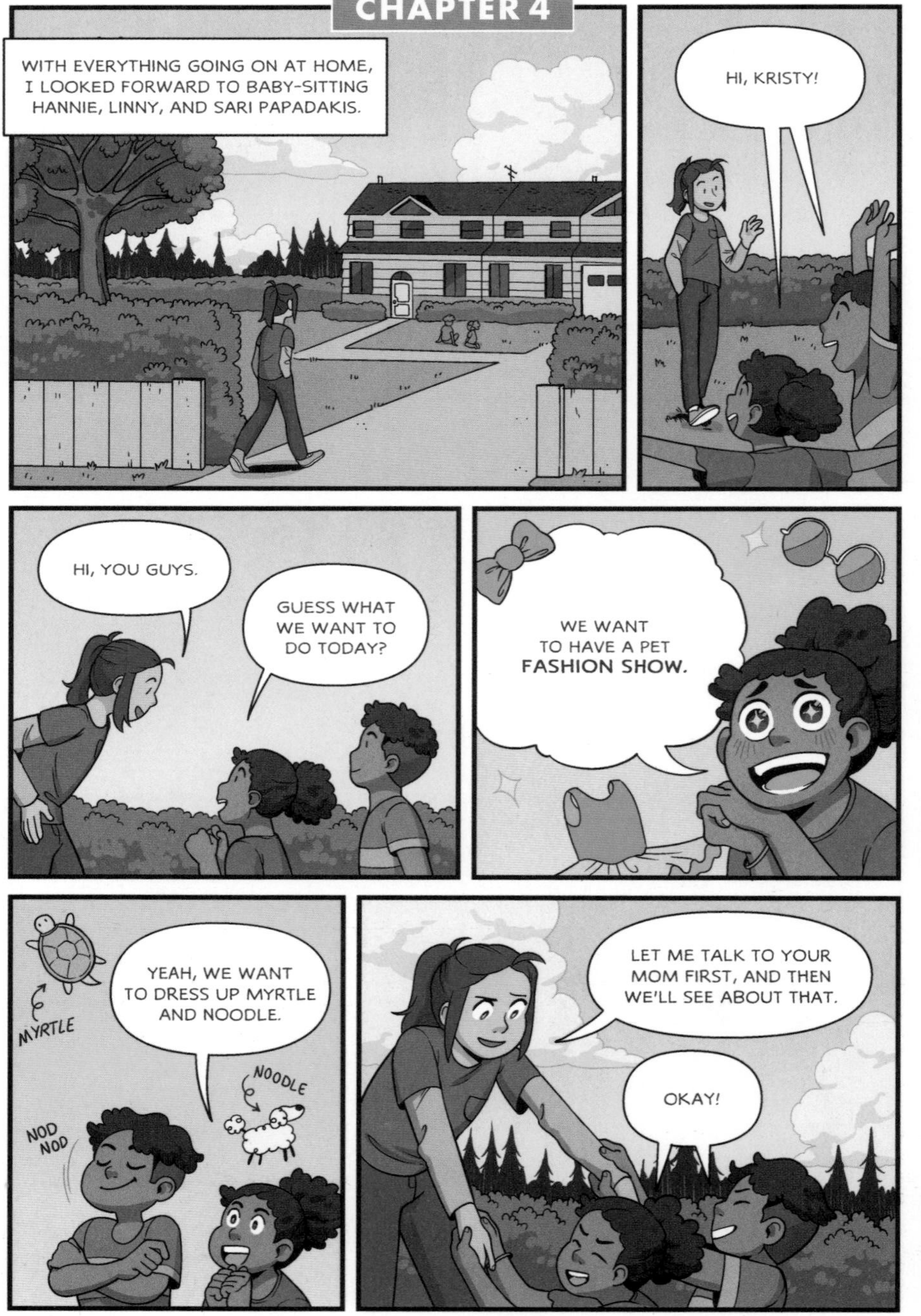
WITH EVERYTHING GOING ON AT HOME, I LOOKED FORWARD TO BABY-SITTING HANNIE, LINNY, AND SARI PAPADAKIS.
HI, KRISTY!
HI, YOU GUYS.
GUESS WHAT WE WANT TO DO TODAY?
WE WANT TO HAVE A PET **FASHION SHOW.**
MYRTLE
YEAH, WE WANT TO DRESS UP MYRTLE AND NOODLE.
NOODLE
NOD NOD
LET ME TALK TO YOUR MOM FIRST, AND THEN WE'LL SEE ABOUT THAT.
OKAY!

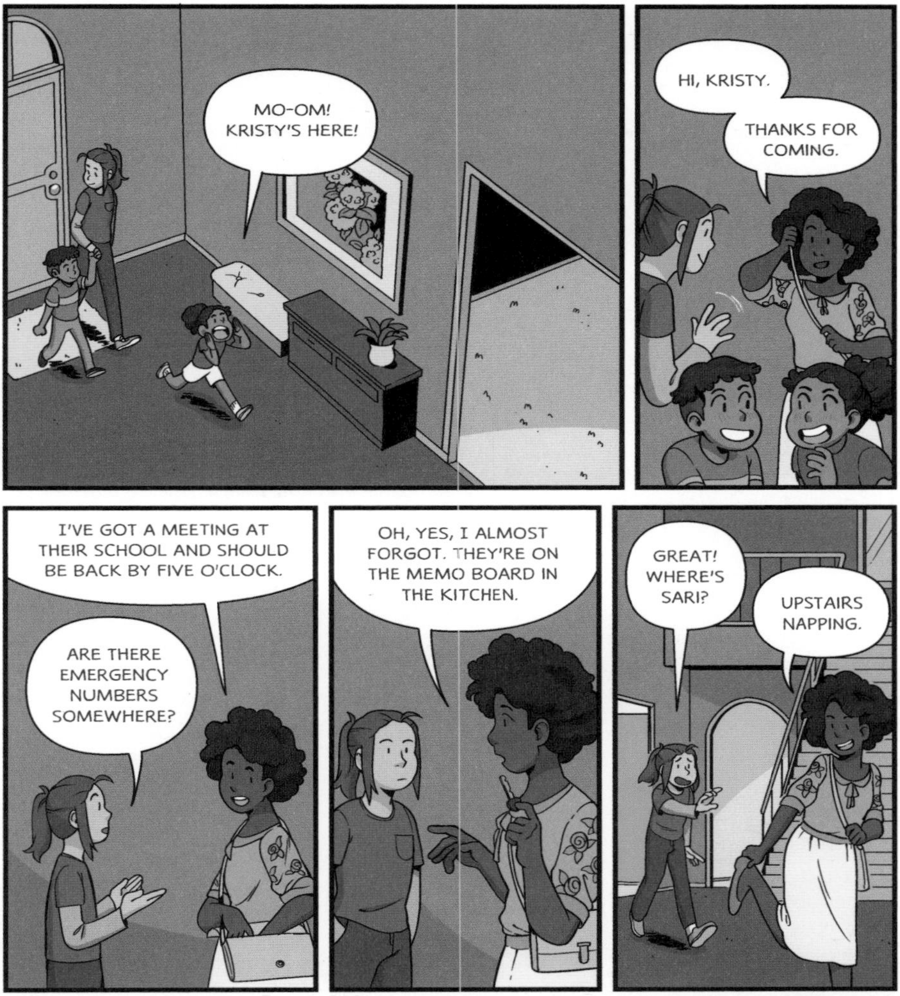
MO-OM! KRISTY'S HERE!
HI, KRISTY.
THANKS FOR COMING.
I'VE GOT A MEETING AT THEIR SCHOOL AND SHOULD BE BACK BY FIVE O'CLOCK.
ARE THERE EMERGENCY NUMBERS SOMEWHERE?
OH, YES, I ALMOST FORGOT. THEY'RE ON THE MEMO BOARD IN THE KITCHEN.
GREAT! WHERE'S SARI?
UPSTAIRS NAPPING.
THERE'S APPLE JUICE IN THE FRIDGE FOR WHEN SHE WAKES UP, BUT NO SNACKS FOR THE KIDS.
GOT IT.
CLACK

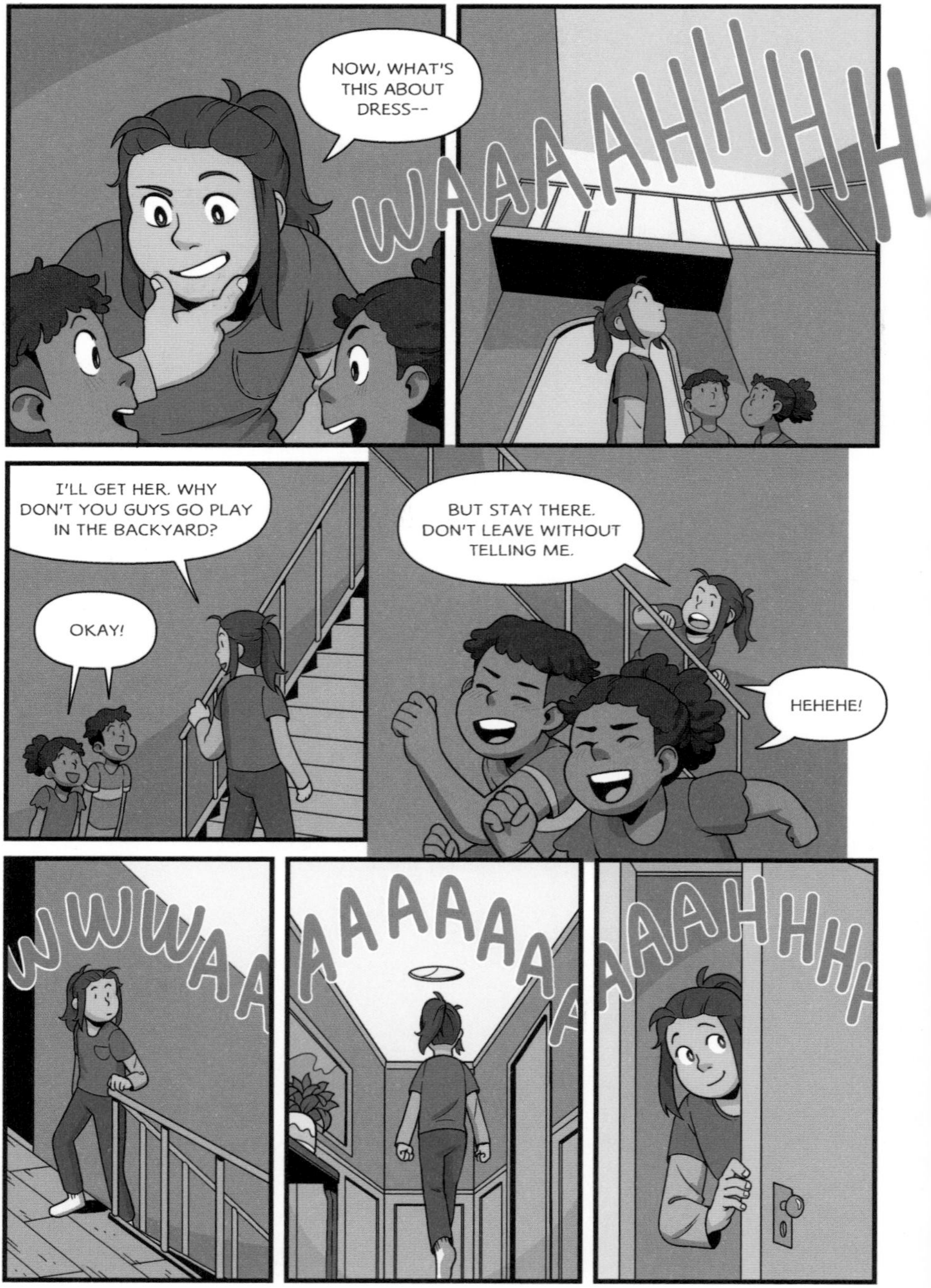

NOW, WHAT'S THIS ABOUT DRESS--
WAAAAHHHH
I'LL GET HER. WHY DON'T YOU GUYS GO PLAY IN THE BACKYARD?
OKAY!
BUT STAY THERE. DON'T LEAVE WITHOUT TELLING ME.
HEHEHE!
WWWAAA
AAAAAA
AAAAHHHH

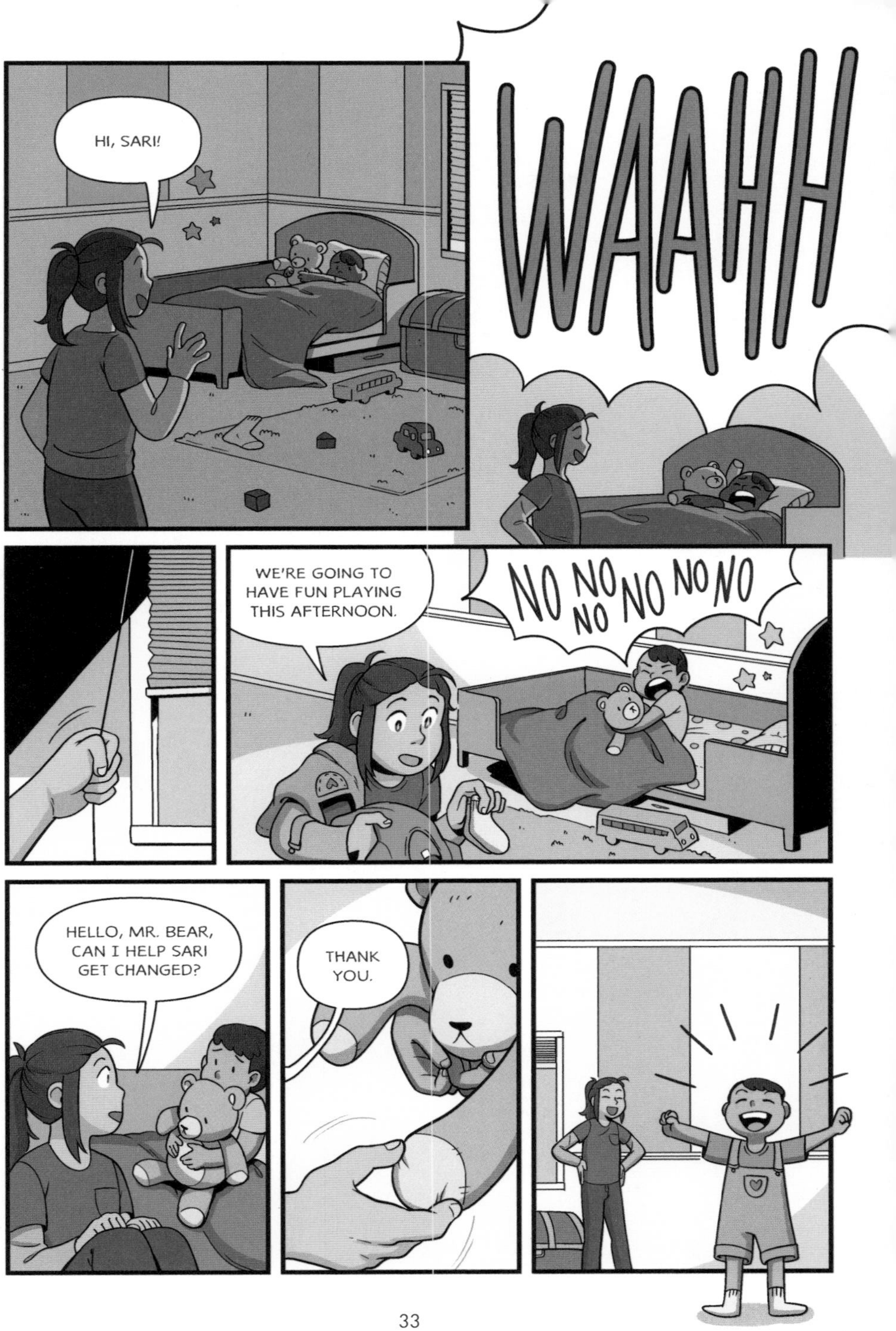
HI, SARI!
WAAHH
WE'RE GOING TO HAVE FUN PLAYING THIS AFTERNOON.
NO NO NO NO NO NO NO
HELLO, MR. BEAR, CAN I HELP SARI GET CHANGED?
THANK YOU.

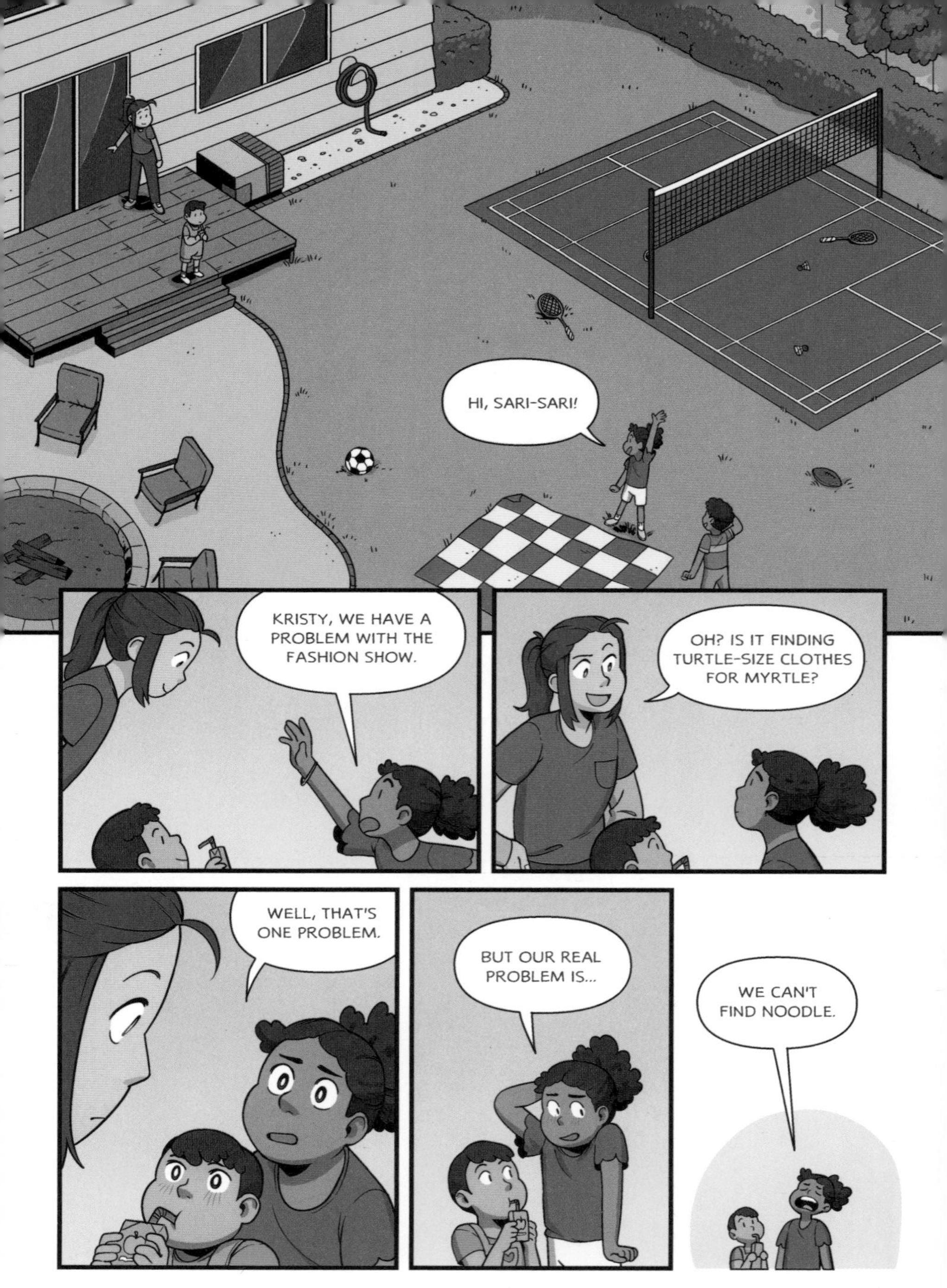
HI, SARI-SARI!
KRISTY, WE HAVE A PROBLEM WITH THE FASHION SHOW.
OH? IS IT FINDING TURTLE-SIZE CLOTHES FOR MYRTLE?
WELL, THAT'S ONE PROBLEM.
BUT OUR REAL PROBLEM IS...
WE CAN'T FIND NOODLE.

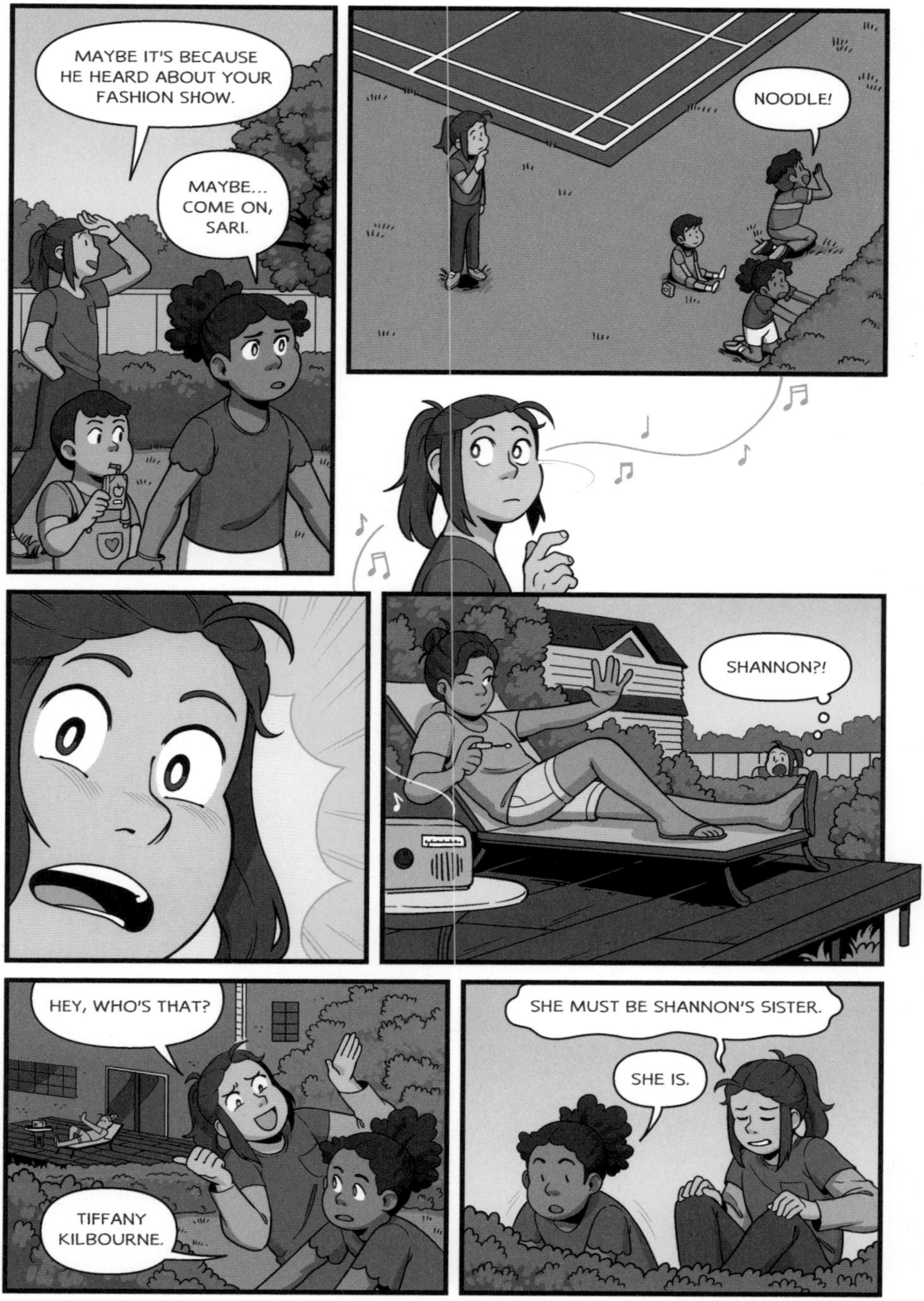
MAYBE IT'S BECAUSE HE HEARD ABOUT YOUR FASHION SHOW.
MAYBE... COME ON, SARI.
NOODLE!
SHANNON?!
HEY, WHO'S THAT?
TIFFANY KILBOURNE.
SHE MUST BE SHANNON'S SISTER.
SHE IS.

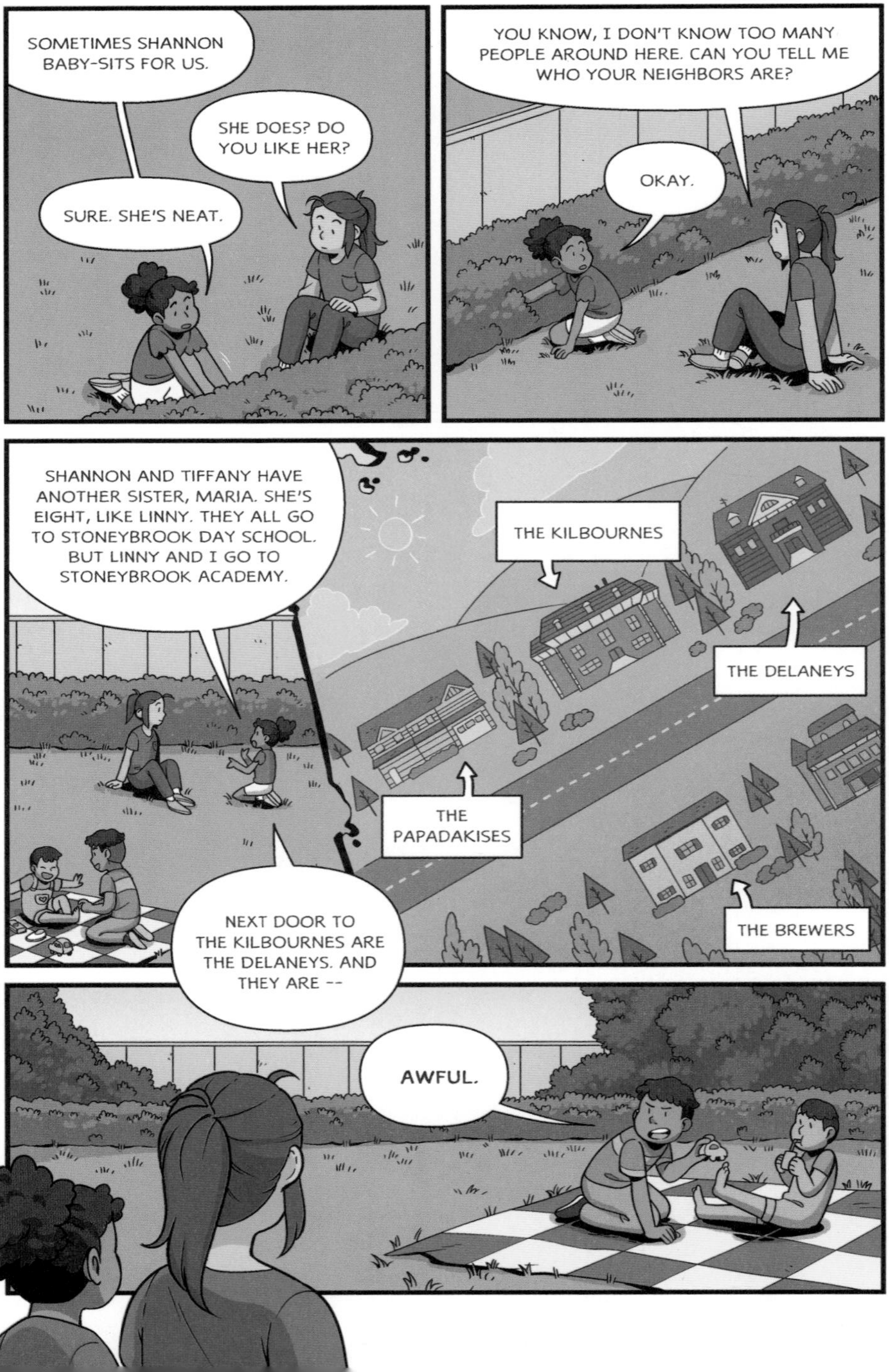
SOMETIMES SHANNON BABY-SITS FOR US.
SHE DOES? DO YOU LIKE HER?
SURE. SHE'S NEAT.
YOU KNOW, I DON'T KNOW TOO MANY PEOPLE AROUND HERE. CAN YOU TELL ME WHO YOUR NEIGHBORS ARE?
OKAY.
SHANNON AND TIFFANY HAVE ANOTHER SISTER, MARIA. SHE'S EIGHT, LIKE LINNY. THEY ALL GO TO STONEYBROOK DAY SCHOOL. BUT LINNY AND I GO TO STONEYBROOK ACADEMY.
THE KILBOURNES
THE DELANEYS
THE PAPADAKISES
THE BREWERS
NEXT DOOR TO THE KILBOURNES ARE THE DELANEYS. AND THEY ARE --
AWFUL.

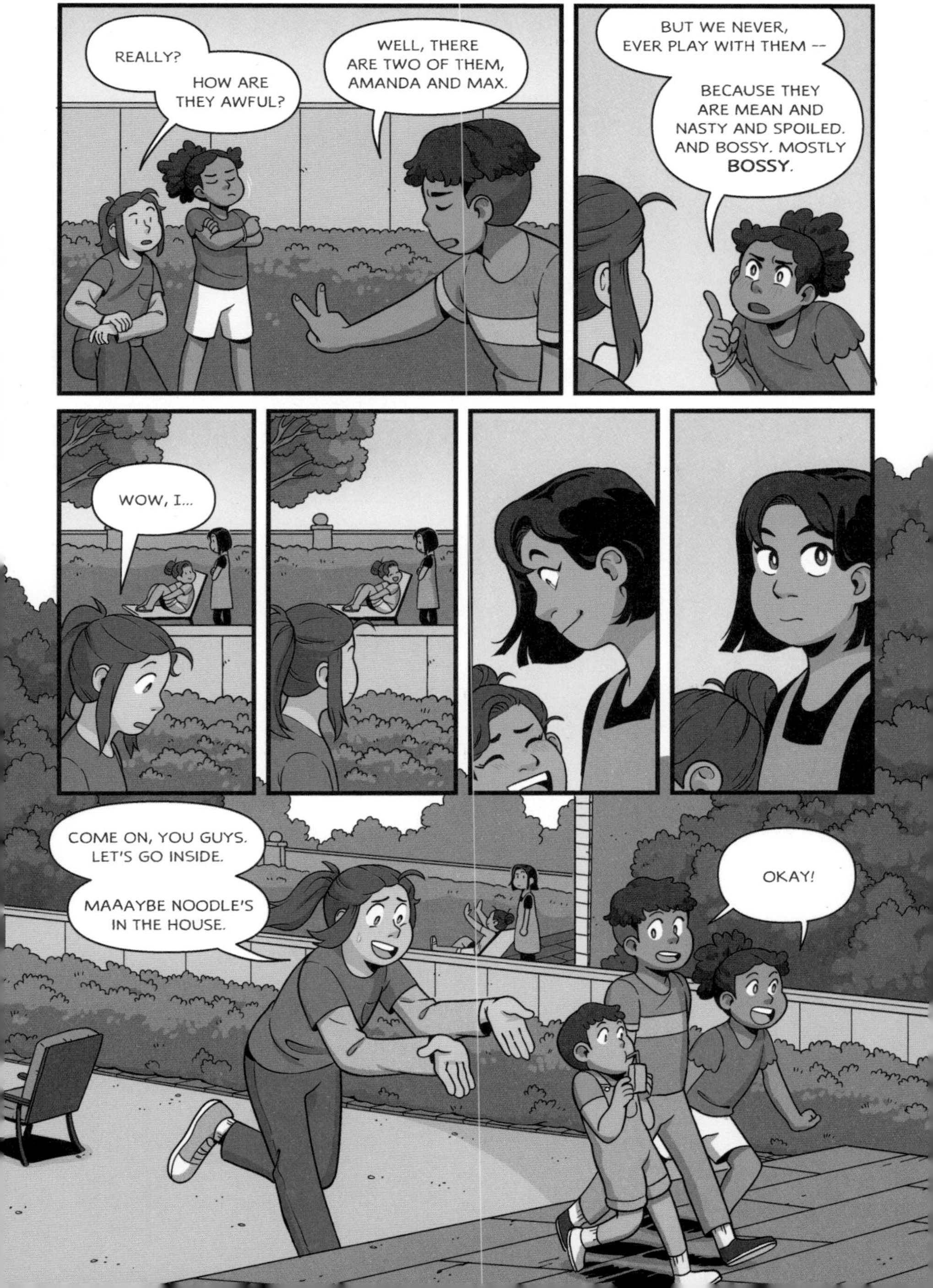
REALLY?
HOW ARE THEY AWFUL?
WELL, THERE ARE TWO OF THEM, AMANDA AND MAX.
BUT WE NEVER, EVER PLAY WITH THEM --
BECAUSE THEY ARE MEAN AND NASTY AND SPOILED. AND BOSSY. MOSTLY **BOSSY**.
WOW, I...
COME ON, YOU GUYS. LET'S GO INSIDE.
MAAAYBE NOODLE'S IN THE HOUSE.
OKAY!

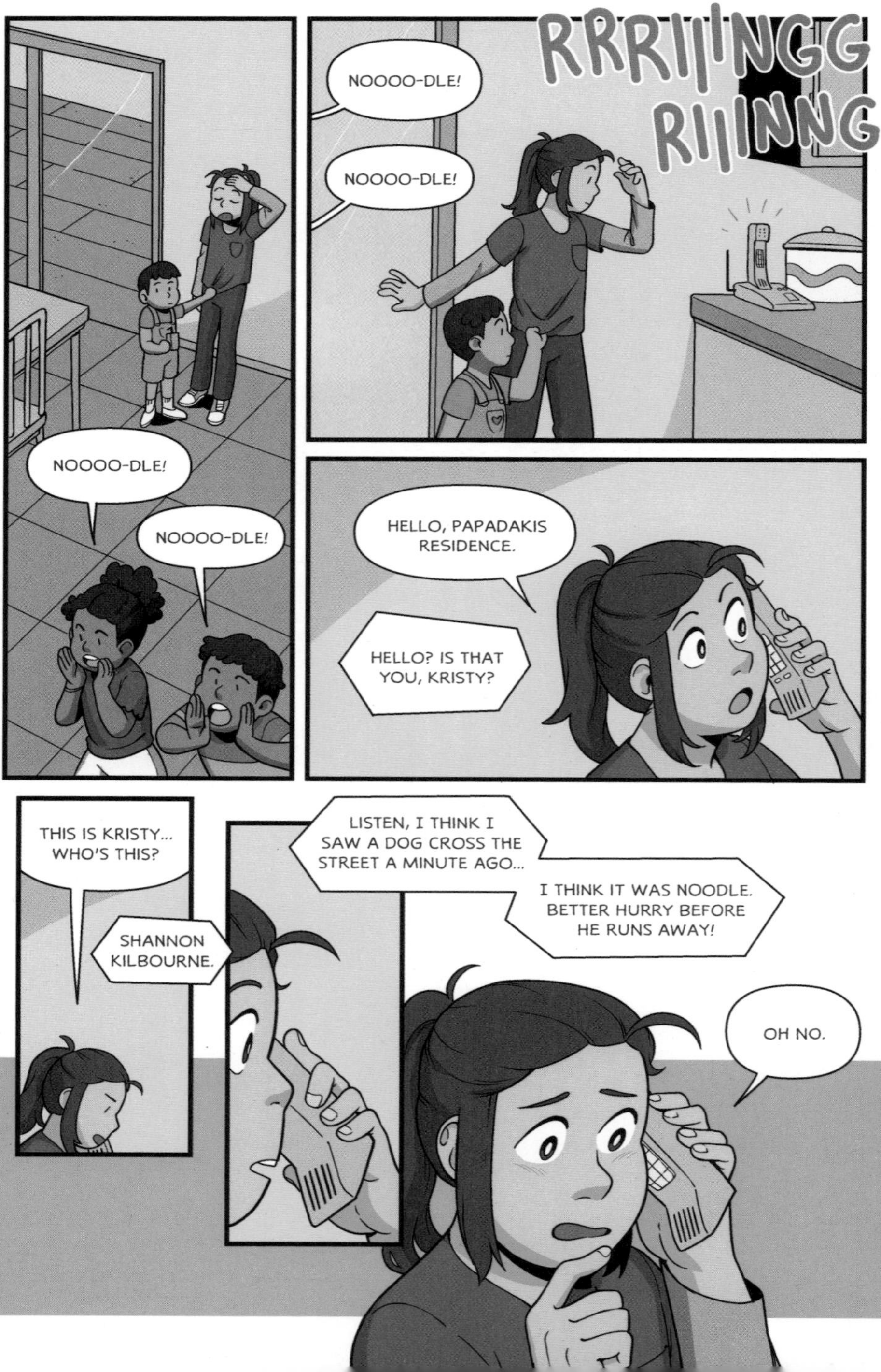
NOOOO-DLE!
NOOOO-DLE!
RRRIIINGG
RIIINNG
NOOOO-DLE!
NOOOO-DLE!
HELLO, PAPADAKIS RESIDENCE.
HELLO? IS THAT YOU, KRISTY?
THIS IS KRISTY... WHO'S THIS?
SHANNON KILBOURNE.
LISTEN, I THINK I SAW A DOG CROSS THE STREET A MINUTE AGO...
I THINK IT WAS NOODLE. BETTER HURRY BEFORE HE RUNS AWAY!
OH NO.

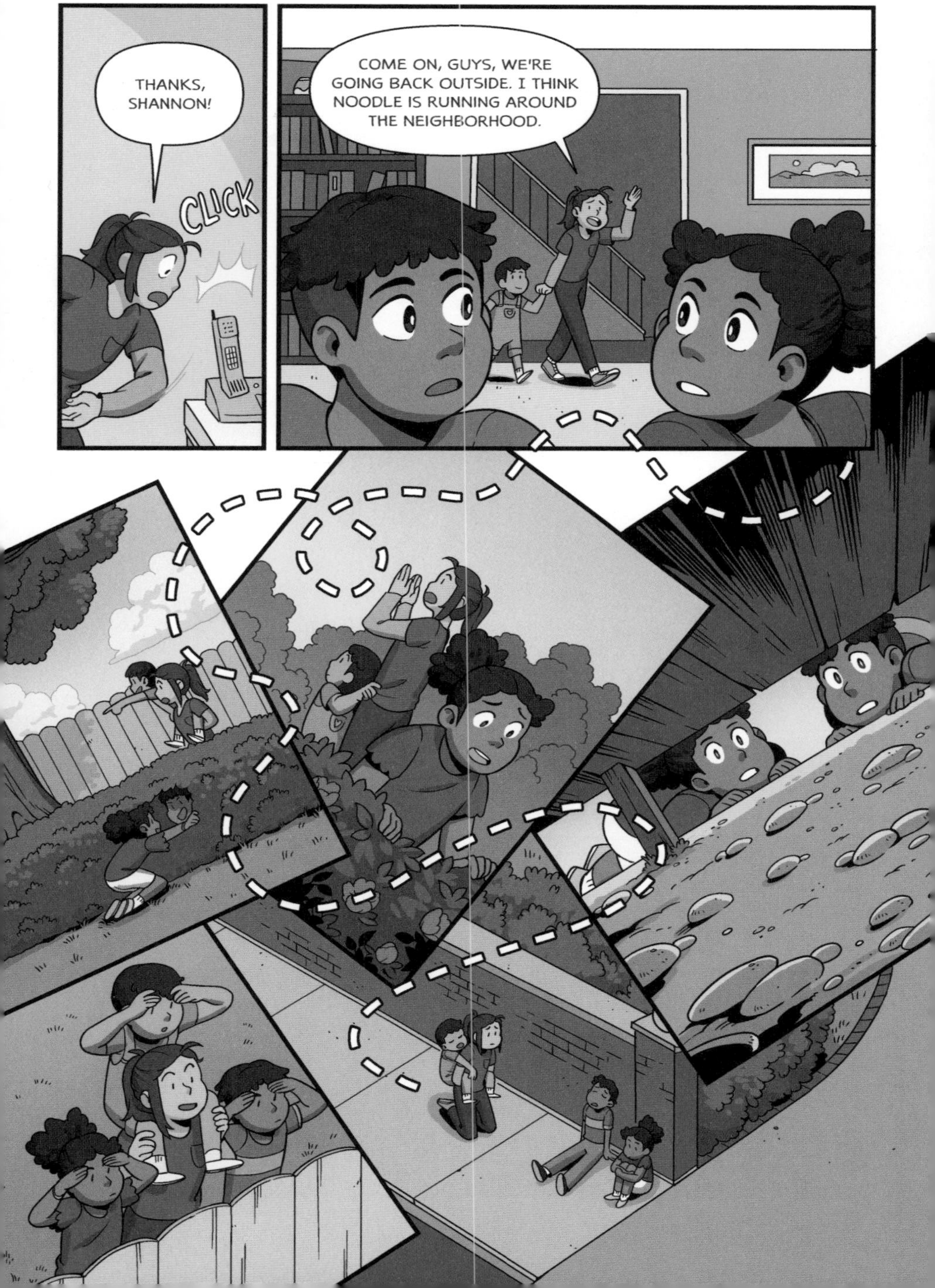
THANKS, SHANNON!
CLICK
COME ON, GUYS, WE'RE GOING BACK OUTSIDE. I THINK NOODLE IS RUNNING AROUND THE NEIGHBORHOOD.

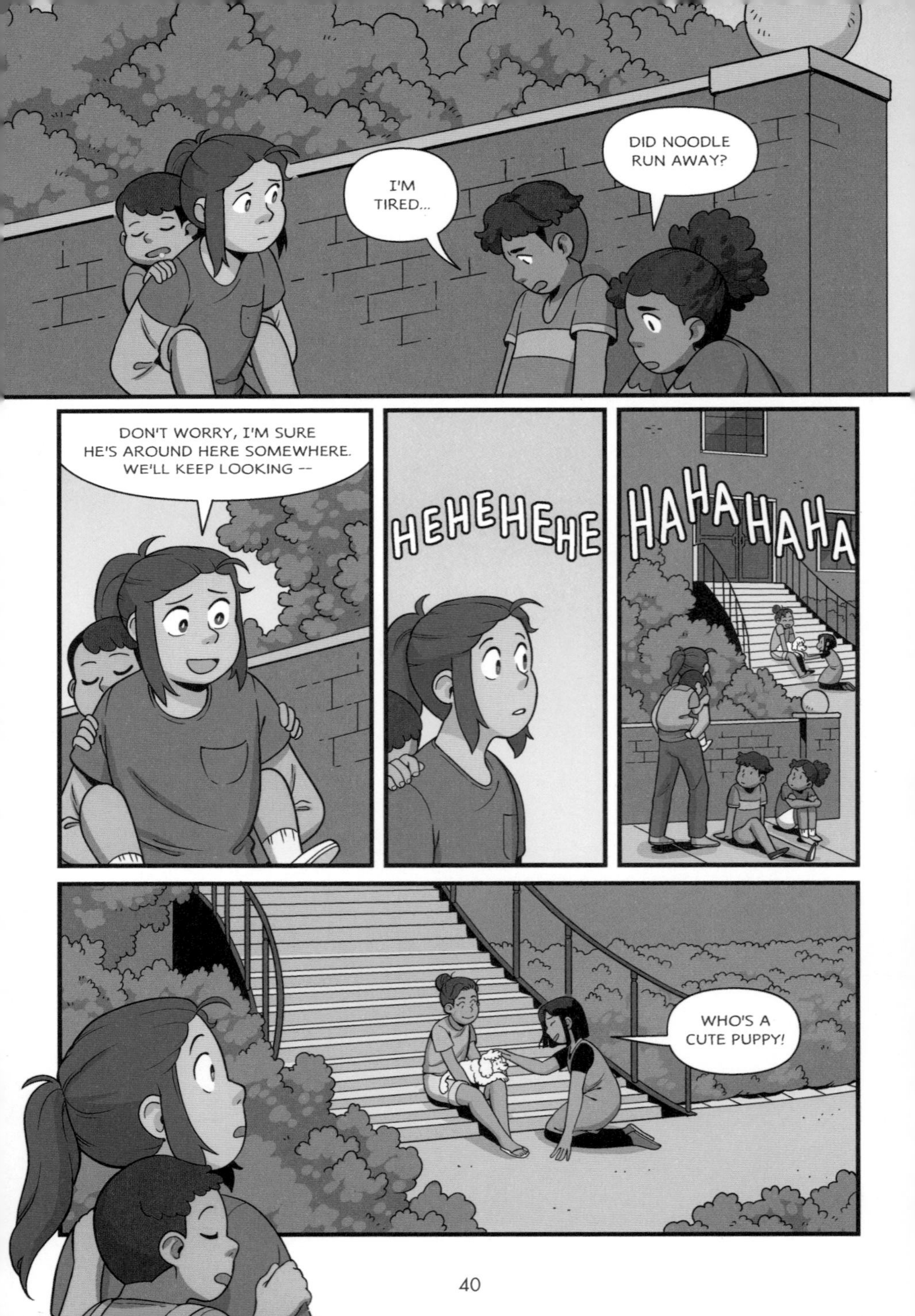
I'M TIRED...
DID NOODLE RUN AWAY?
DON'T WORRY, I'M SURE HE'S AROUND HERE SOMEWHERE. WE'LL KEEP LOOKING --
HEHEHEHEHE
HAHAHAHAHA
WHO'S A CUTE PUPPY!

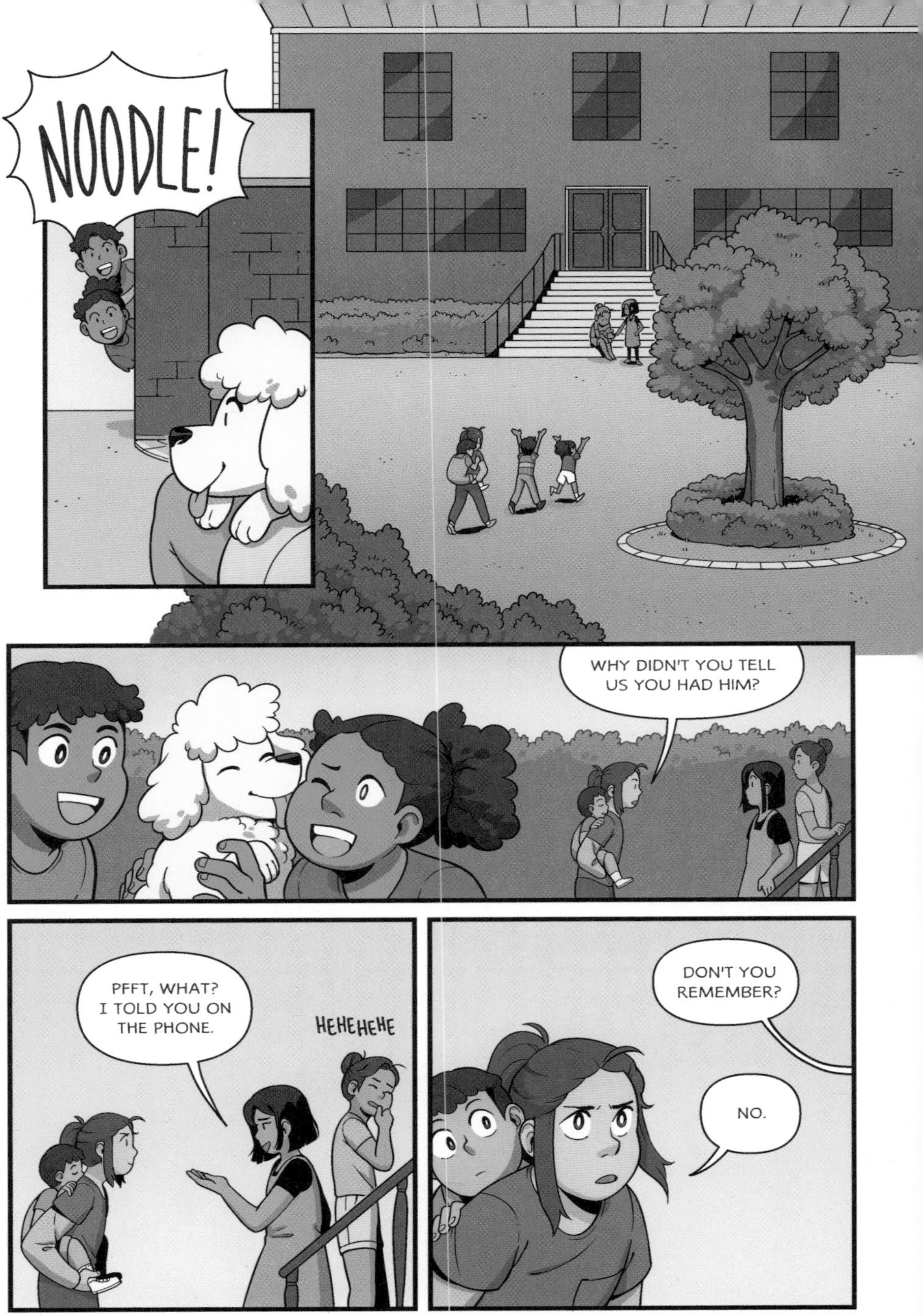
NOODLE!
WHY DIDN'T YOU TELL US YOU HAD HIM?
PFFT, WHAT? I TOLD YOU ON THE PHONE.
HEHEHEHE
DON'T YOU REMEMBER?
NO.

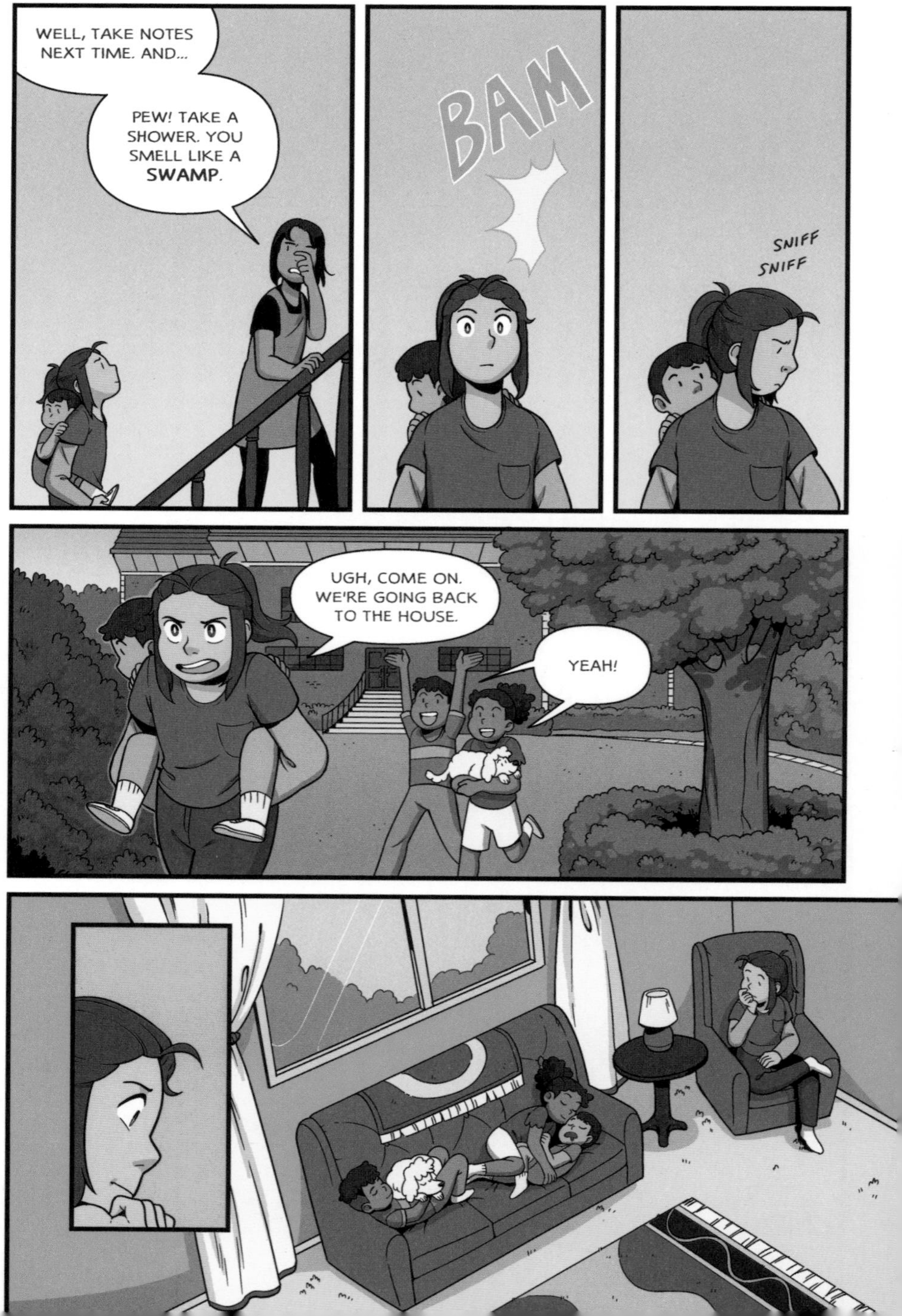
WELL, TAKE NOTES NEXT TIME. AND...
PEW! TAKE A SHOWER. YOU SMELL LIKE A **SWAMP**.
BAM
SNIFF SNIFF
UGH, COME ON. WE'RE GOING BACK TO THE HOUSE.
YEAH!

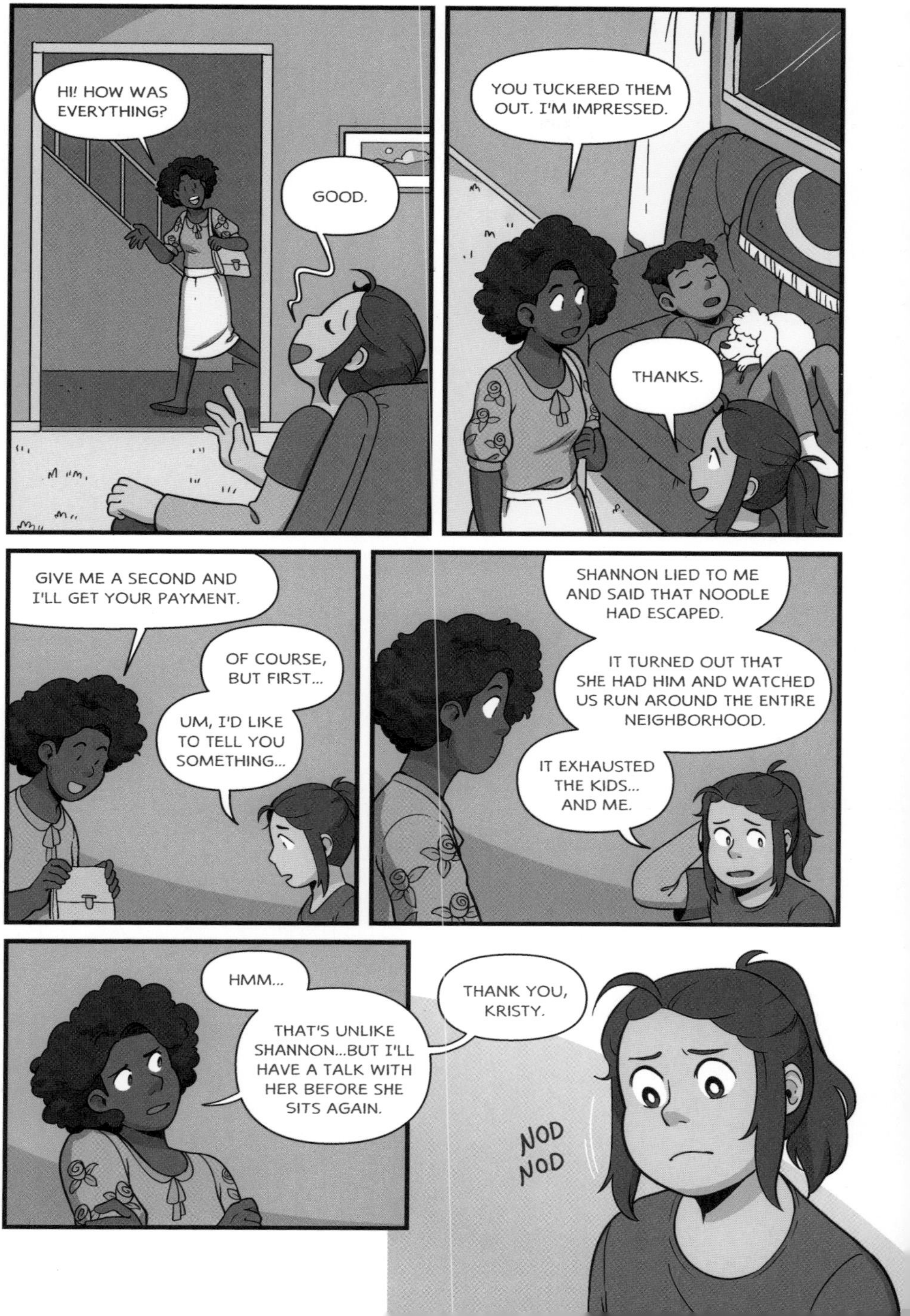
HI! HOW WAS EVERYTHING?
GOOD.
YOU TUCKERED THEM OUT. I'M IMPRESSED.
THANKS.
GIVE ME A SECOND AND I'LL GET YOUR PAYMENT.
OF COURSE, BUT FIRST...
UM, I'D LIKE TO TELL YOU SOMETHING...
SHANNON LIED TO ME AND SAID THAT NOODLE HAD ESCAPED.
IT TURNED OUT THAT SHE HAD HIM AND WATCHED US RUN AROUND THE ENTIRE NEIGHBORHOOD.
IT EXHAUSTED THE KIDS... AND ME.
HMM...
THAT'S UNLIKE SHANNON...BUT I'LL HAVE A TALK WITH HER BEFORE SHE SITS AGAIN.
THANK YOU, KRISTY.
NOD NOD

UP

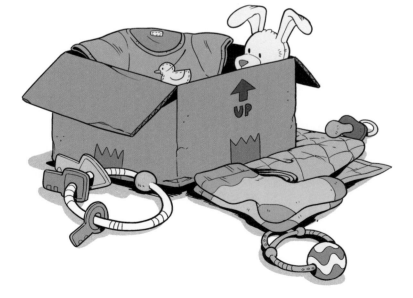

Thursday

I baby-sat for Myriah and Gabbie this afternoon, and we had a little trouble. Mrs. Perkins is getting ready for the new baby. She's fixing up the room that used to be David Michael's. (You guys should see it. There are bunnies and alphabet letters everywhere!) Mrs. Perkins is also sorting through Myriah and Gabbie's baby toys and clothes. The kids have been helping out, but Gabbie is so excited that she doesn't understand why anyone wouldn't be. So when Jamie Newton came over to play, he started to tell Gabbie how he felt about his sister. Poor Gabbie didn't understand at all...

Mary Anne

CHAPTER 5

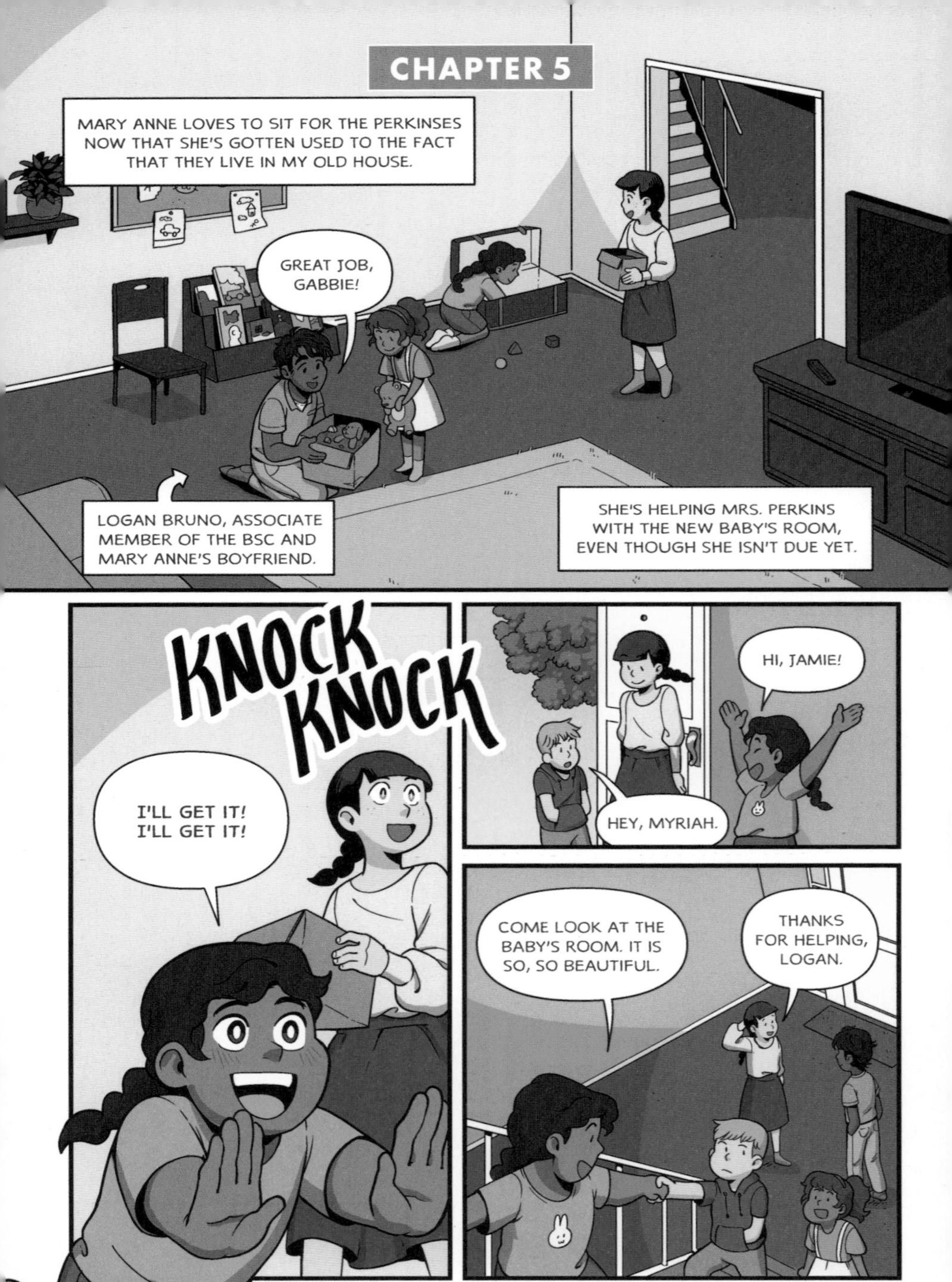
MARY ANNE LOVES TO SIT FOR THE PERKINSES NOW THAT SHE'S GOTTEN USED TO THE FACT THAT THEY LIVE IN MY OLD HOUSE.
GREAT JOB, GABBIE!
LOGAN BRUNO, ASSOCIATE MEMBER OF THE BSC AND MARY ANNE'S BOYFRIEND.
SHE'S HELPING MRS. PERKINS WITH THE NEW BABY'S ROOM, EVEN THOUGH SHE ISN'T DUE YET.
KNOCK KNOCK
I'LL GET IT! I'LL GET IT!
HI, JAMIE!
HEY, MYRIAH.
COME LOOK AT THE BABY'S ROOM. IT IS SO, SO BEAUTIFUL.
THANKS FOR HELPING, LOGAN.

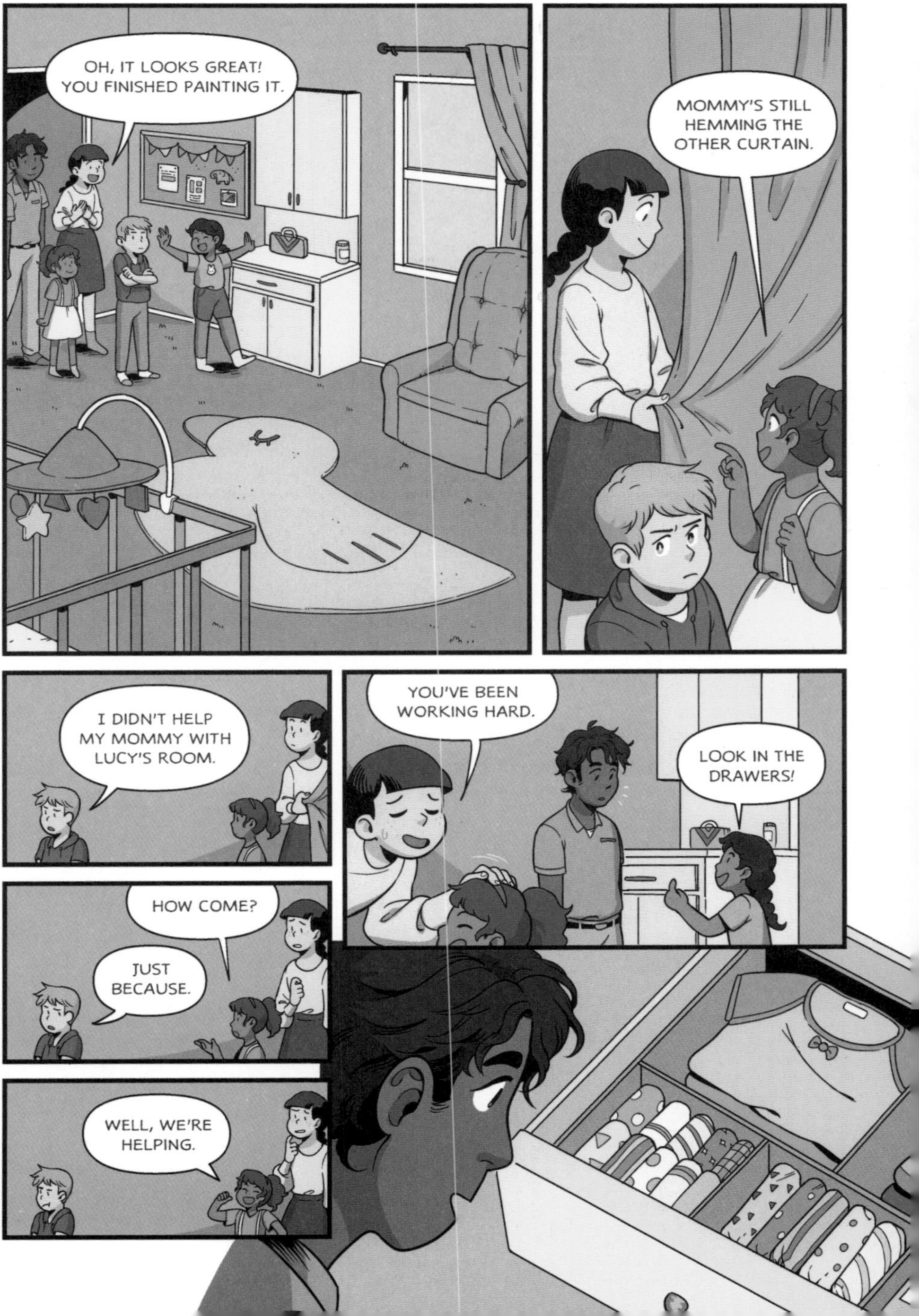
OH, IT LOOKS GREAT! YOU FINISHED PAINTING IT.
MOMMY'S STILL HEMMING THE OTHER CURTAIN.
I DIDN'T HELP MY MOMMY WITH LUCY'S ROOM.
HOW COME?
JUST BECAUSE.
WELL, WE'RE HELPING.
YOU'VE BEEN WORKING HARD.
LOOK IN THE DRAWERS!

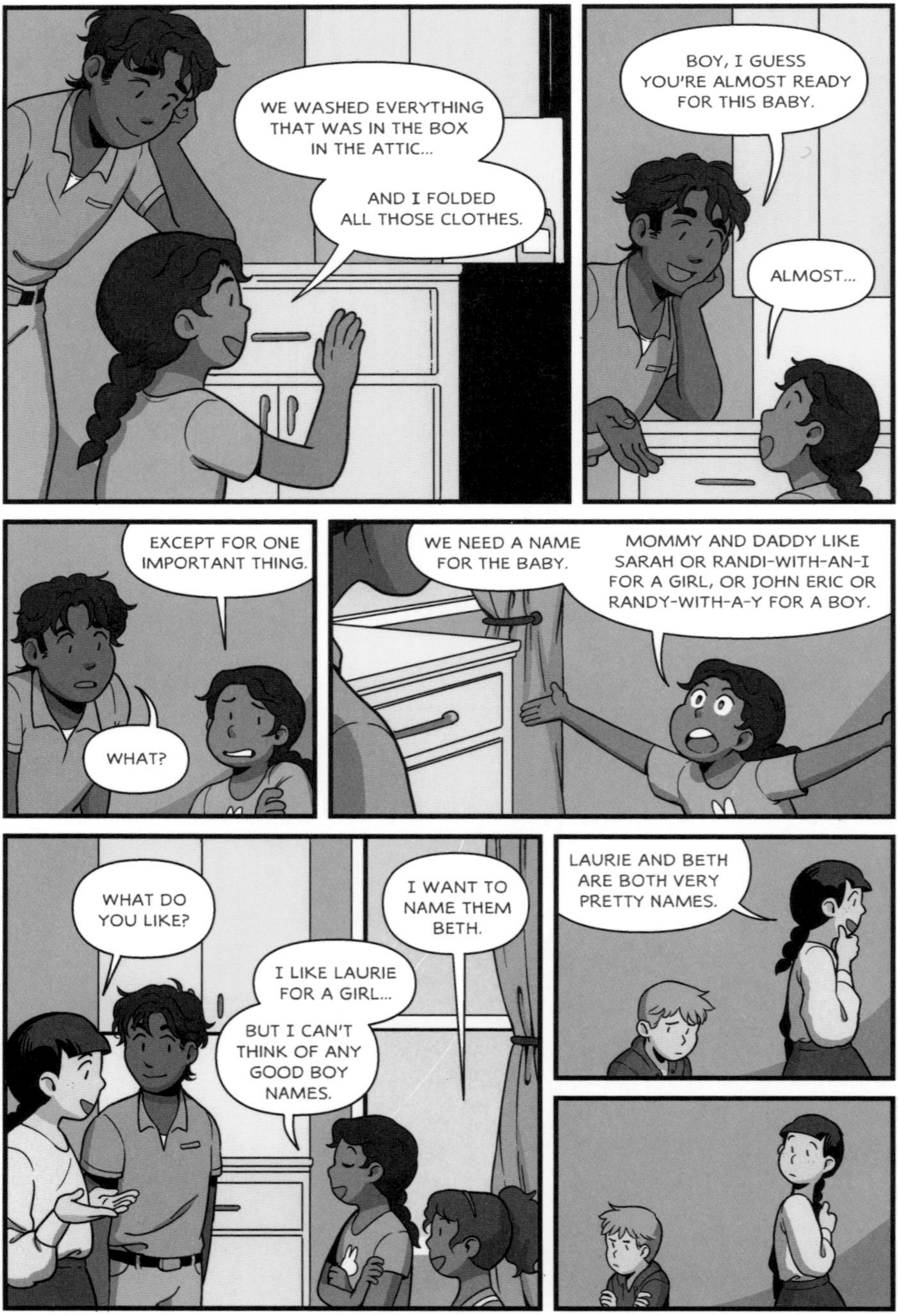
WE WASHED EVERYTHING THAT WAS IN THE BOX IN THE ATTIC...
AND I FOLDED ALL THOSE CLOTHES.
BOY, I GUESS YOU'RE ALMOST READY FOR THIS BABY.
ALMOST...
EXCEPT FOR ONE IMPORTANT THING.
WHAT?
WE NEED A NAME FOR THE BABY.
MOMMY AND DADDY LIKE SARAH OR RANDI-WITH-AN-I FOR A GIRL, OR JOHN ERIC OR RANDY-WITH-A-Y FOR A BOY.
WHAT DO YOU LIKE?
I LIKE LAURIE FOR A GIRL...
BUT I CAN'T THINK OF ANY GOOD BOY NAMES.
I WANT TO NAME THEM BETH.
LAURIE AND BETH ARE BOTH VERY PRETTY NAMES.

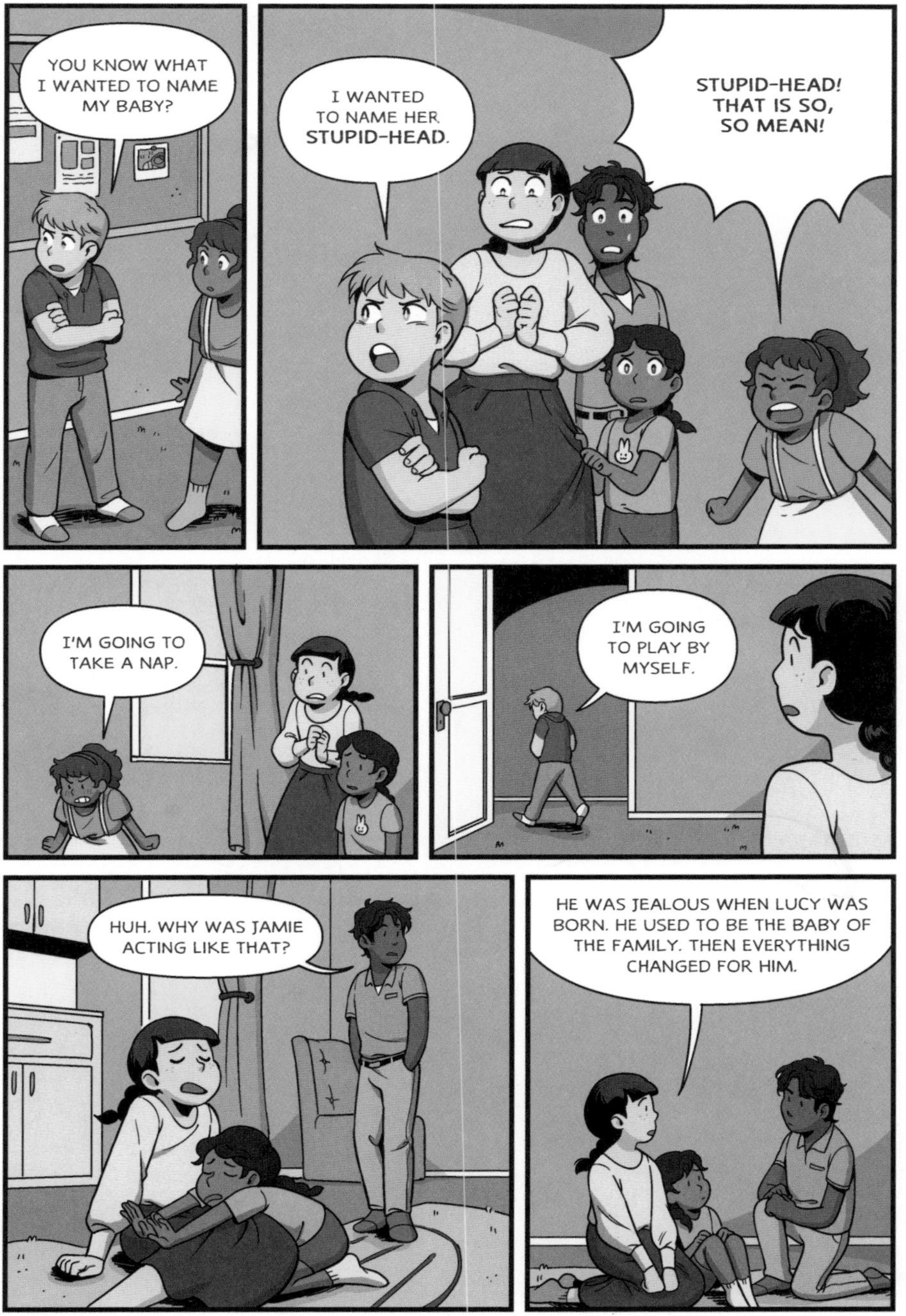
YOU KNOW WHAT I WANTED TO NAME MY BABY?
I WANTED TO NAME HER STUPID-HEAD.
STUPID-HEAD! THAT IS SO, SO MEAN!
I'M GOING TO TAKE A NAP.
I'M GOING TO PLAY BY MYSELF.
HUH. WHY WAS JAMIE ACTING LIKE THAT?
HE WAS JEALOUS WHEN LUCY WAS BORN. HE USED TO BE THE BABY OF THE FAMILY. THEN EVERYTHING CHANGED FOR HIM.

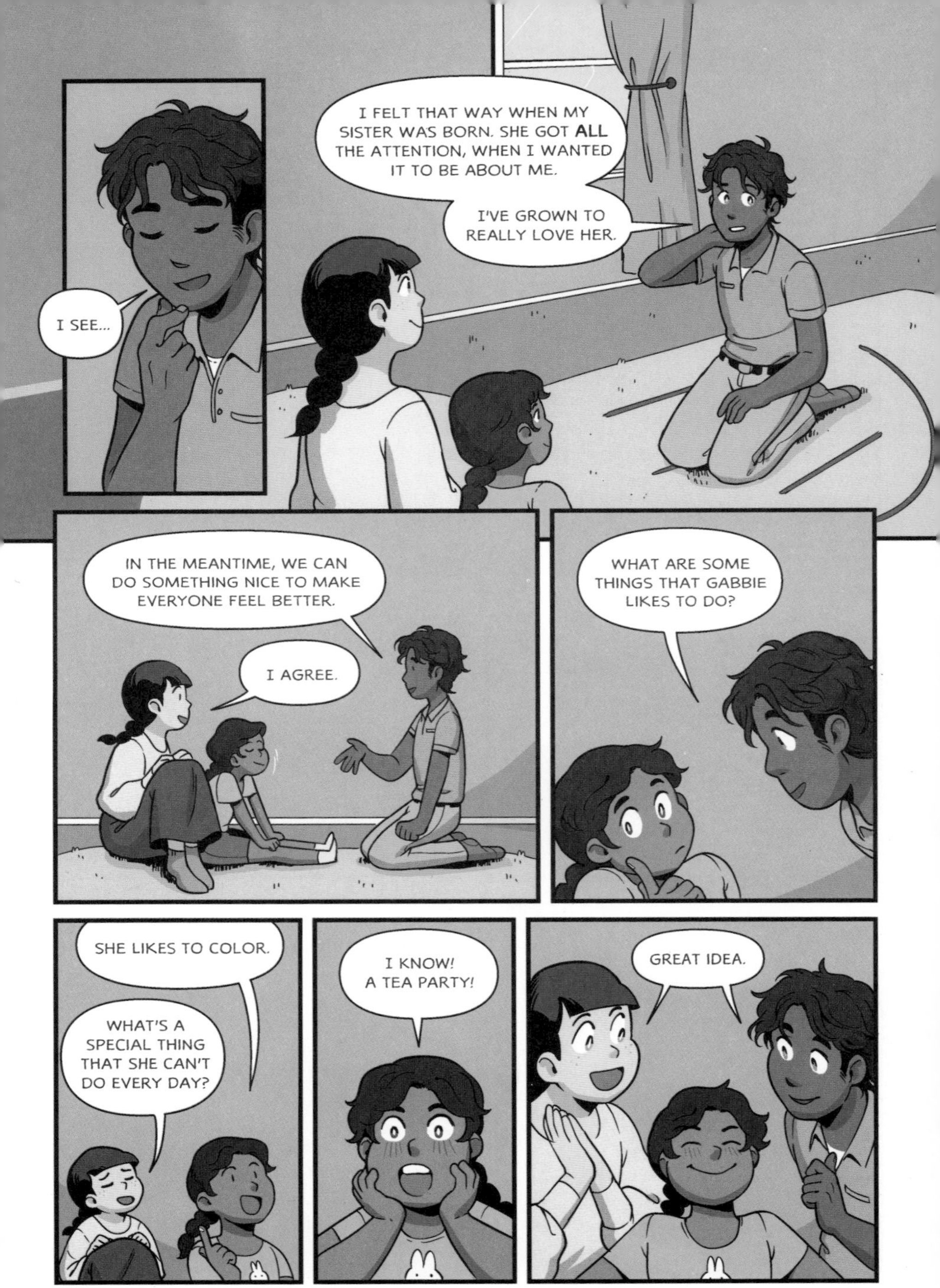
I FELT THAT WAY WHEN MY SISTER WAS BORN. SHE GOT **ALL** THE ATTENTION, WHEN I WANTED IT TO BE ABOUT ME.
I'VE GROWN TO REALLY LOVE HER.
I SEE...
IN THE MEANTIME, WE CAN DO SOMETHING NICE TO MAKE EVERYONE FEEL BETTER.
I AGREE.
WHAT ARE SOME THINGS THAT GABBIE LIKES TO DO?
SHE LIKES TO COLOR.
WHAT'S A SPECIAL THING THAT SHE CAN'T DO EVERY DAY?
I KNOW! A TEA PARTY!
GREAT IDEA.

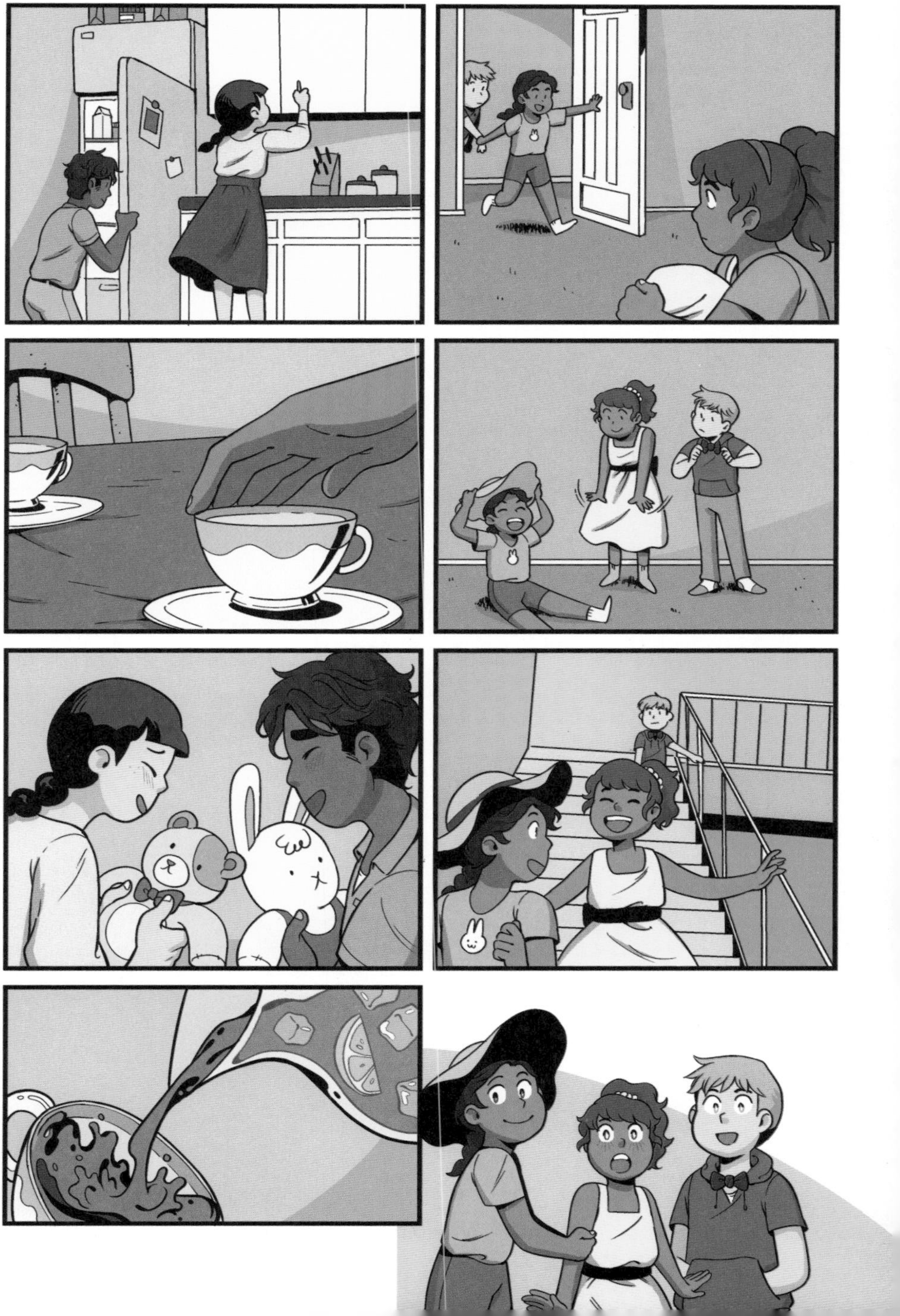

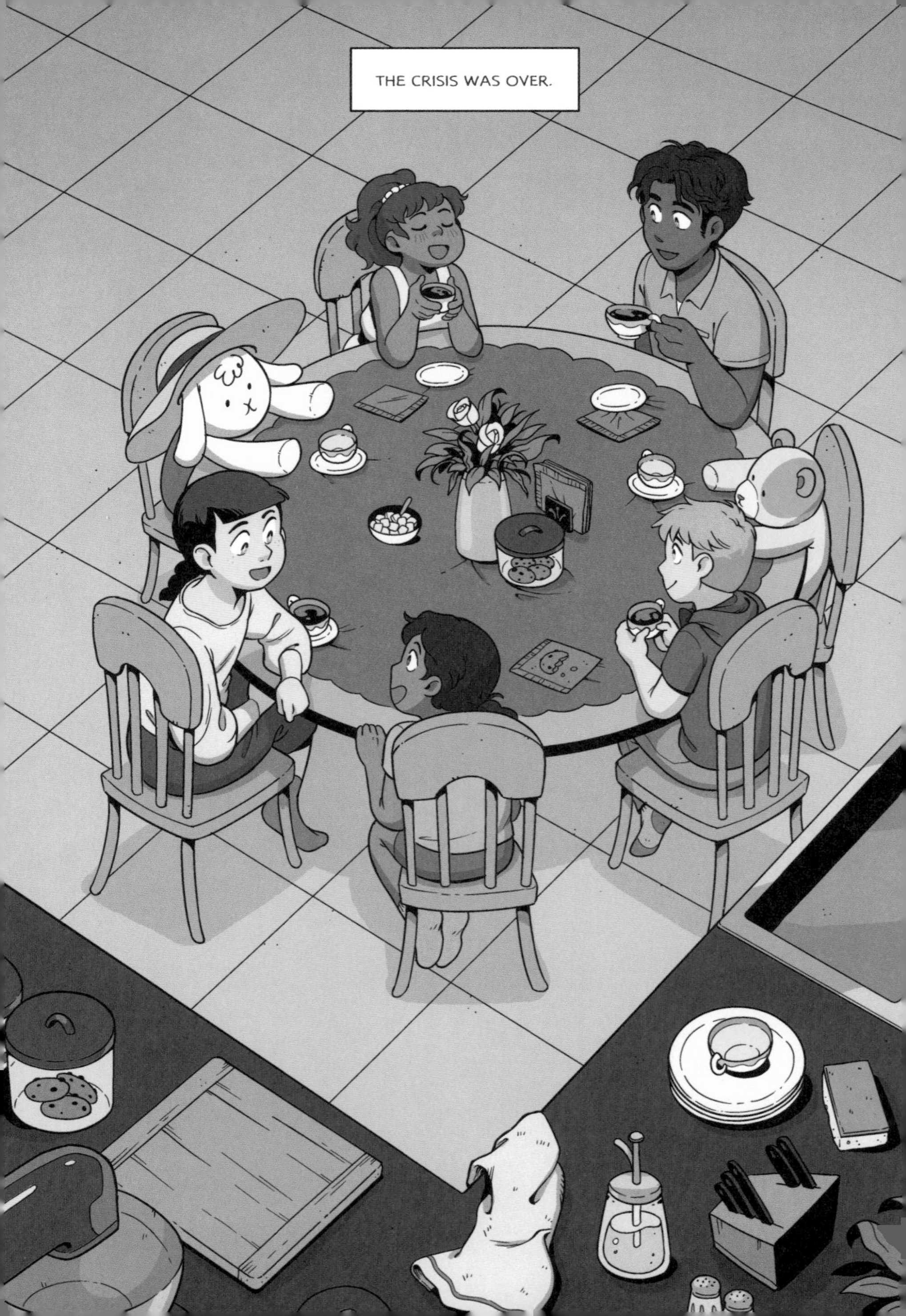
THE CRISIS WAS OVER.

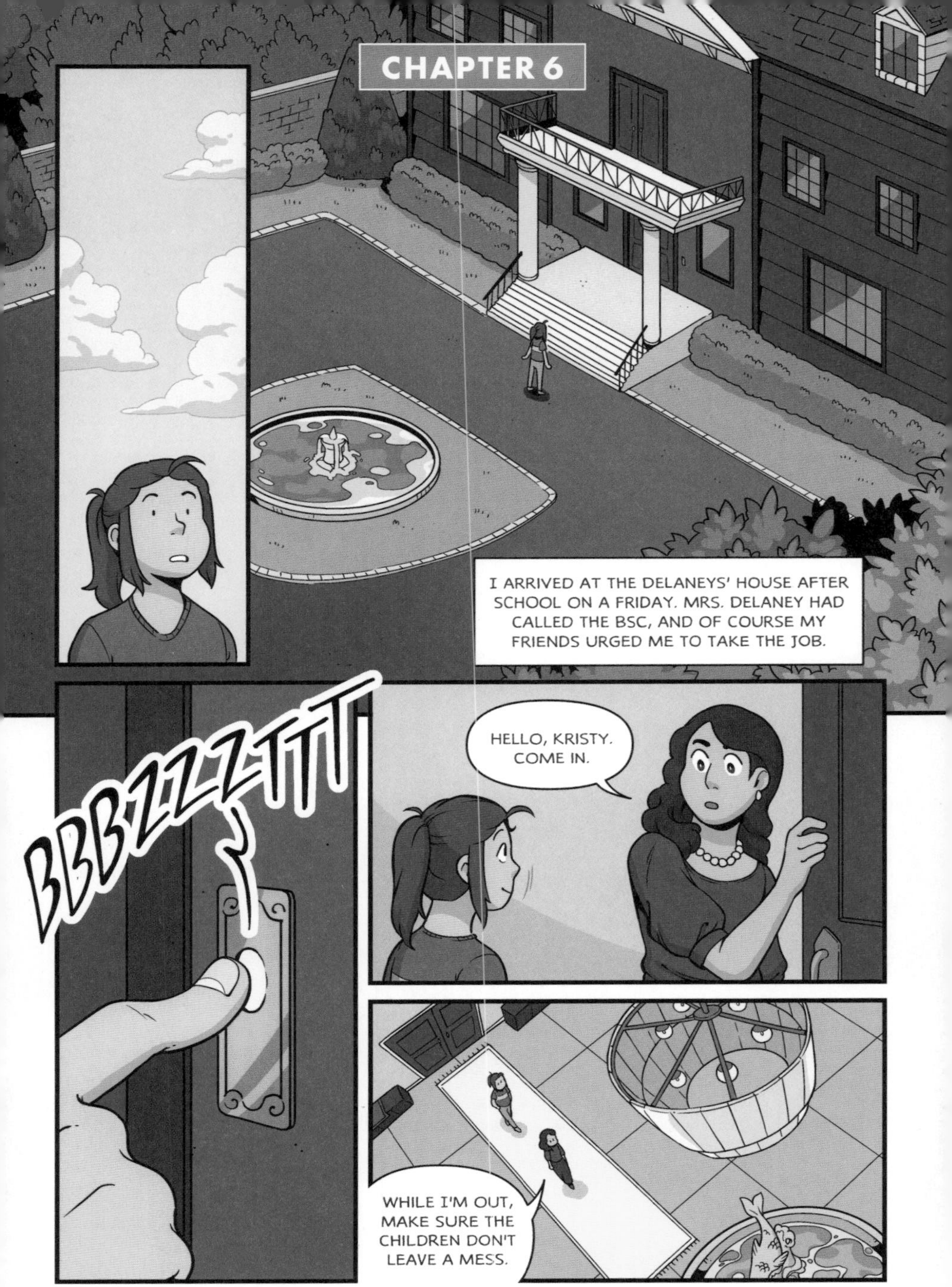
CHAPTER 6
I ARRIVED AT THE DELANEYS' HOUSE AFTER SCHOOL ON A FRIDAY. MRS. DELANEY HAD CALLED THE BSC, AND OF COURSE MY FRIENDS URGED ME TO TAKE THE JOB.
BBBZZZZTTT
HELLO, KRISTY. COME IN.
WHILE I'M OUT, MAKE SURE THE CHILDREN DON'T LEAVE A MESS.

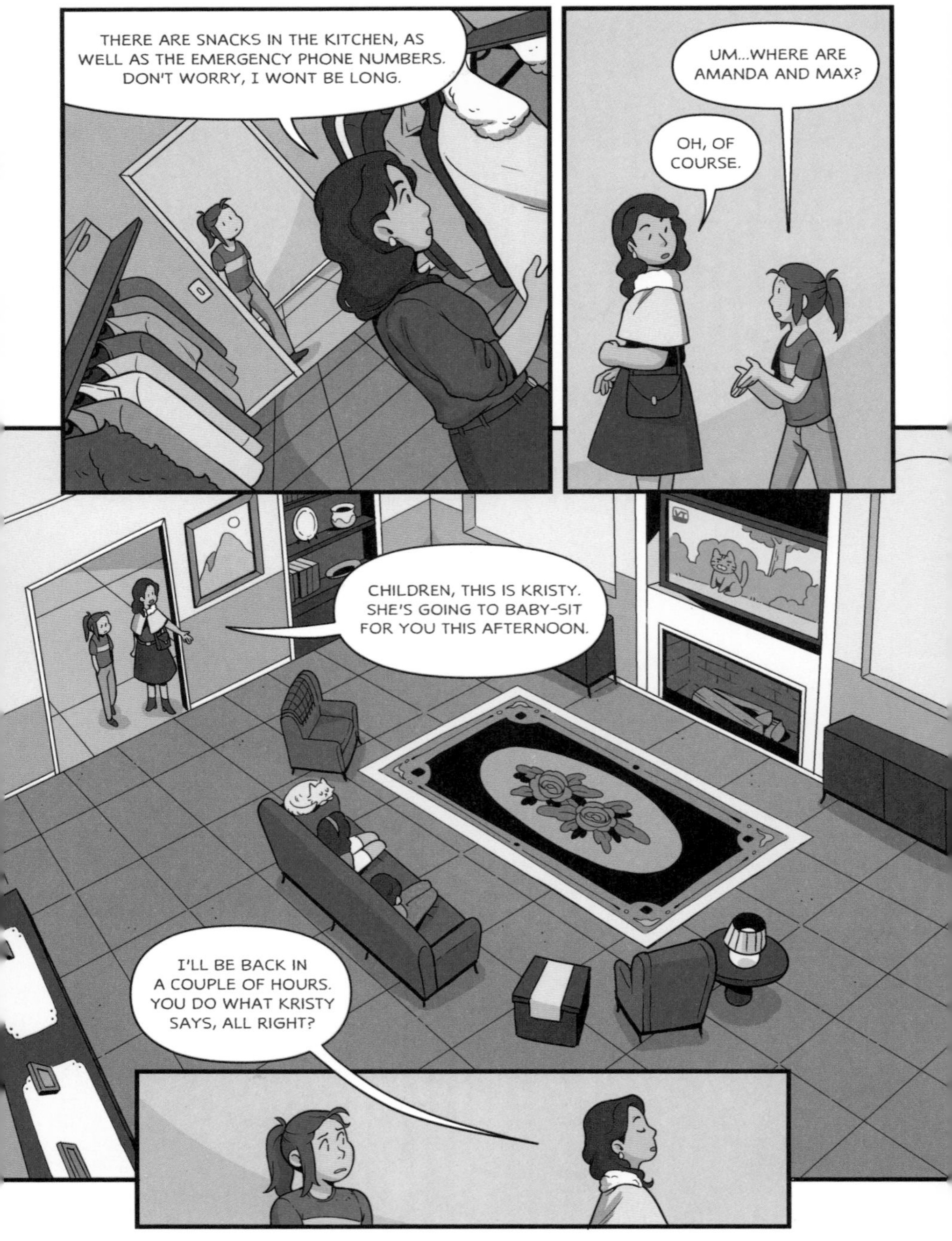
THERE ARE SNACKS IN THE KITCHEN, AS WELL AS THE EMERGENCY PHONE NUMBERS. DON'T WORRY, I WONT BE LONG.
UM...WHERE ARE AMANDA AND MAX?
OH, OF COURSE.
CHILDREN, THIS IS KRISTY. SHE'S GOING TO BABY-SIT FOR YOU THIS AFTERNOON.
I'LL BE BACK IN A COUPLE OF HOURS. YOU DO WHAT KRISTY SAYS, ALL RIGHT?

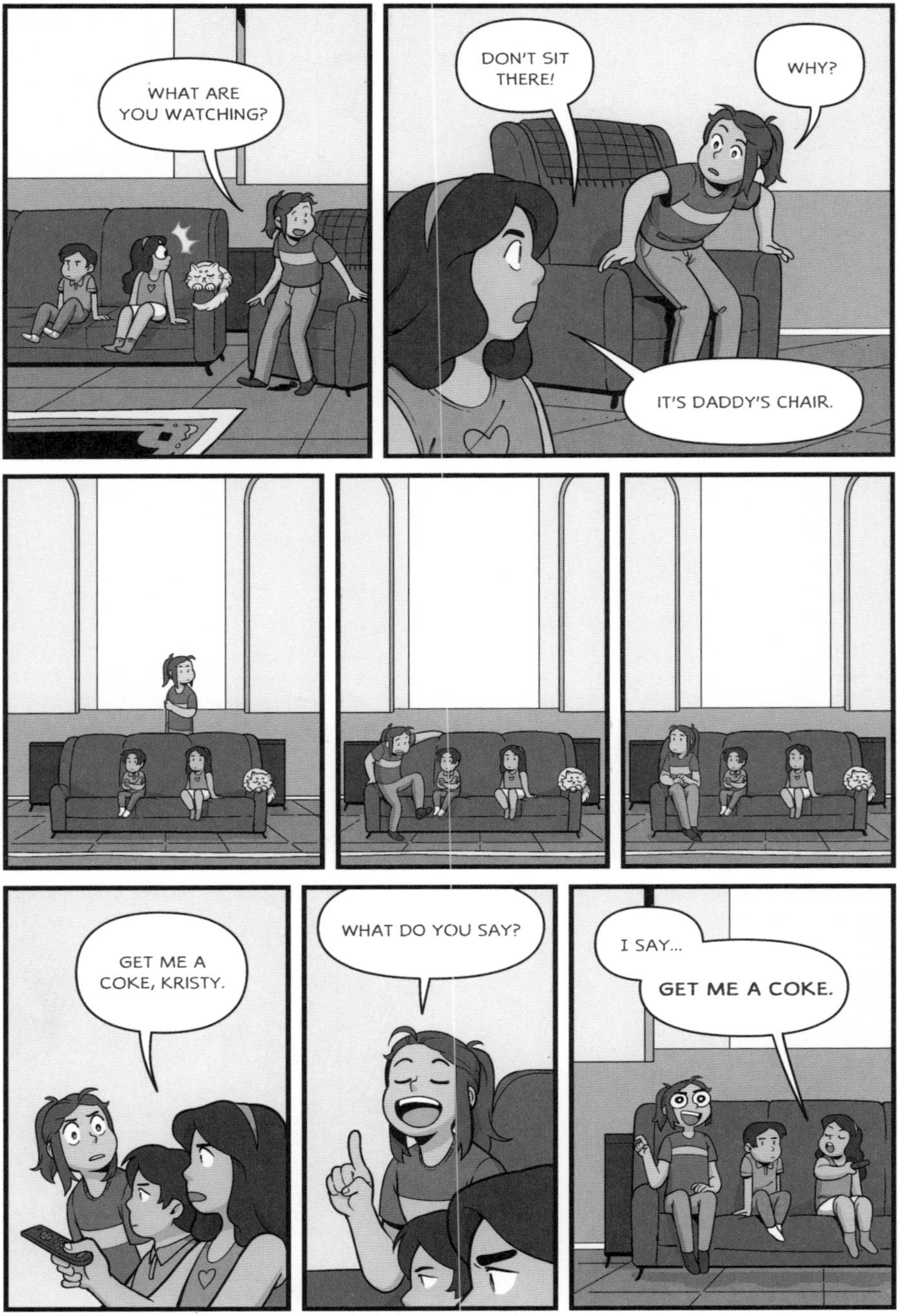
WHAT ARE YOU WATCHING?
DON'T SIT THERE!
WHY?
IT'S DADDY'S CHAIR.
GET ME A COKE, KRISTY.
WHAT DO YOU SAY?
I SAY...
GET ME A COKE.

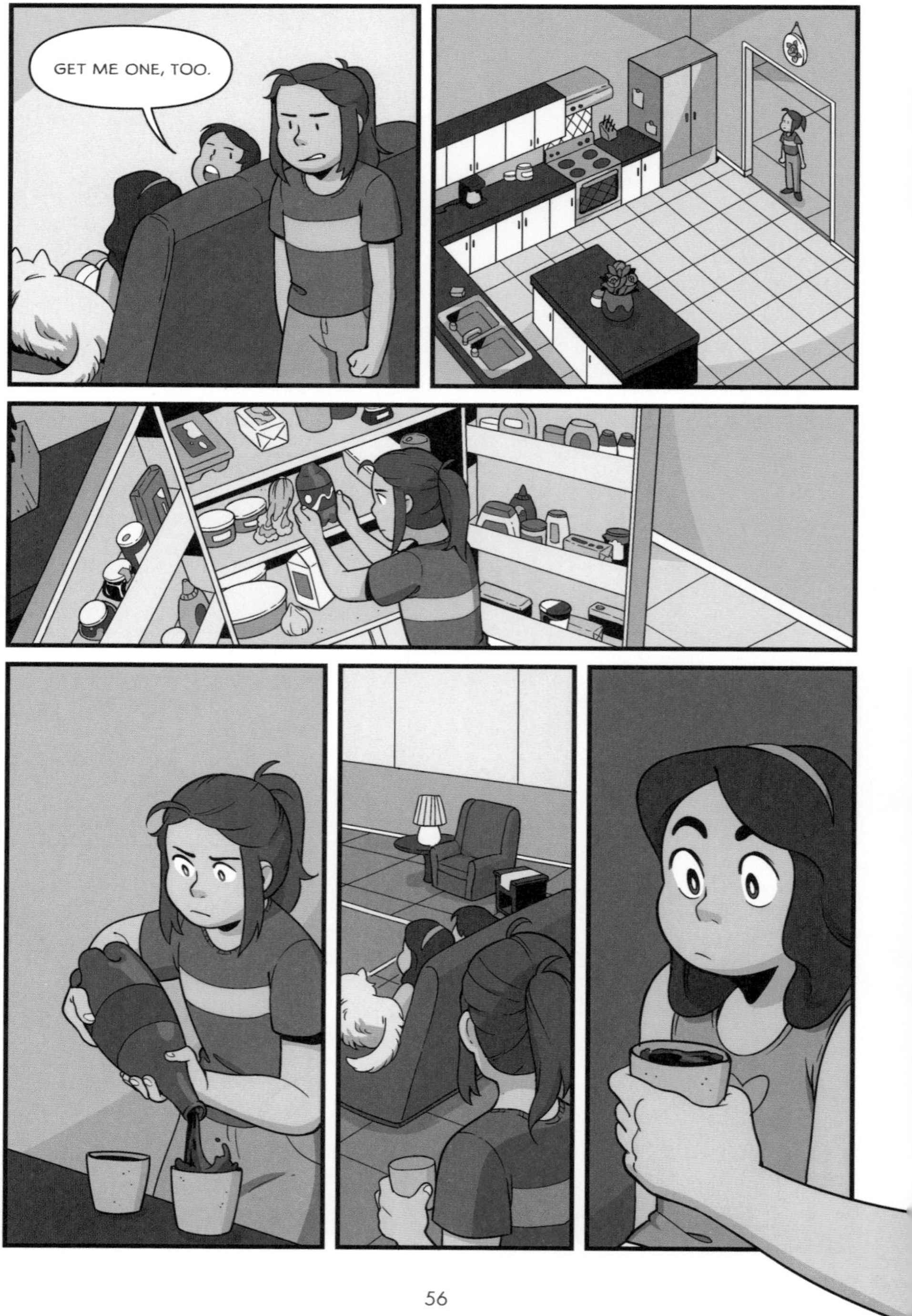
GET ME ONE, TOO.

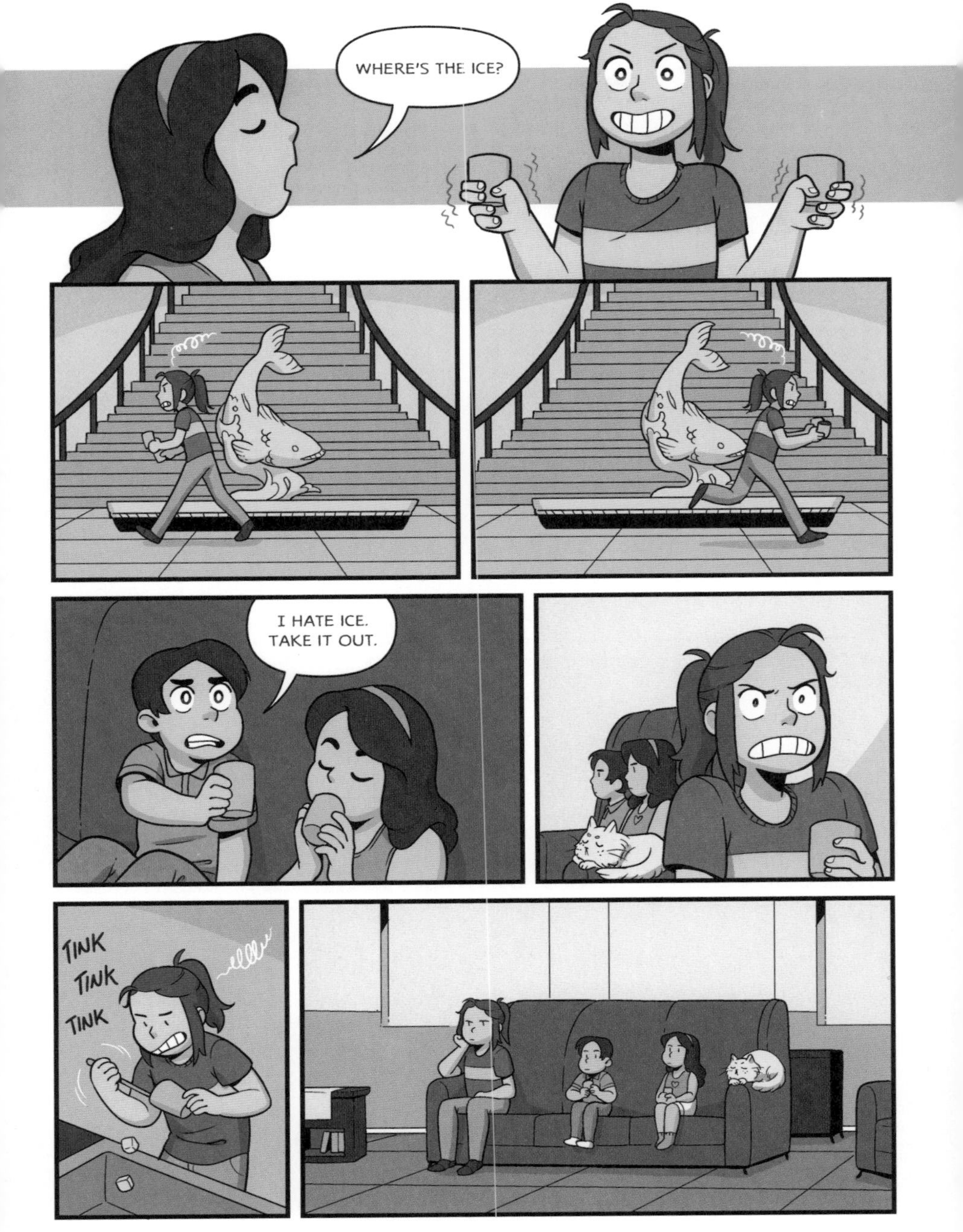
WHERE'S THE ICE?
I HATE ICE. TAKE IT OUT.
TINK TINK TINK

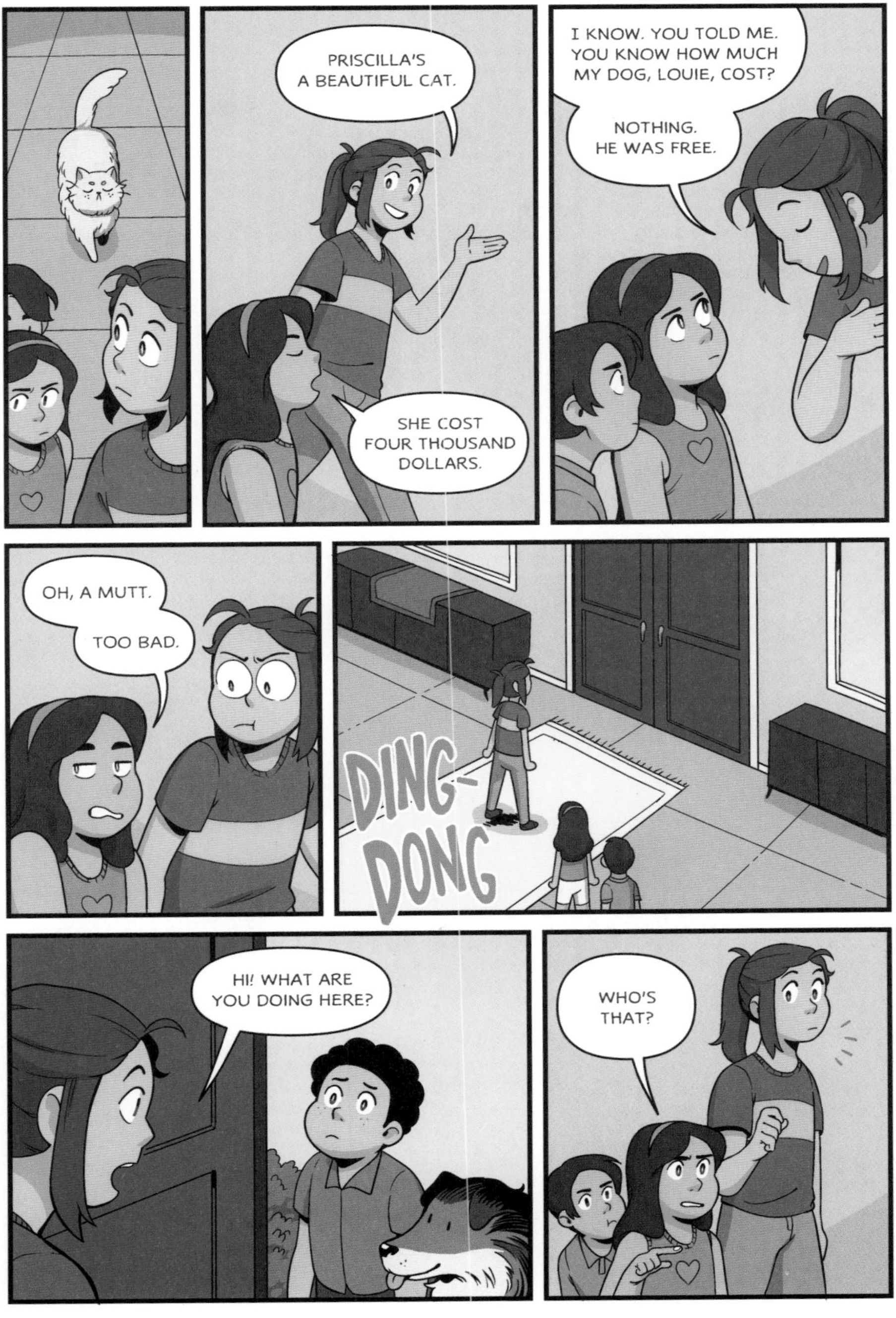
PRISCILLA'S A BEAUTIFUL CAT.
SHE COST FOUR THOUSAND DOLLARS.
I KNOW. YOU TOLD ME. YOU KNOW HOW MUCH MY DOG, LOUIE, COST?
NOTHING. HE WAS FREE.
OH, A MUTT.
TOO BAD.
DING-DONG
HI! WHAT ARE YOU DOING HERE?
WHO'S THAT?

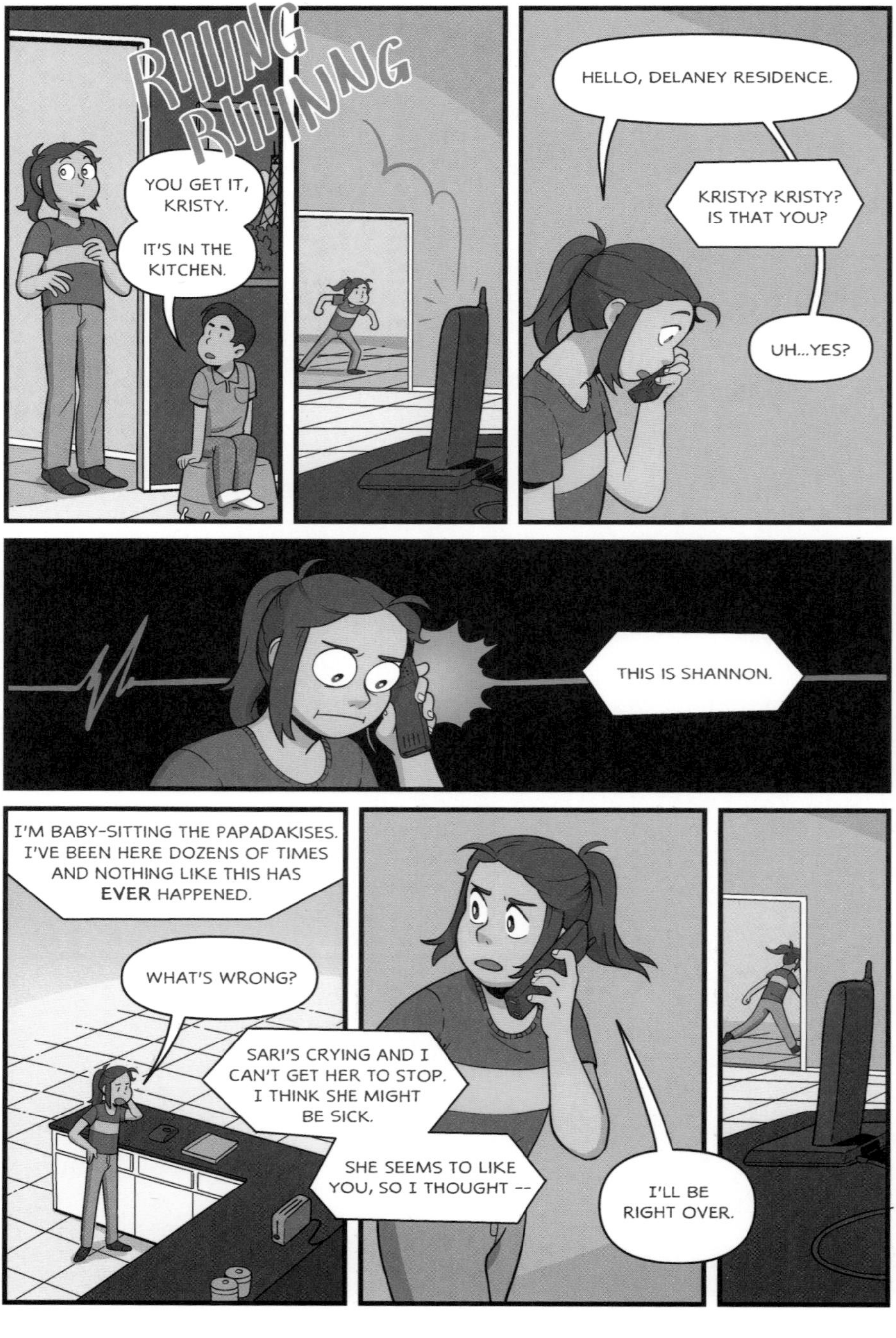
RIIIING
BRIIINNG
YOU GET IT, KRISTY.
IT'S IN THE KITCHEN.
HELLO, DELANEY RESIDENCE.
KRISTY? KRISTY? IS THAT YOU?
UH...YES?
THIS IS SHANNON.
I'M BABY-SITTING THE PAPADAKISES. I'VE BEEN HERE DOZENS OF TIMES AND NOTHING LIKE THIS HAS **EVER** HAPPENED.
WHAT'S WRONG?
SARI'S CRYING AND I CAN'T GET HER TO STOP. I THINK SHE MIGHT BE SICK.
SHE SEEMS TO LIKE YOU, SO I THOUGHT --
I'LL BE RIGHT OVER.

AMANDA, MAX, COME ON. WE HAVE TO GO TO THE PAPADAKISES'.
NOW.
URGHHHHH
UURRGGHHHHHHHH
DING-DONG
YES?
HERE I AM. WHERE'S SARI?

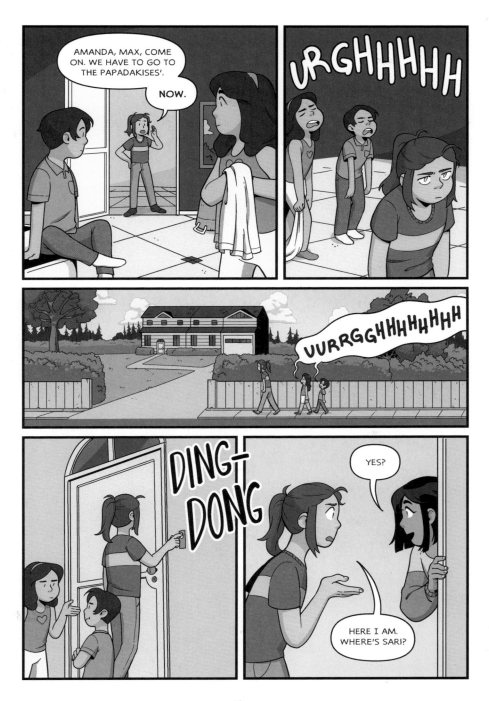

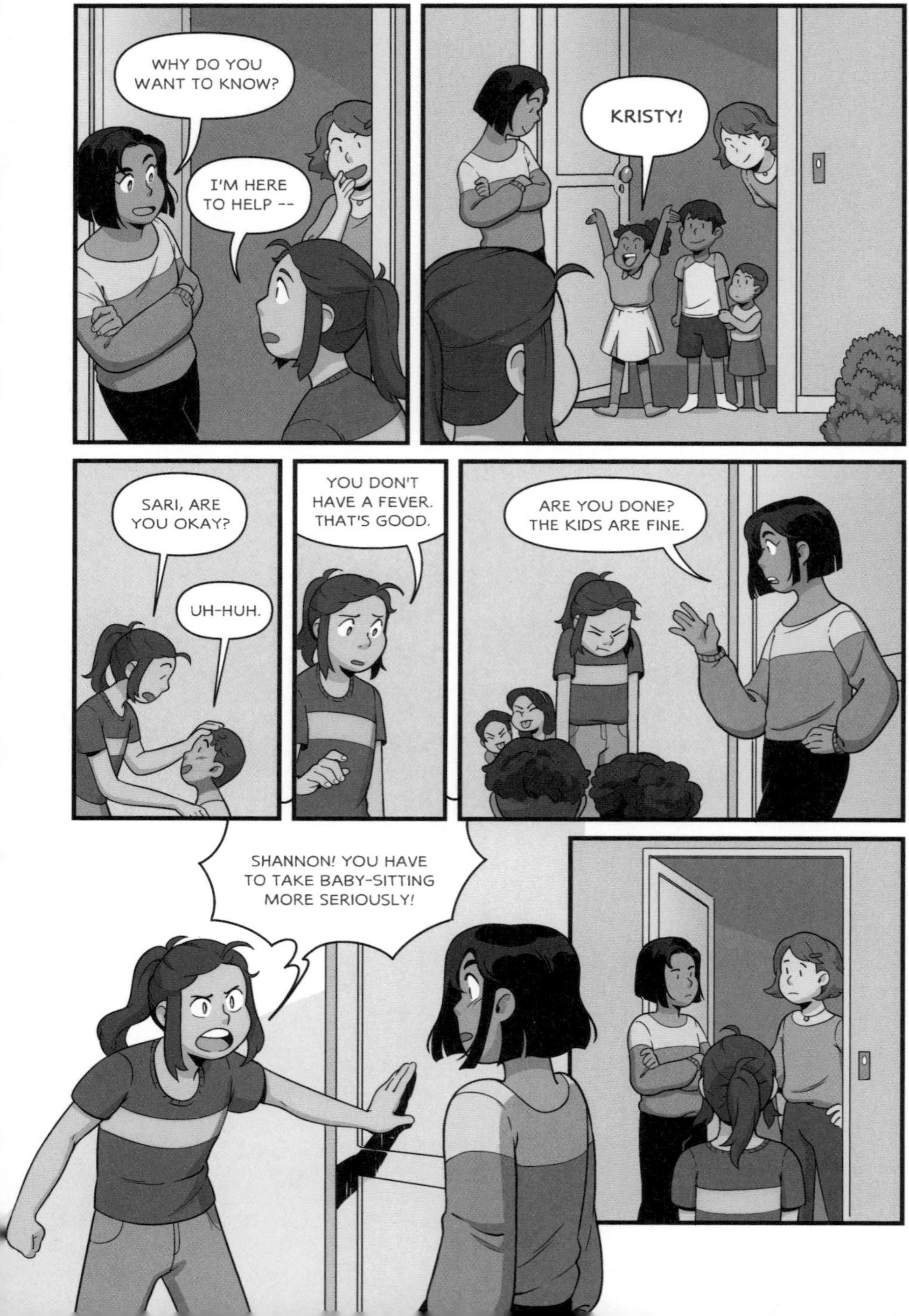
WHY DO YOU WANT TO KNOW?
I'M HERE TO HELP --
KRISTY!
SARI, ARE YOU OKAY?
UH-HUH.
YOU DON'T HAVE A FEVER. THAT'S GOOD.
ARE YOU DONE? THE KIDS ARE FINE.
SHANNON! YOU HAVE TO TAKE BABY-SITTING MORE SERIOUSLY!

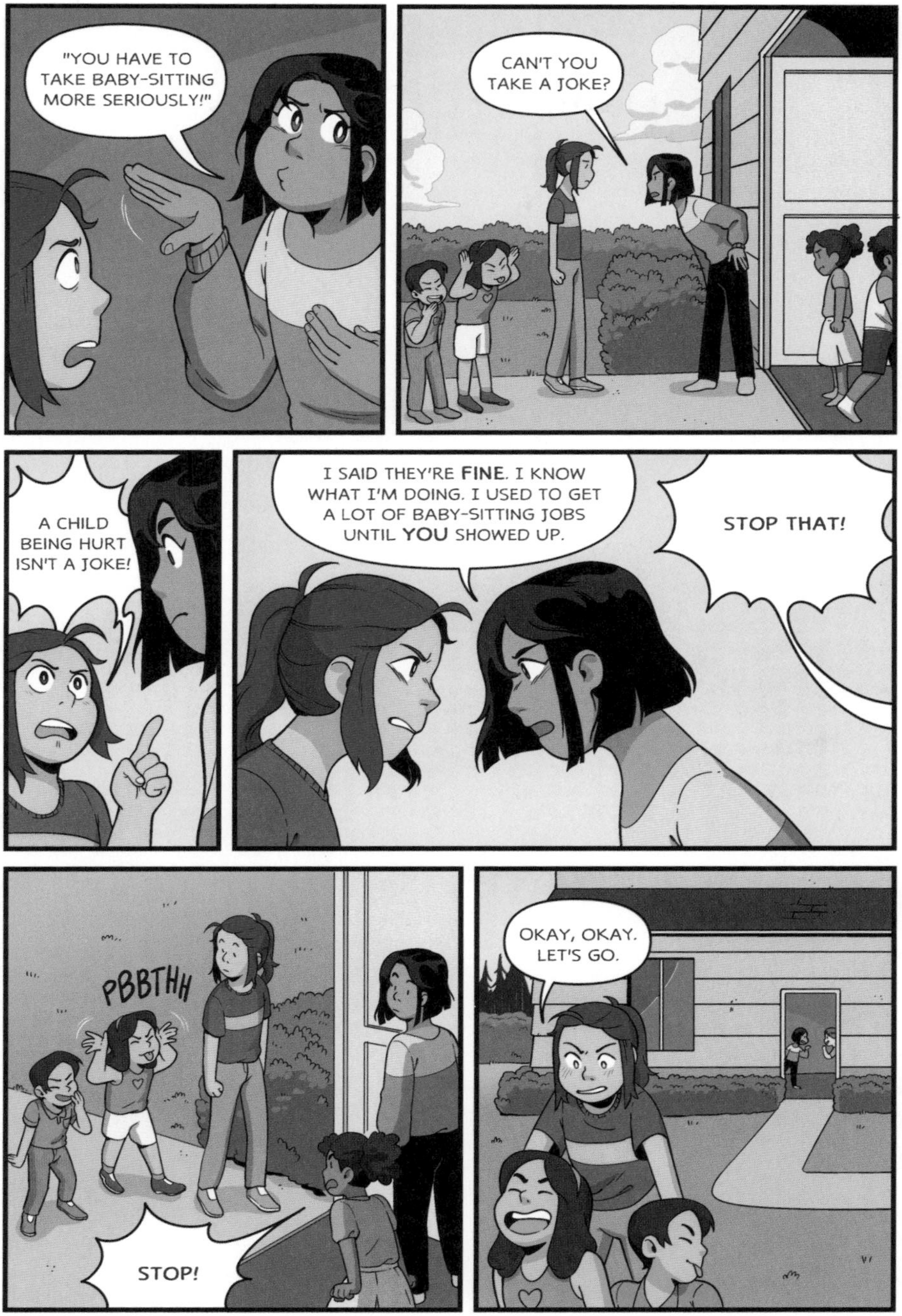
"YOU HAVE TO TAKE BABY-SITTING MORE SERIOUSLY!"
CAN'T YOU TAKE A JOKE?
A CHILD BEING HURT ISN'T A JOKE!
I SAID THEY'RE **FINE**. I KNOW WHAT I'M DOING. I USED TO GET A LOT OF BABY-SITTING JOBS UNTIL **YOU** SHOWED UP.
STOP THAT!
PBBTHH
STOP!
OKAY, OKAY. LET'S GO.

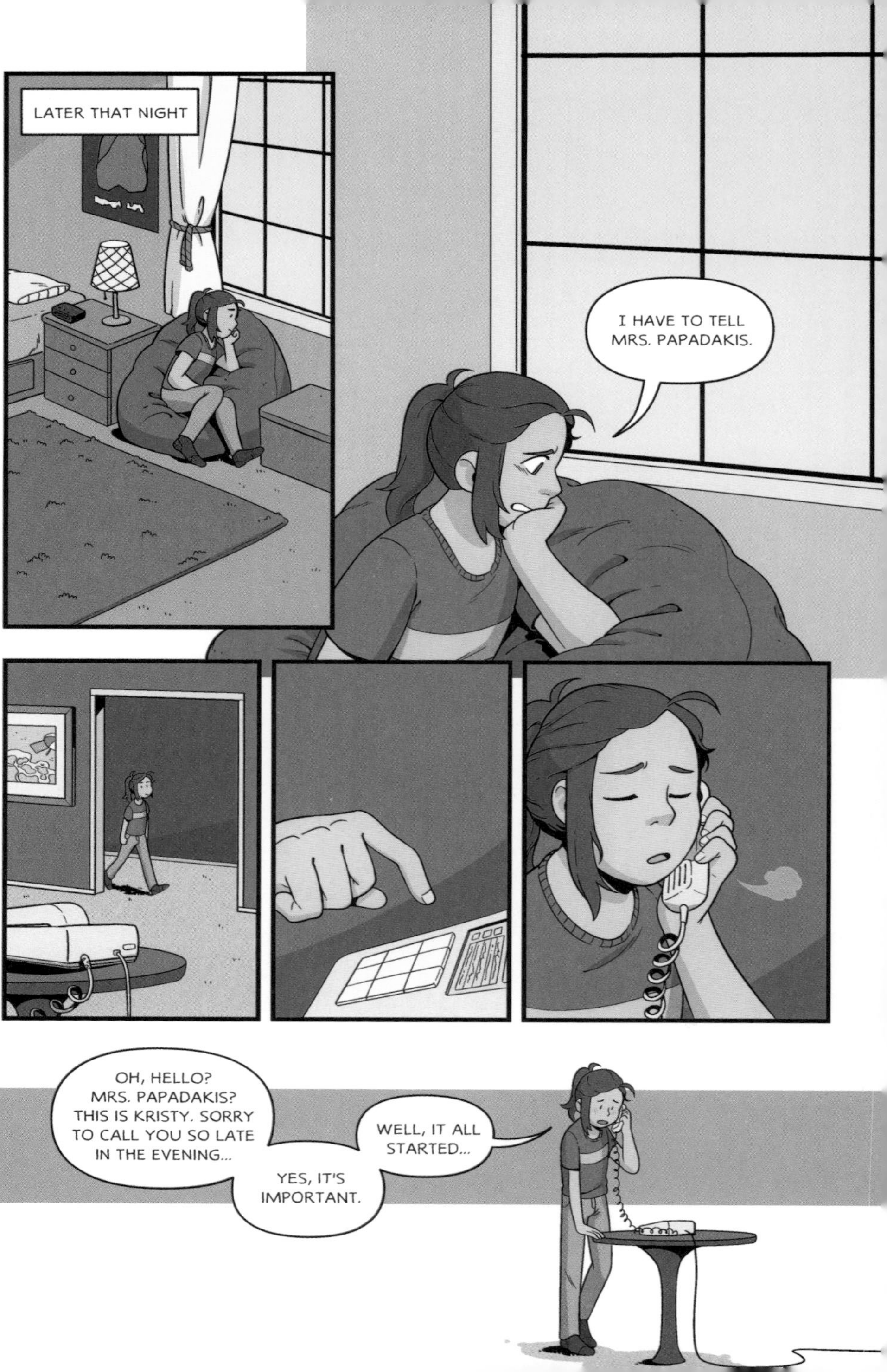
LATER THAT NIGHT
I HAVE TO TELL MRS. PAPADAKIS.
OH, HELLO? MRS. PAPADAKIS? THIS IS KRISTY. SORRY TO CALL YOU SO LATE IN THE EVENING...
YES, IT'S IMPORTANT.
WELL, IT ALL STARTED...

CHAPTER 7

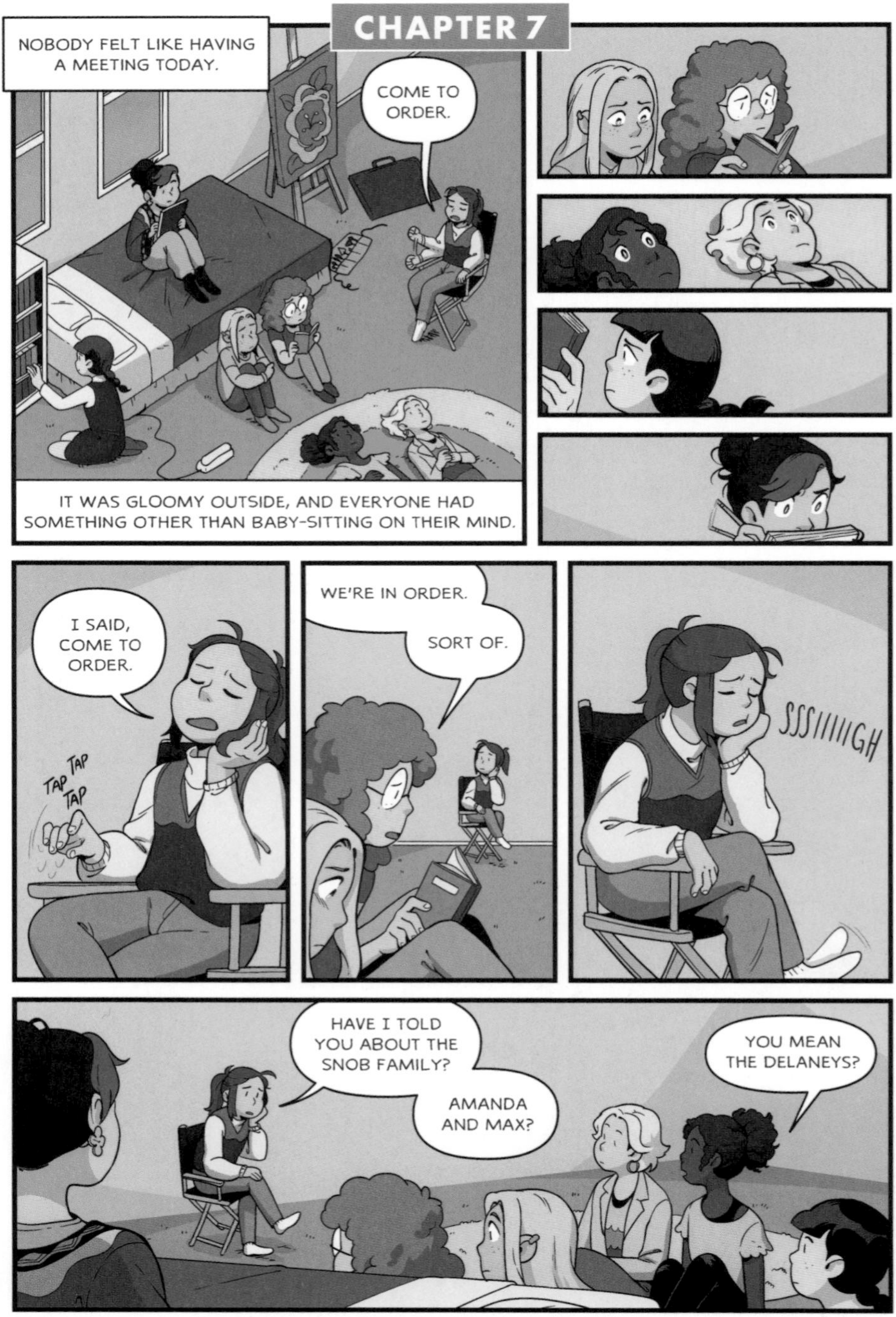

NOBODY FELT LIKE HAVING A MEETING TODAY.
COME TO ORDER.
IT WAS GLOOMY OUTSIDE, AND EVERYONE HAD SOMETHING OTHER THAN BABY-SITTING ON THEIR MIND.
I SAID, COME TO ORDER.
TAP TAP TAP
WE'RE IN ORDER.
SORT OF.
SSSIIIIIGH
HAVE I TOLD YOU ABOUT THE SNOB FAMILY?
AMANDA AND MAX?
YOU MEAN THE DELANEYS?

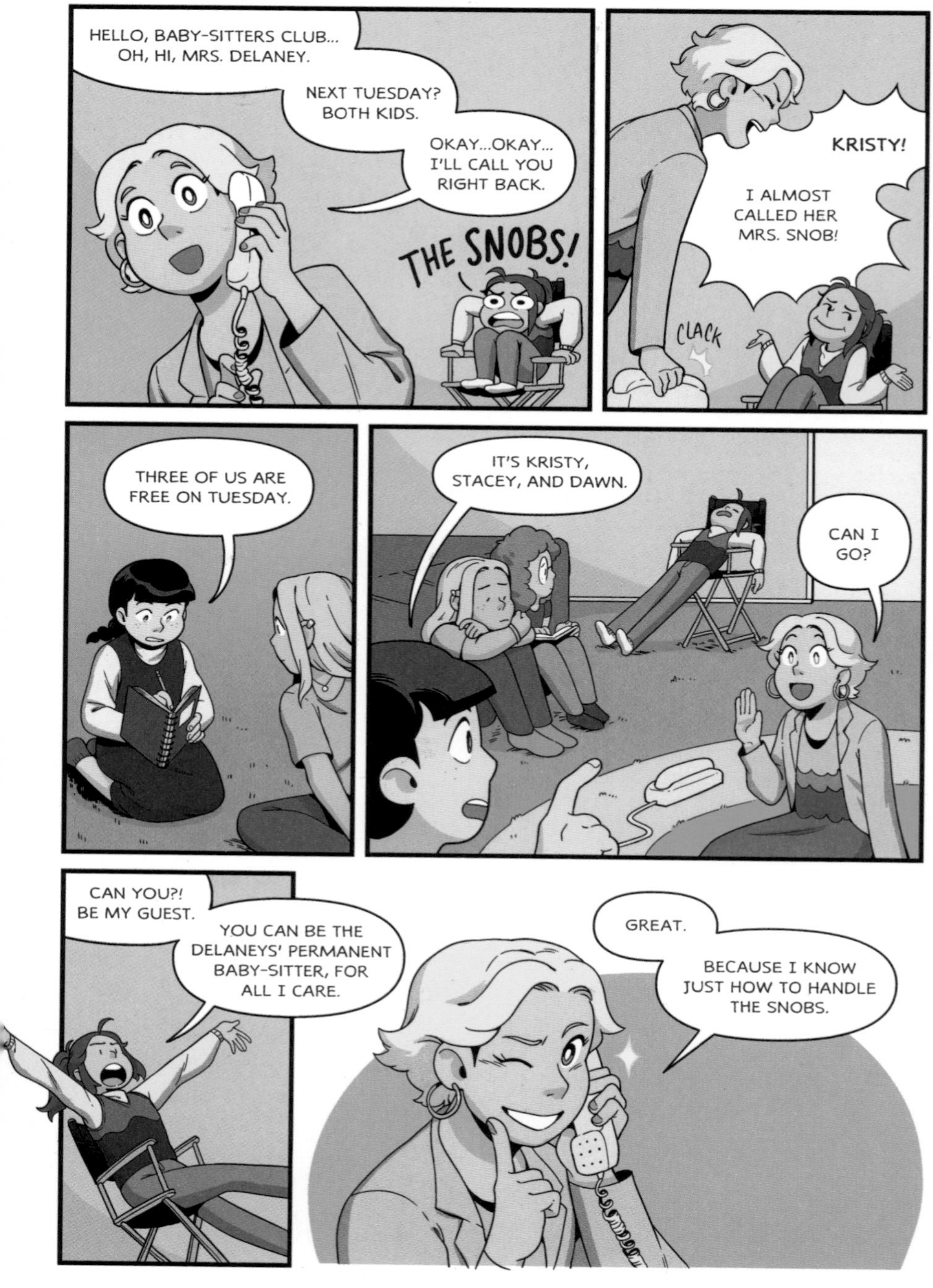
HELLO, BABY-SITTERS CLUB... OH, HI, MRS. DELANEY.
NEXT TUESDAY? BOTH KIDS.
OKAY...OKAY... I'LL CALL YOU RIGHT BACK.
THE SNOBS!
KRISTY!
I ALMOST CALLED HER MRS. SNOB!
CLACK
THREE OF US ARE FREE ON TUESDAY.
IT'S KRISTY, STACEY, AND DAWN.
CAN I GO?
CAN YOU?! BE MY GUEST.
YOU CAN BE THE DELANEYS' PERMANENT BABY-SITTER, FOR ALL I CARE.
GREAT.
BECAUSE I KNOW JUST HOW TO HANDLE THE SNOBS.

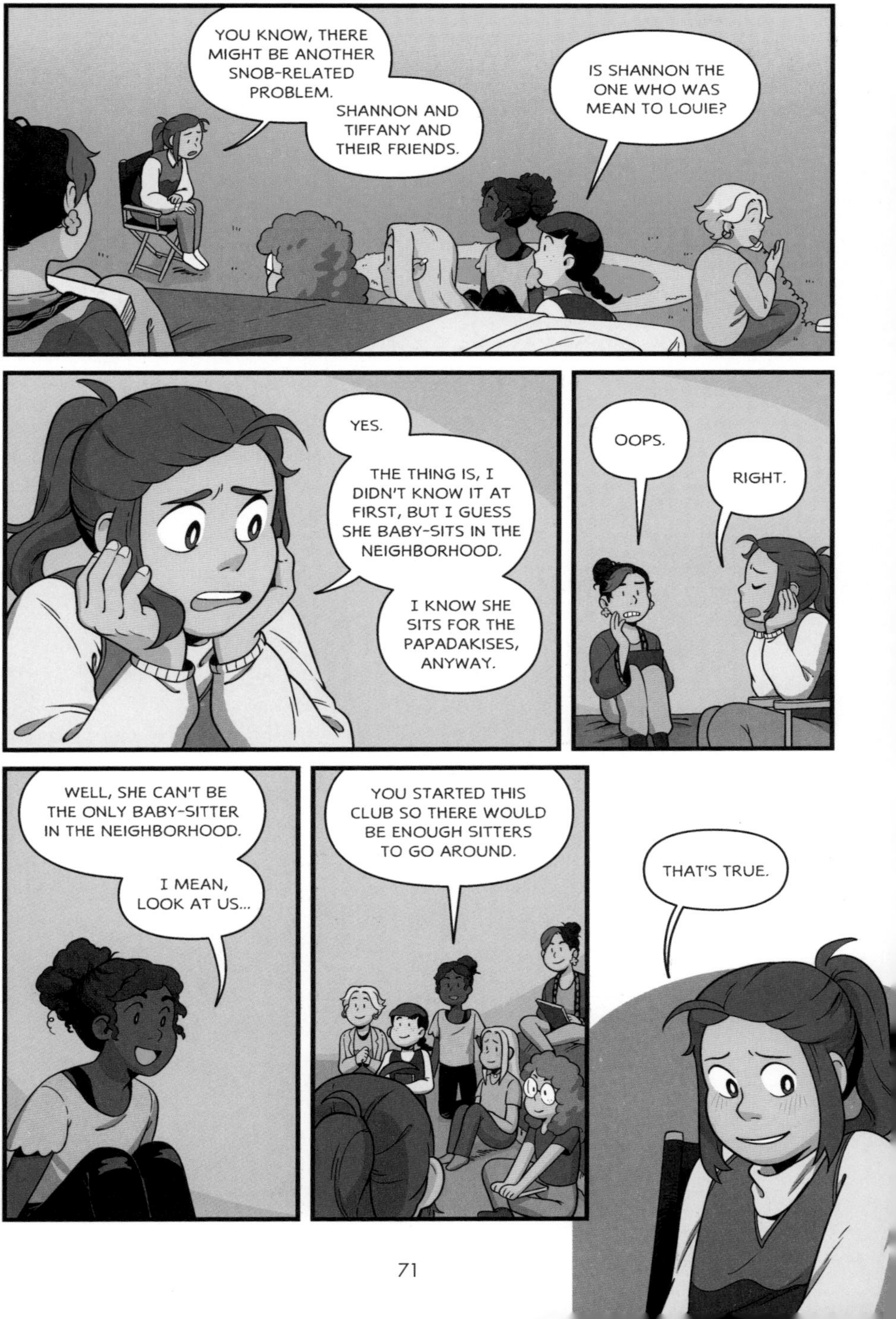
YOU KNOW, THERE MIGHT BE ANOTHER SNOB-RELATED PROBLEM.
SHANNON AND TIFFANY AND THEIR FRIENDS.
IS SHANNON THE ONE WHO WAS MEAN TO LOUIE?
YES.
THE THING IS, I DIDN'T KNOW IT AT FIRST, BUT I GUESS SHE BABY-SITS IN THE NEIGHBORHOOD.
I KNOW SHE SITS FOR THE PAPADAKISES, ANYWAY.
OOPS.
RIGHT.
WELL, SHE CAN'T BE THE ONLY BABY-SITTER IN THE NEIGHBORHOOD.
I MEAN, LOOK AT US...
YOU STARTED THIS CLUB SO THERE WOULD BE ENOUGH SITTERS TO GO AROUND.
THAT'S TRUE.

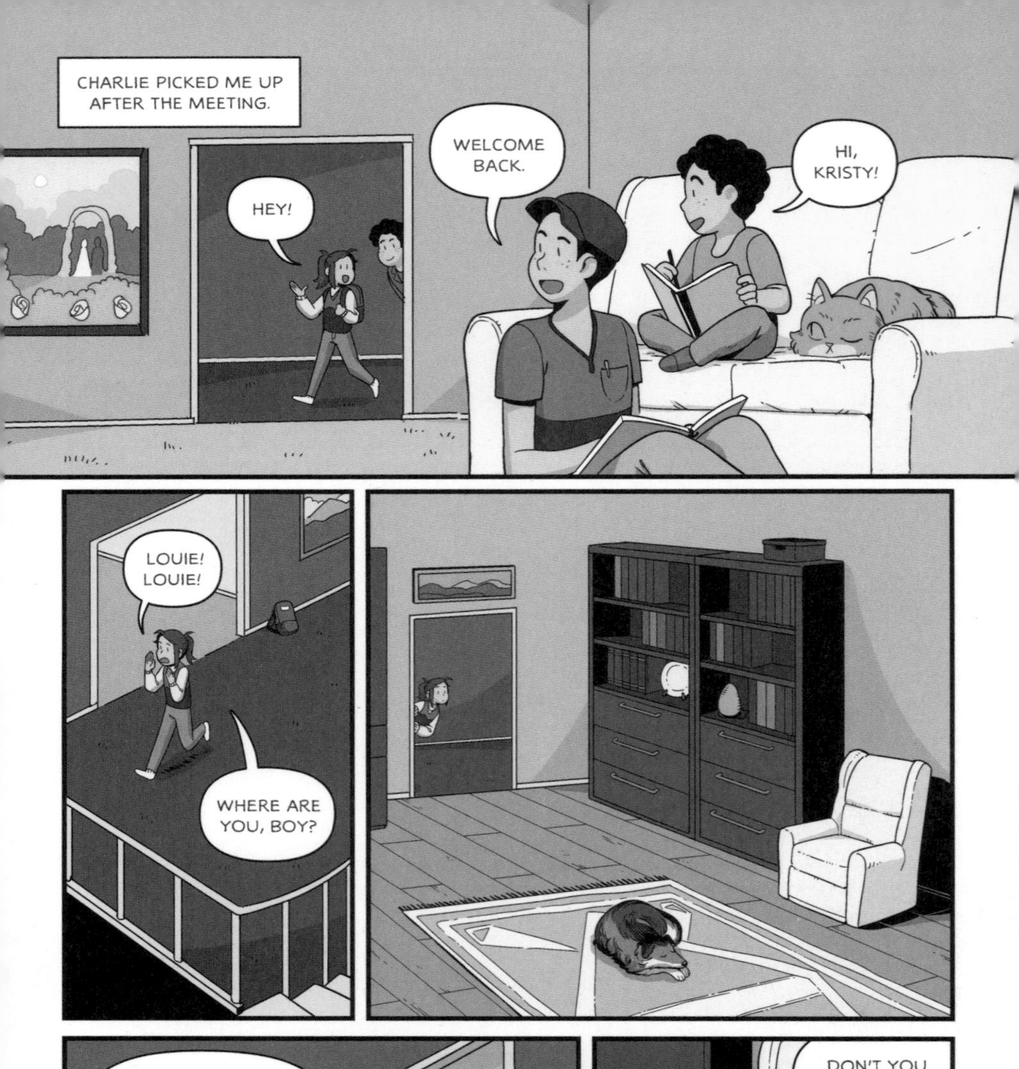
CHARLIE PICKED ME UP AFTER THE MEETING.
HEY!
WELCOME BACK.
HI, KRISTY!
LOUIE! LOUIE!
WHERE ARE YOU, BOY?
HEY, DAVID MICHAEL! DID YOU FEED LOUIE?
I PUT HIS FOOD OUT AND CALLED HIM, BUT HE WOULDN'T COME.
DON'T YOU WANT DINNER?

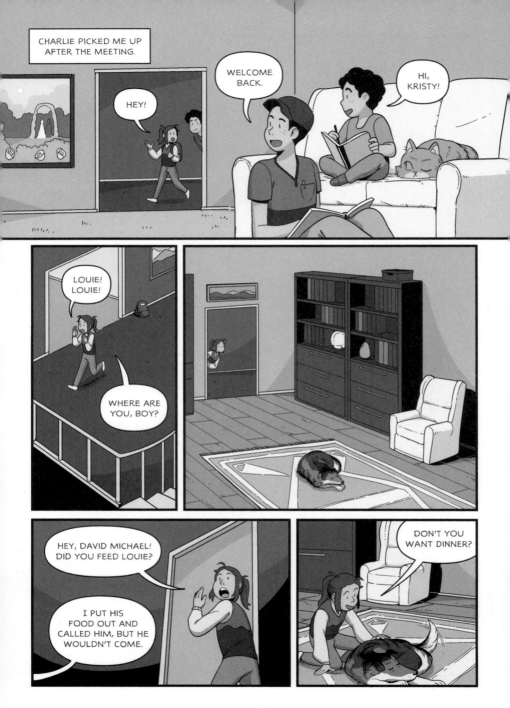

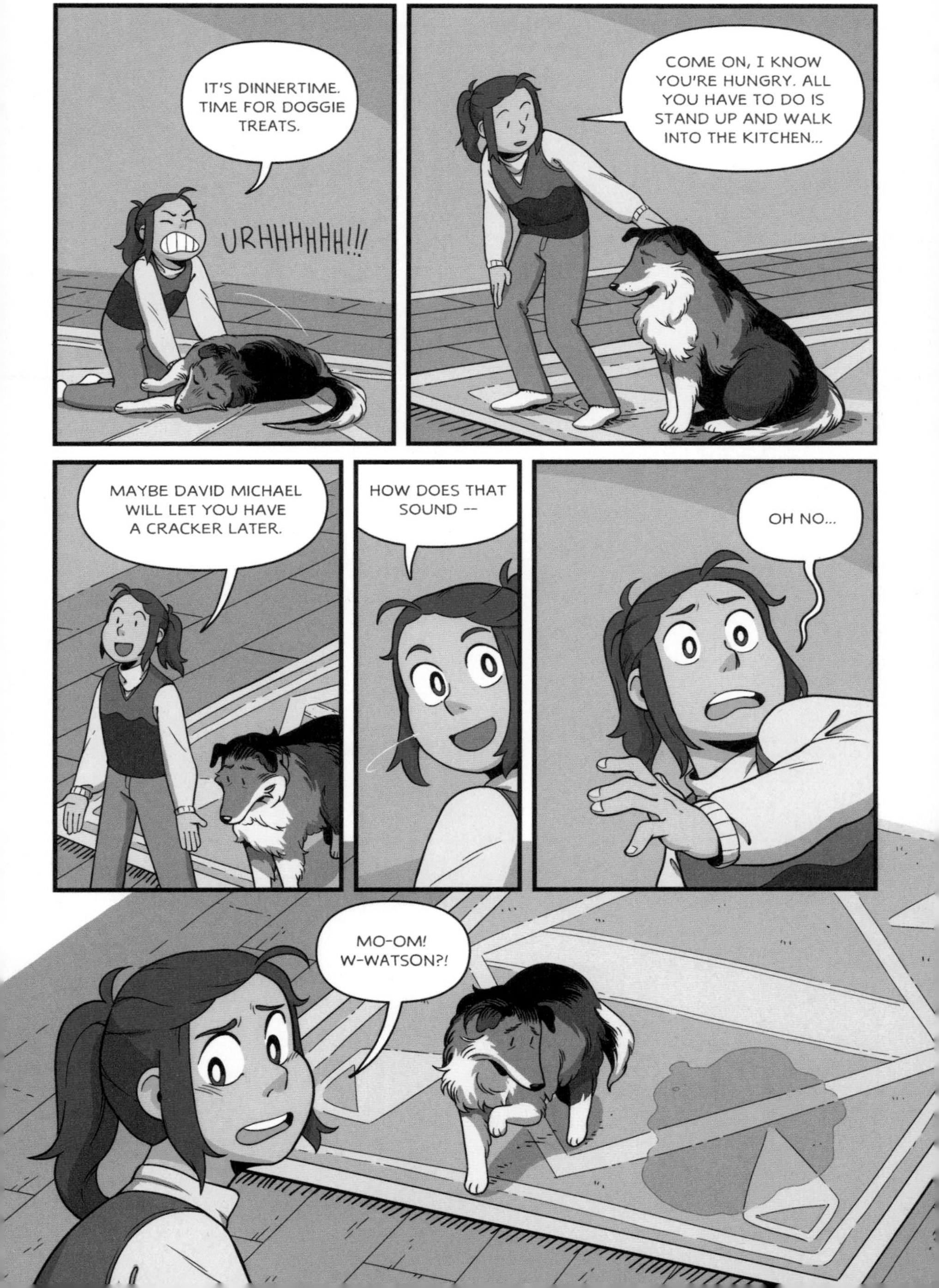
IT'S DINNERTIME. TIME FOR DOGGIE TREATS.
URHHHHHH!!!
COME ON, I KNOW YOU'RE HUNGRY. ALL YOU HAVE TO DO IS STAND UP AND WALK INTO THE KITCHEN...
MAYBE DAVID MICHAEL WILL LET YOU HAVE A CRACKER LATER.
HOW DOES THAT SOUND --
OH NO...
MO-OM! W-WATSON?!

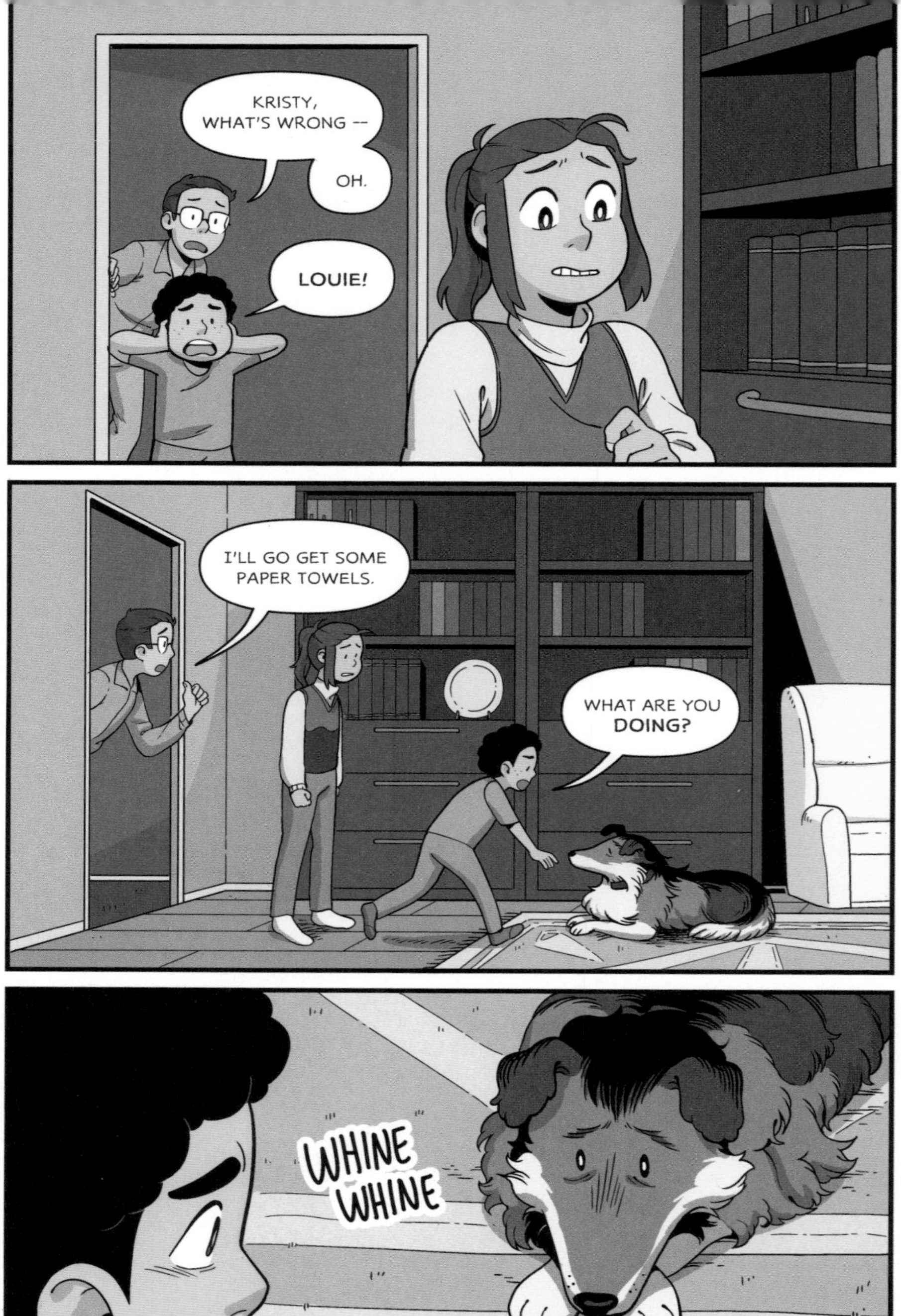
KRISTY, WHAT'S WRONG --
OH.
LOUIE!
I'LL GO GET SOME PAPER TOWELS.
WHAT ARE YOU **DOING?**
WHINE WHINE

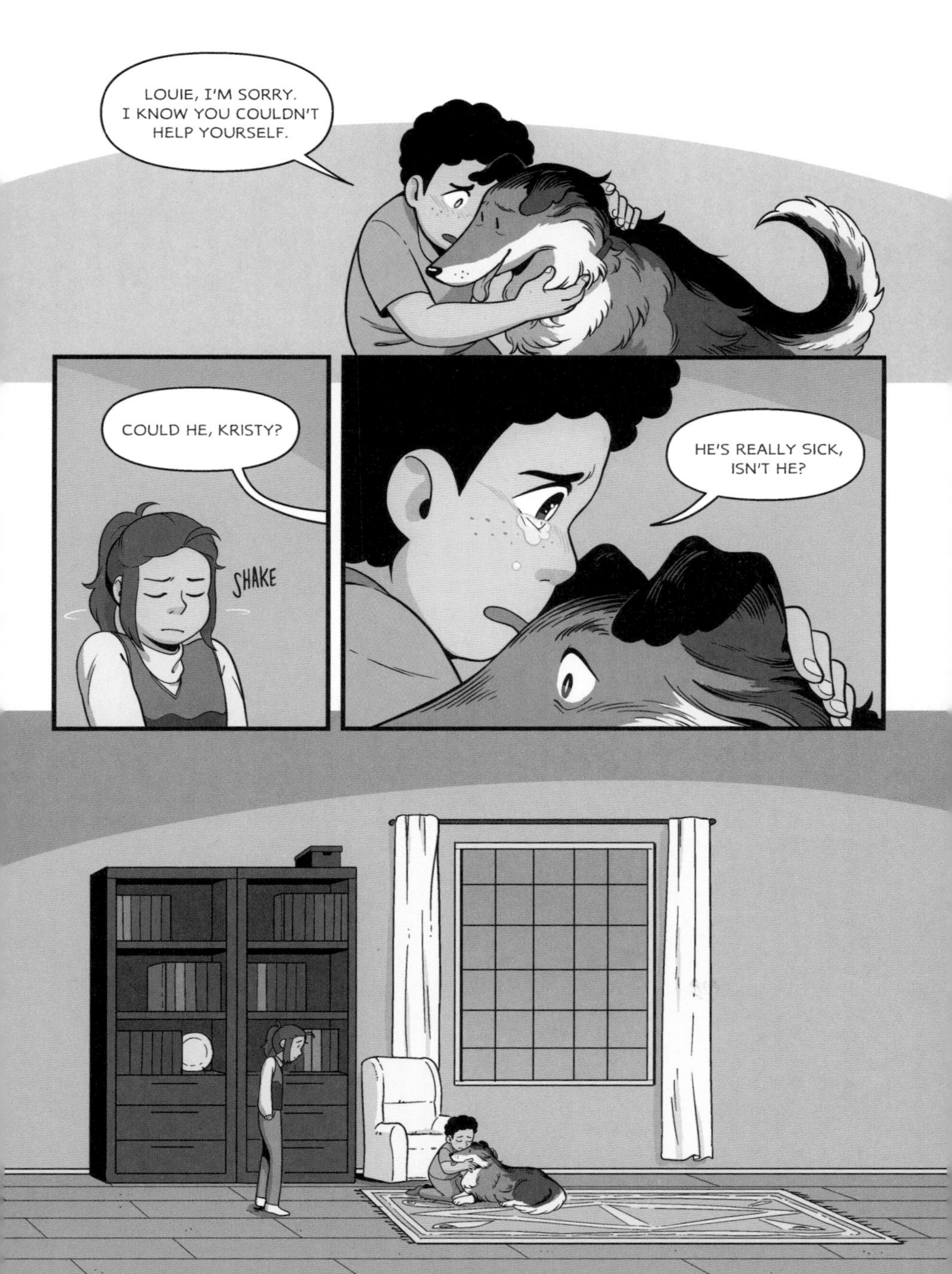

LOUIE, I'M SORRY. I KNOW YOU COULDN'T HELP YOURSELF.
COULD HE, KRISTY?
SHAKE
HE'S REALLY SICK, ISN'T HE?

Tuesday

    Okay, so I sat for the Snobs today, and it was no big deal. You just have to know how to handle them. You have to know a little psychology. I read this magazine article called "Getting What You Want: Dealing with Difficult People the Easy Way." It's kind of hard to explain what you're supposed to do, so I'll just give you some examples of how I dealt with the Snobs. I found that once you have tamed them, they're pretty nice little kids.

    By the way, my parents have a book called The Taming of the Shrew. I think it might be a play. Now I could write a play called The Taming of the Snobs!

                      Stacey

CHAPTER 8

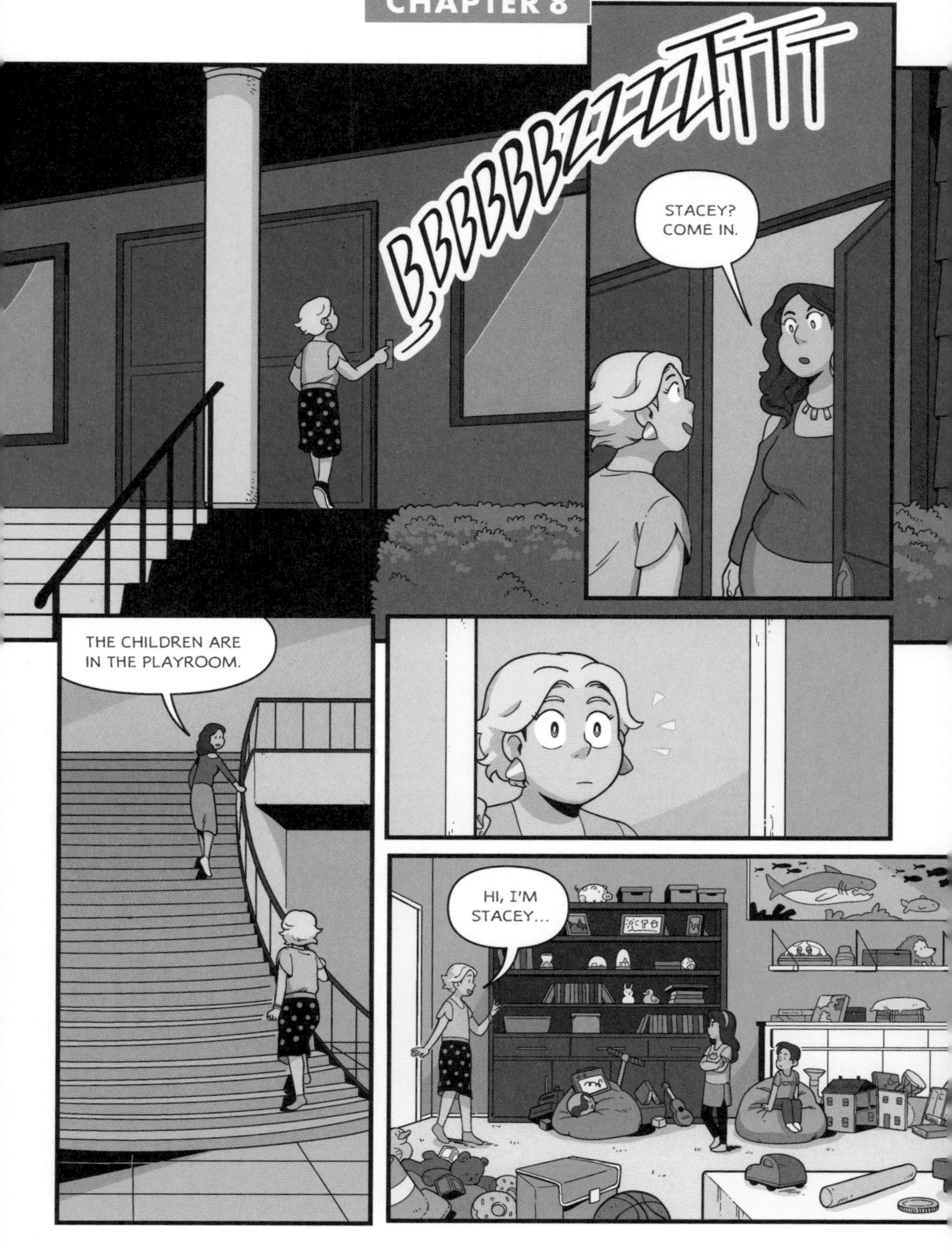
BBBBBBZZZZZATTT
STACEY? COME IN.
THE CHILDREN ARE IN THE PLAYROOM.
HI, I'M STACEY...

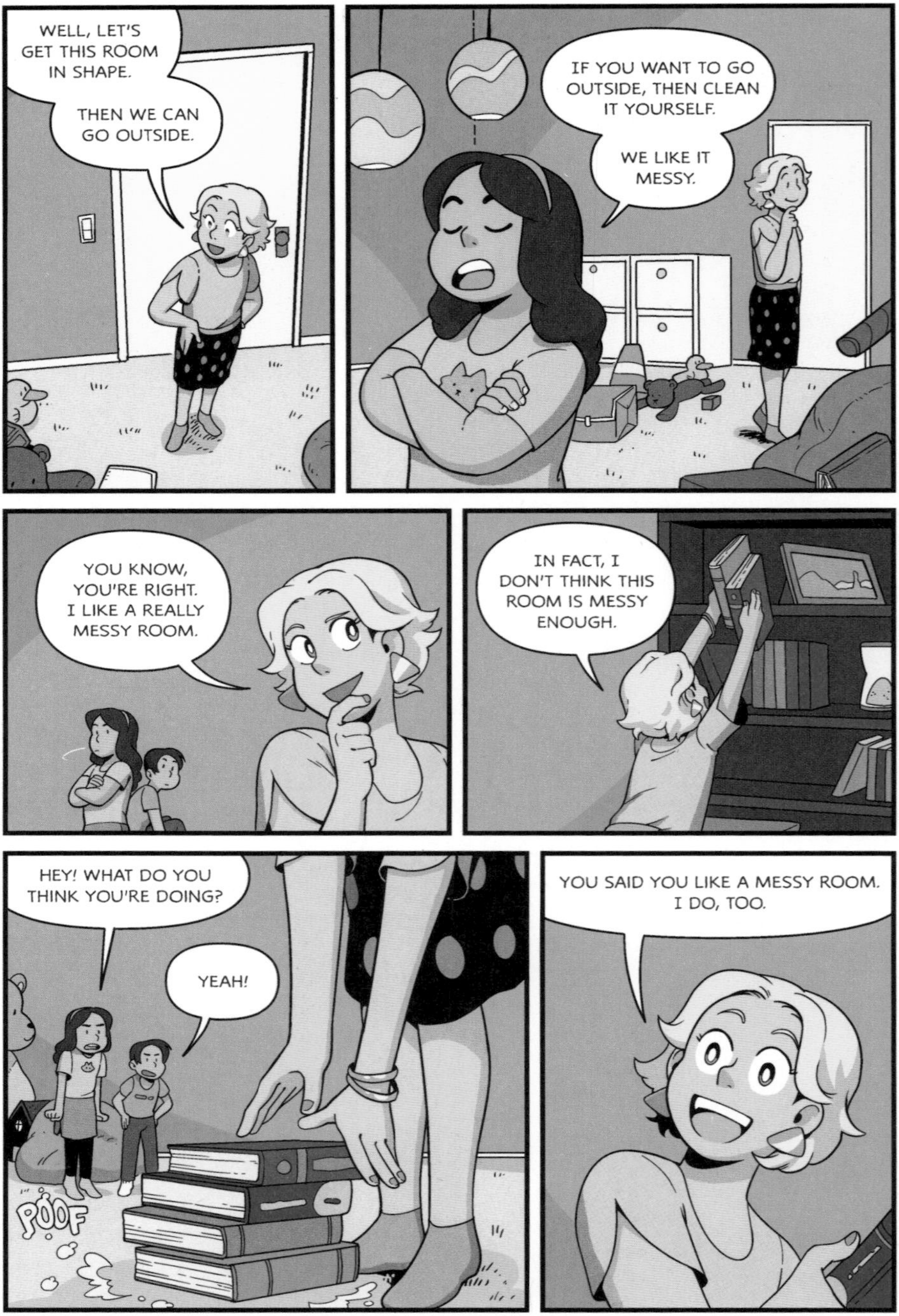
WELL, LET'S GET THIS ROOM IN SHAPE.
THEN WE CAN GO OUTSIDE.
IF YOU WANT TO GO OUTSIDE, THEN CLEAN IT YOURSELF.
WE LIKE IT MESSY.
YOU KNOW, YOU'RE RIGHT. I LIKE A REALLY MESSY ROOM.
IN FACT, I DON'T THINK THIS ROOM IS MESSY ENOUGH.
HEY! WHAT DO YOU THINK YOU'RE DOING?
YEAH!
POOF
YOU SAID YOU LIKE A MESSY ROOM. I DO, TOO.

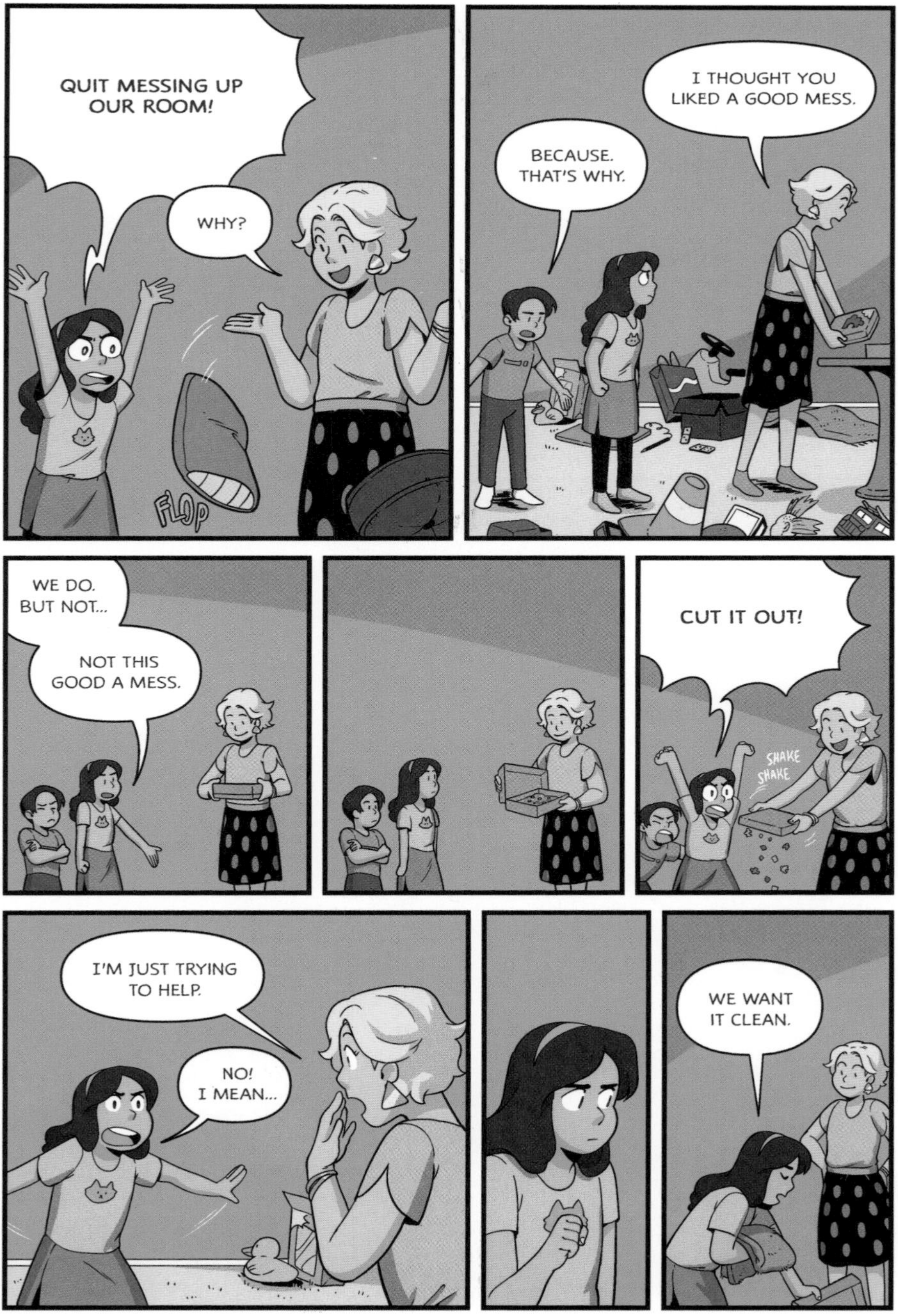
QUIT MESSING UP OUR ROOM!
WHY?
FLOP
BECAUSE. THAT'S WHY.
I THOUGHT YOU LIKED A GOOD MESS.
WE DO. BUT NOT...
NOT THIS GOOD A MESS.
CUT IT OUT!
SHAKE SHAKE
I'M JUST TRYING TO HELP.
NO! I MEAN...
WE WANT IT CLEAN.

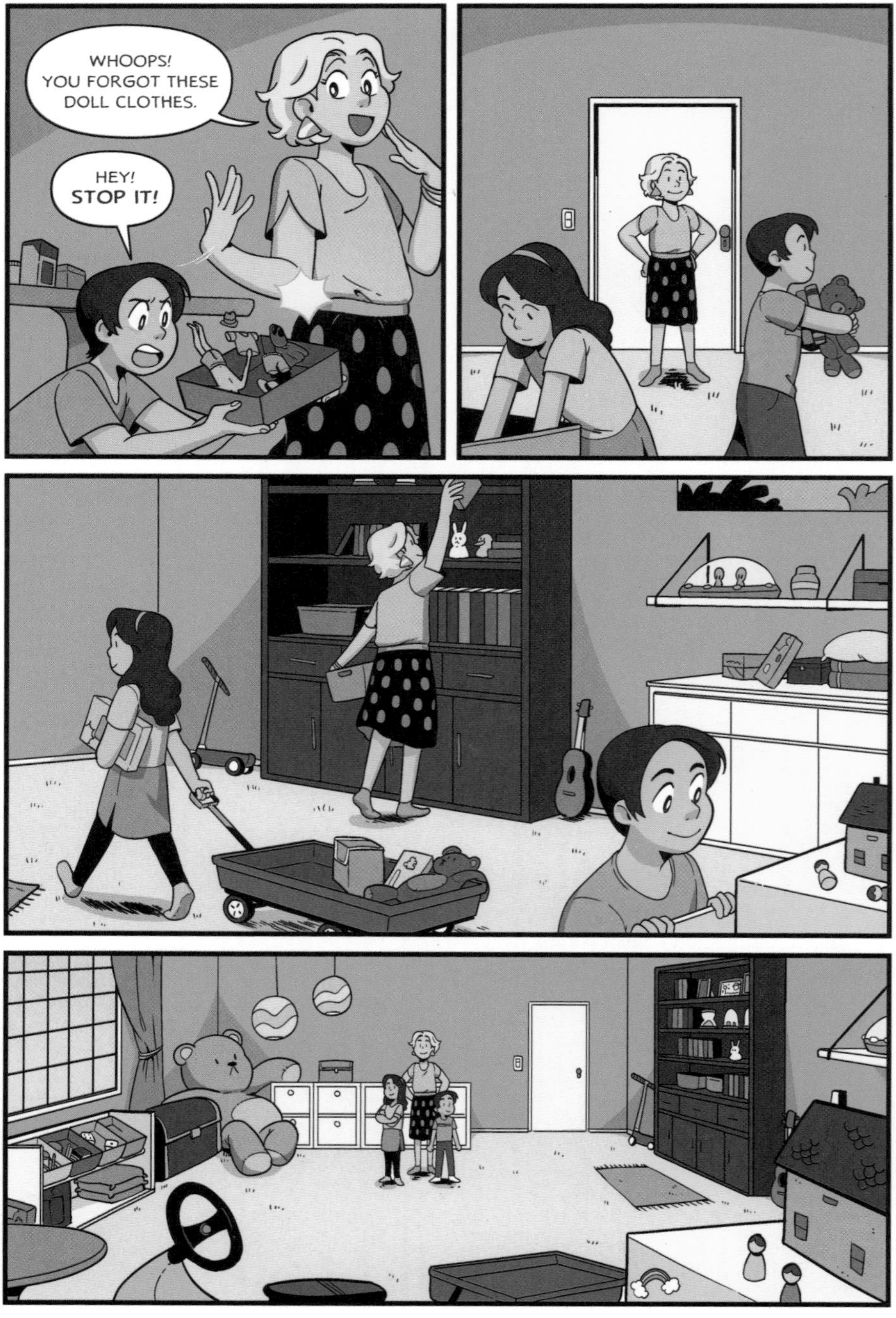
WHOOPS! YOU FORGOT THESE DOLL CLOTHES.
HEY! STOP IT!

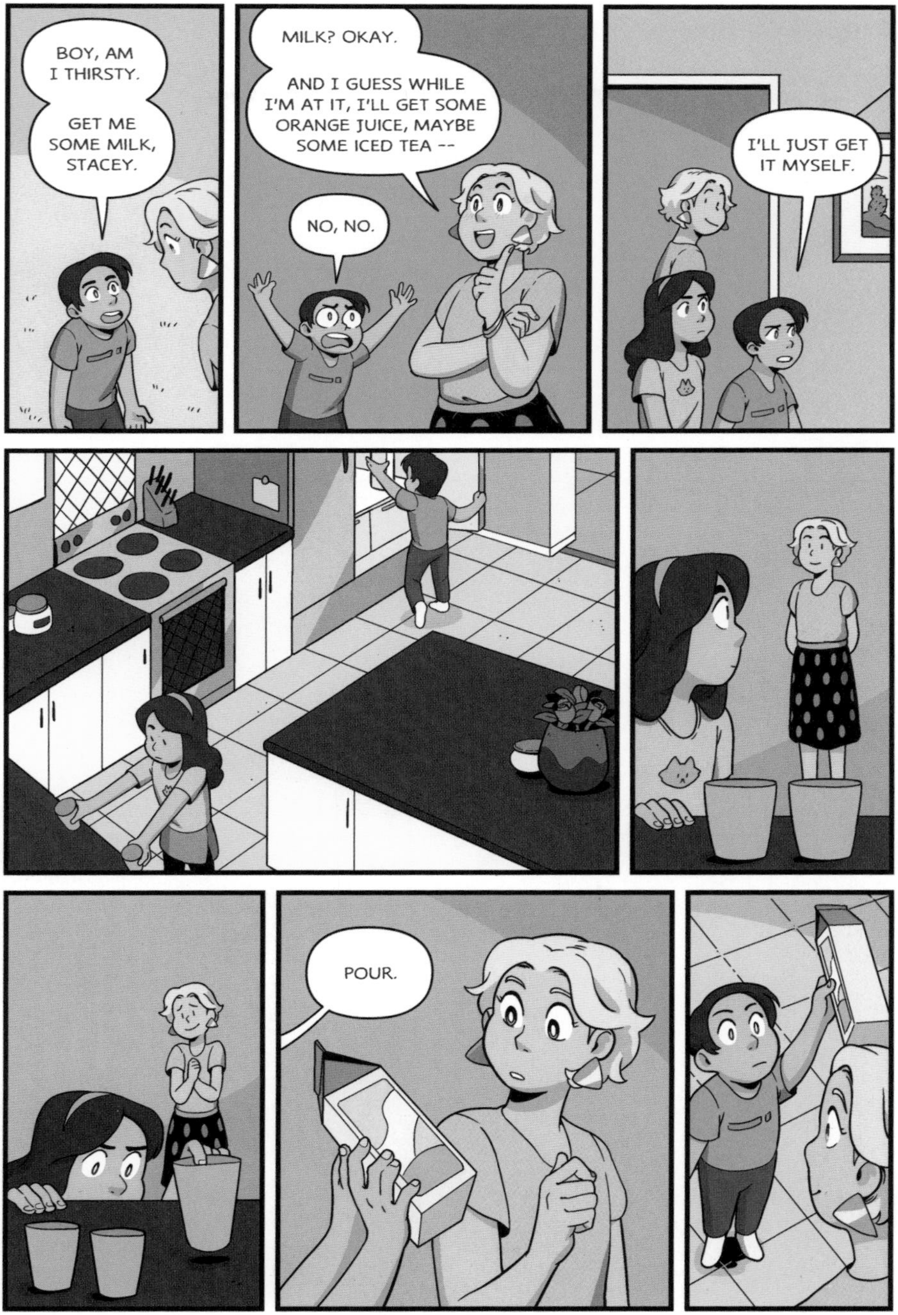
BOY, AM I THIRSTY.
GET ME SOME MILK, STACEY.
MILK? OKAY.
AND I GUESS WHILE I'M AT IT, I'LL GET SOME ORANGE JUICE, MAYBE SOME ICED TEA --
NO, NO.
I'LL JUST GET IT MYSELF.
POUR.

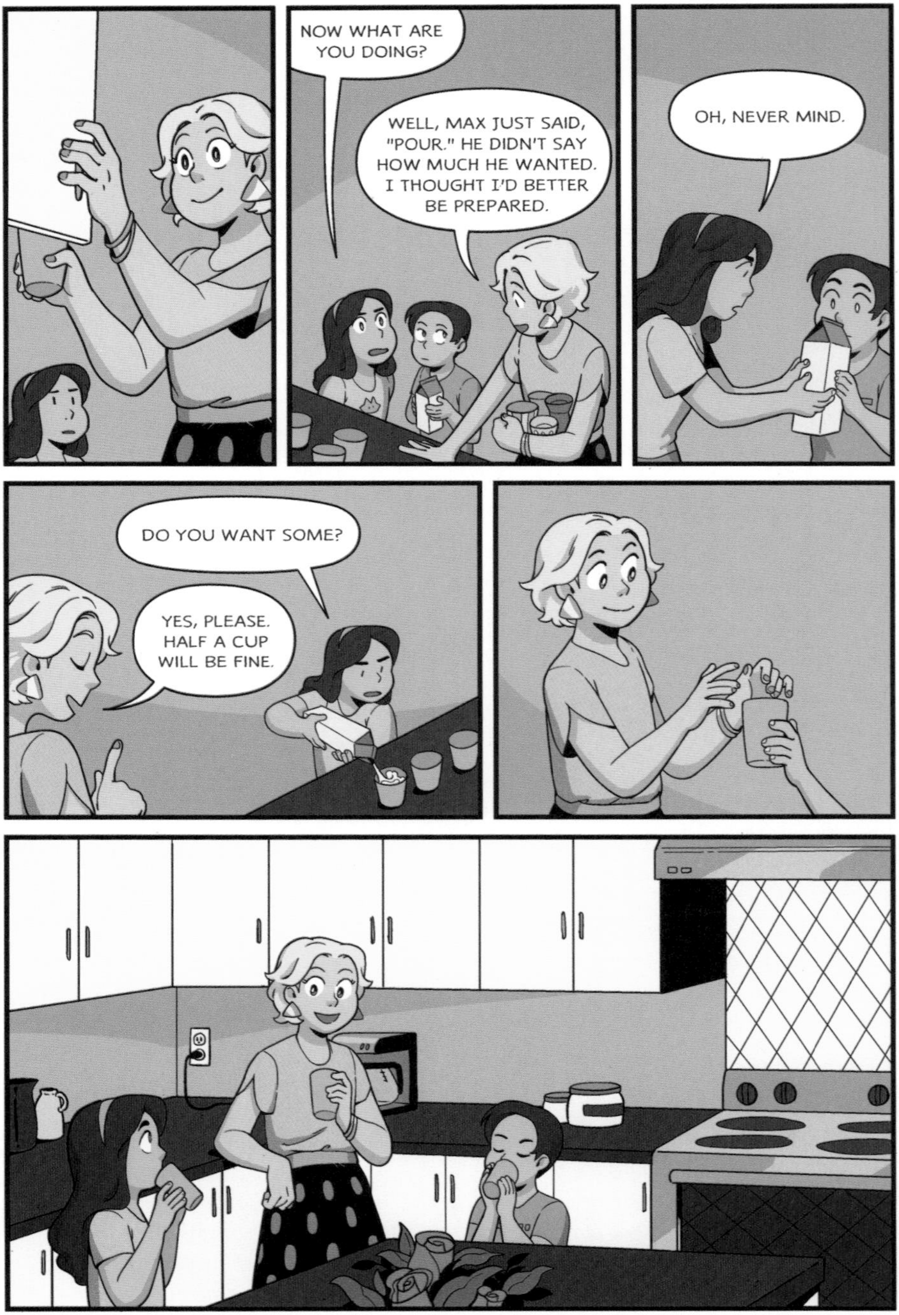
NOW WHAT ARE YOU DOING?
WELL, MAX JUST SAID, "POUR." HE DIDN'T SAY HOW MUCH HE WANTED. I THOUGHT I'D BETTER BE PREPARED.
OH, NEVER MIND.
DO YOU WANT SOME?
YES, PLEASE. HALF A CUP WILL BE FINE.

84

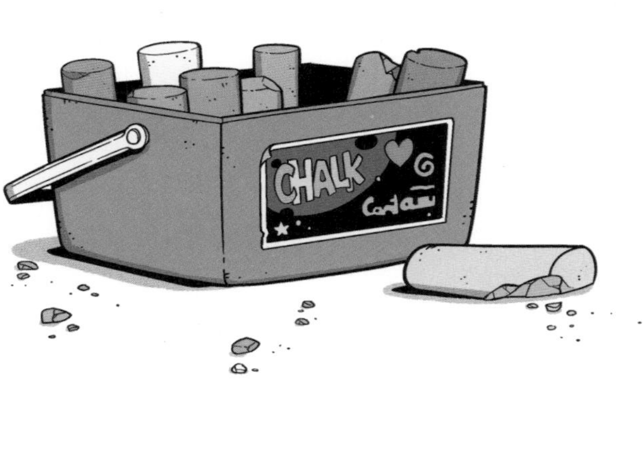
CHALK

CHAPTER 9

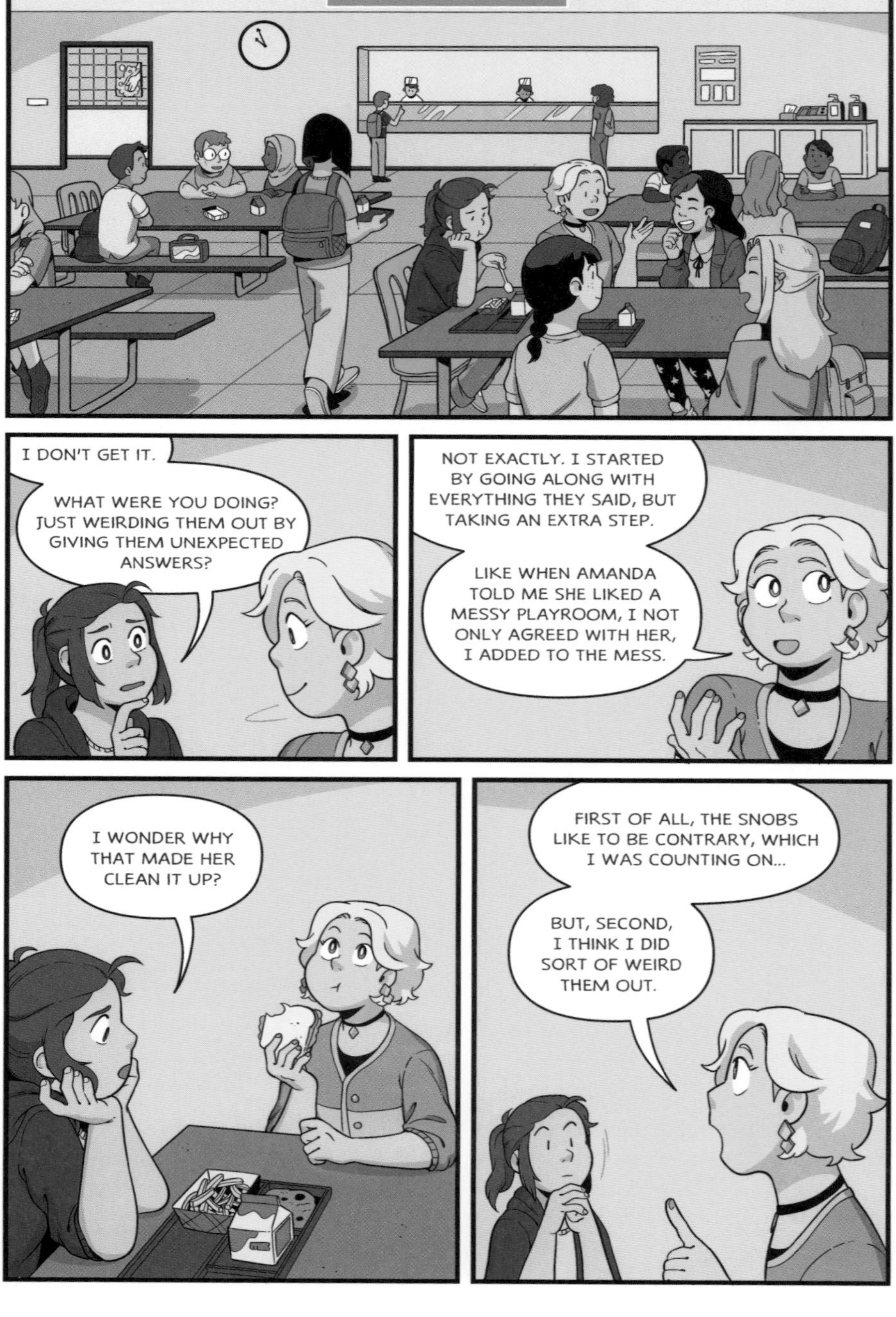
I DON'T GET IT.
WHAT WERE YOU DOING? JUST WEIRDING THEM OUT BY GIVING THEM UNEXPECTED ANSWERS?
NOT EXACTLY. I STARTED BY GOING ALONG WITH EVERYTHING THEY SAID, BUT TAKING AN EXTRA STEP.
LIKE WHEN AMANDA TOLD ME SHE LIKED A MESSY PLAYROOM, I NOT ONLY AGREED WITH HER, I ADDED TO THE MESS.
I WONDER WHY THAT MADE HER CLEAN IT UP?
FIRST OF ALL, THE SNOBS LIKE TO BE CONTRARY, WHICH I WAS COUNTING ON...
BUT, SECOND, I THINK I DID SORT OF WEIRD THEM OUT.

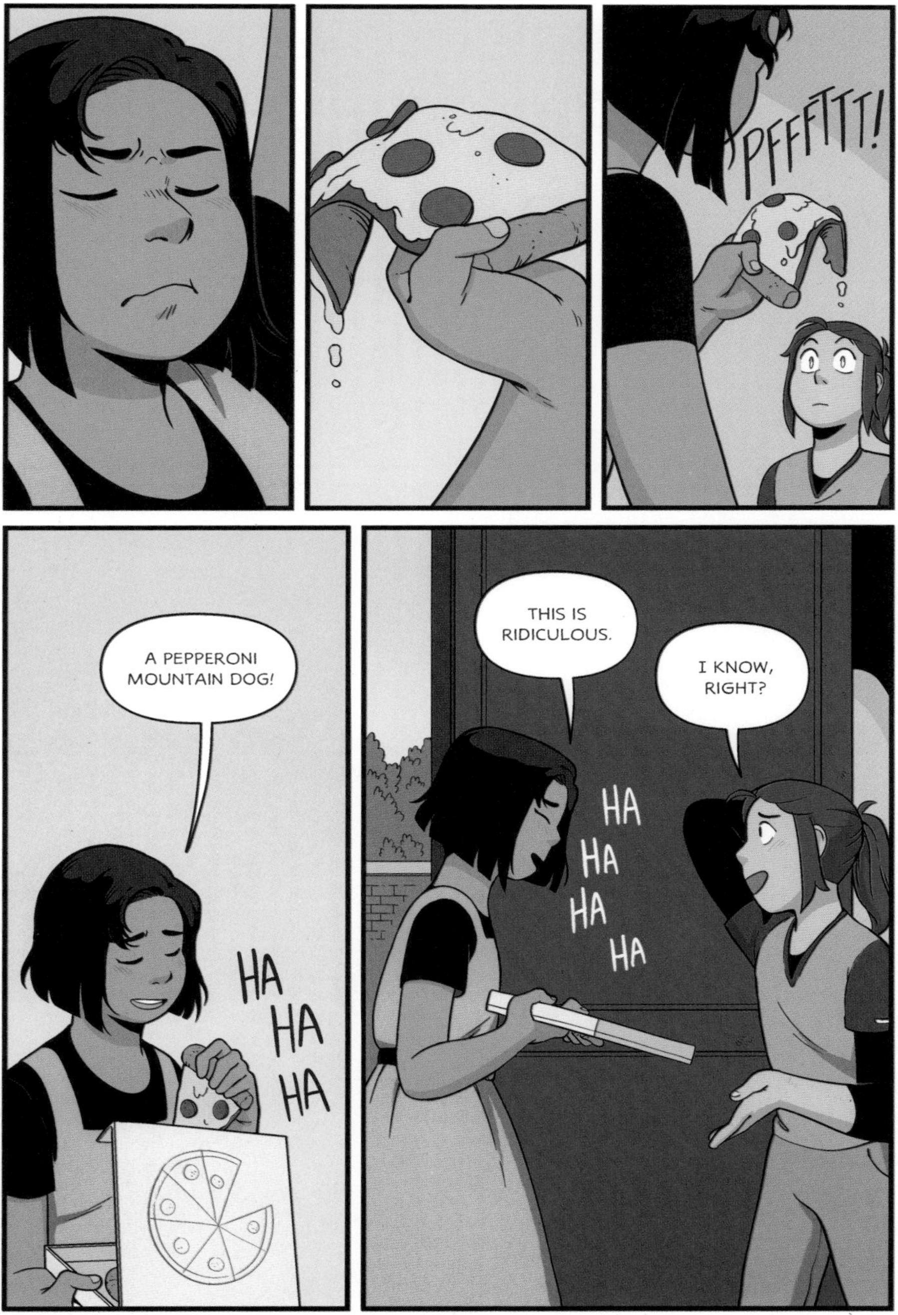
PFFFTTT!
A PEPPERONI MOUNTAIN DOG!
HA HA HA
THIS IS RIDICULOUS.
HA HA HA HA
I KNOW, RIGHT?

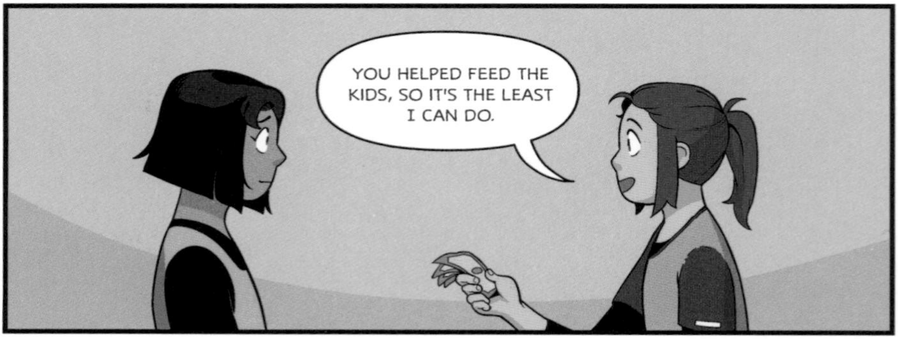
YOU HELPED FEED THE KIDS, SO IT'S THE LEAST I CAN DO.

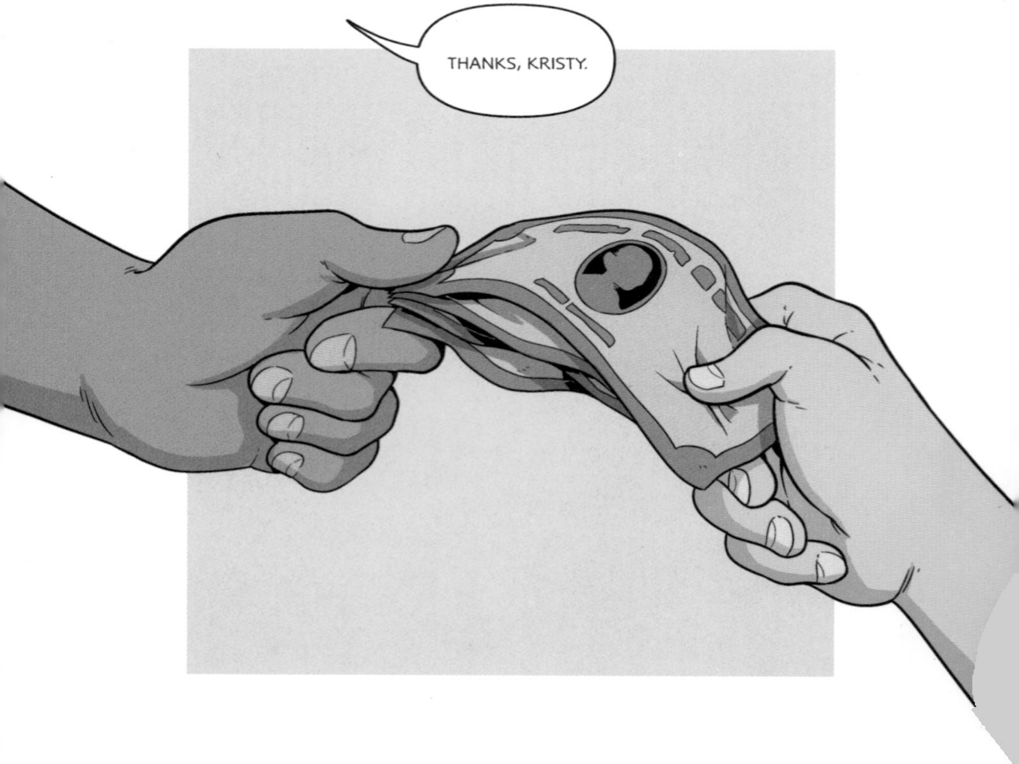
THANKS, KRISTY.

Saturday

   Chicken pocks! The only way your going
to apreciat what I wright here is if you
rember how it felt to have the chicken
pocks. I do sort of. I was seven when I
had them and it was not plesent. I itched
and had a feever and my mom said Don't
scratch but it was the only thing I
wanted to do. So keep that in mind.
   OK so Malory, Jessi, and I sat for
Malory's brothers and sisters. The triplets
and Margo and Claire were all ~~rek~~ ~~recov~~
getting over the chicken pox. They were
not felling very good. What a night we had.
Orders, orders, orders...

                              * Claudia *

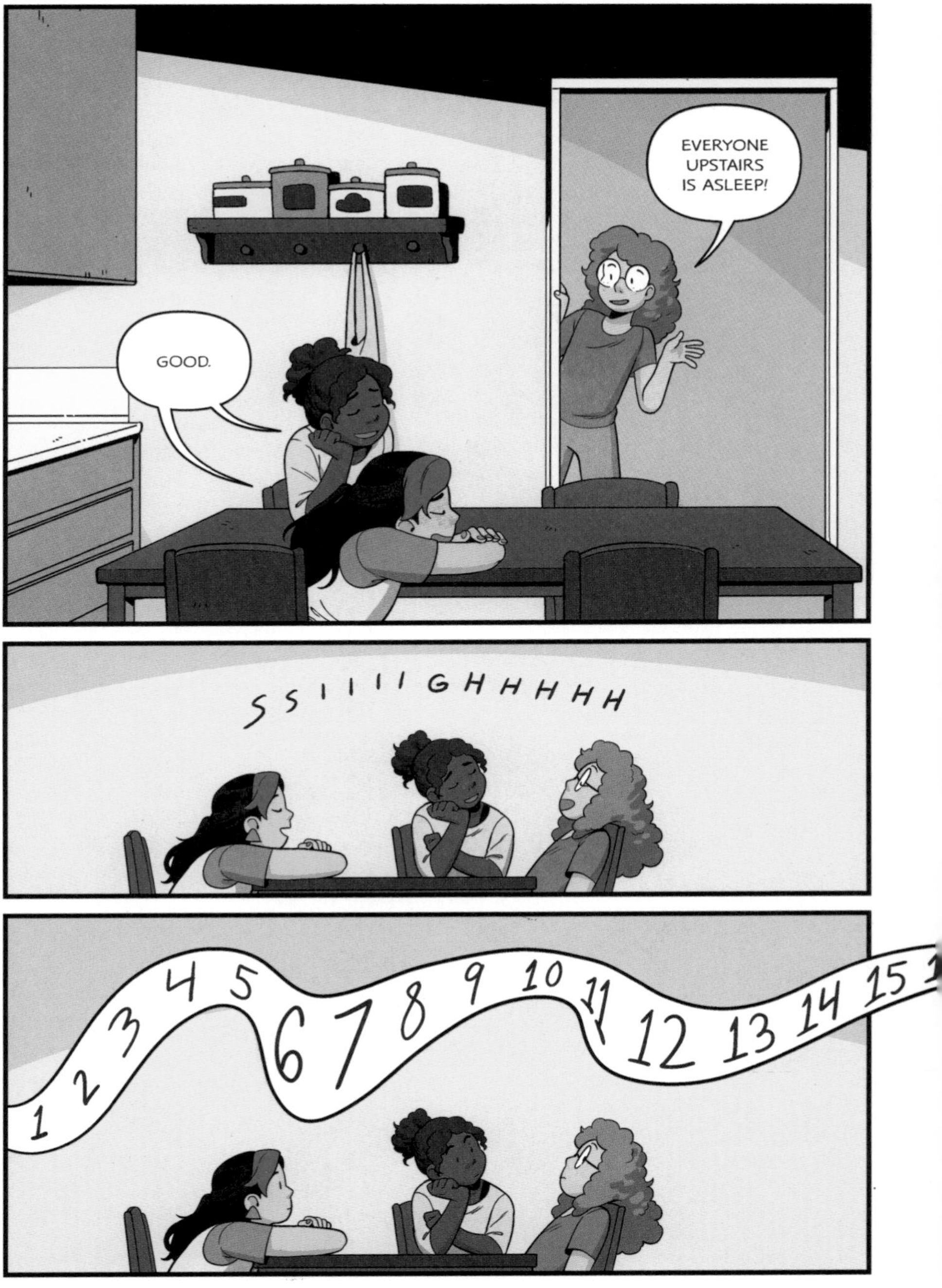
EVERYONE UPSTAIRS IS ASLEEP!
GOOD.
SSIIIIGHHHHHH
1 2 3 4 5 6 7 8 9 10 11 12 13 14 15

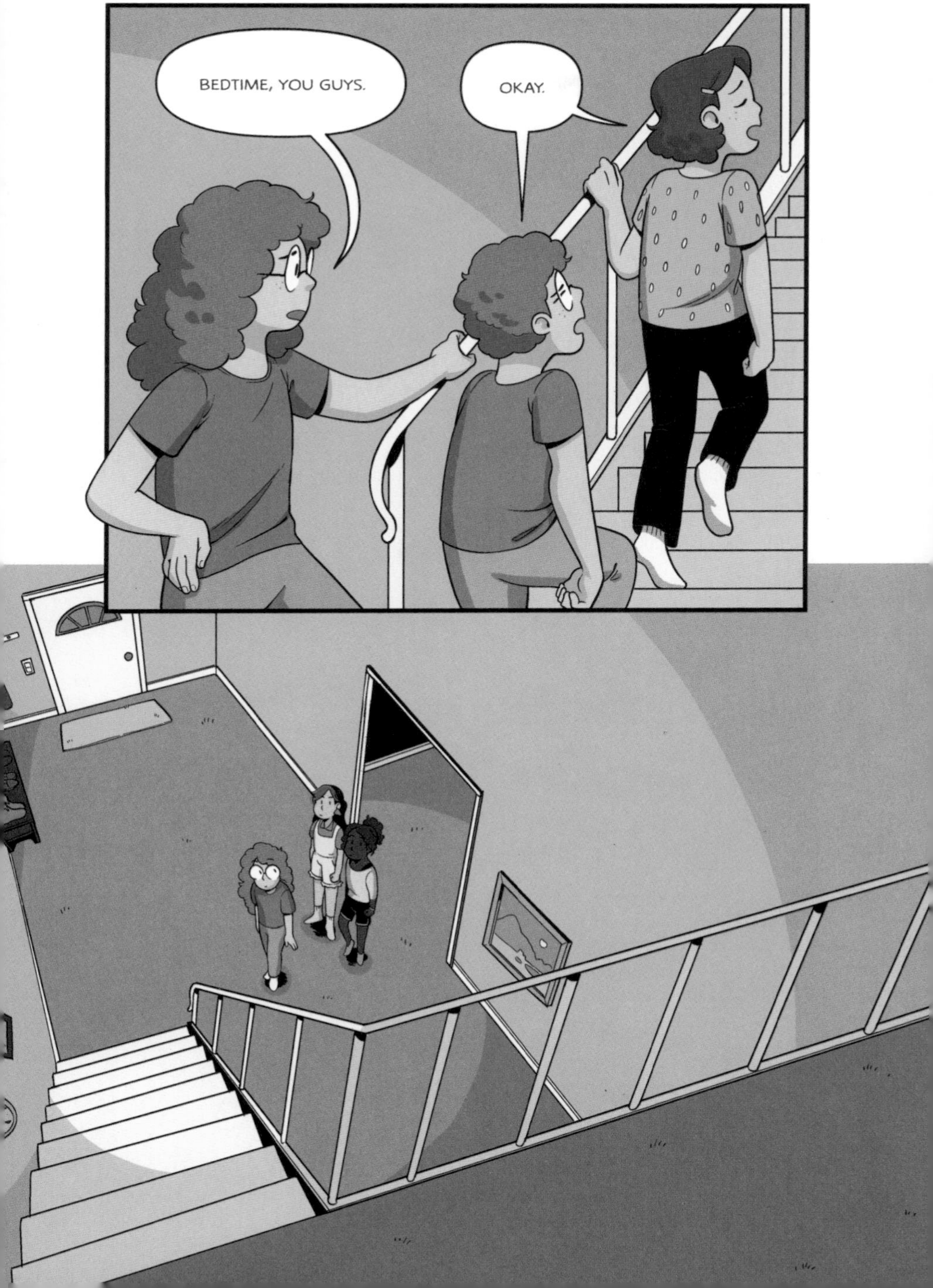
BEDTIME, YOU GUYS.
OKAY.

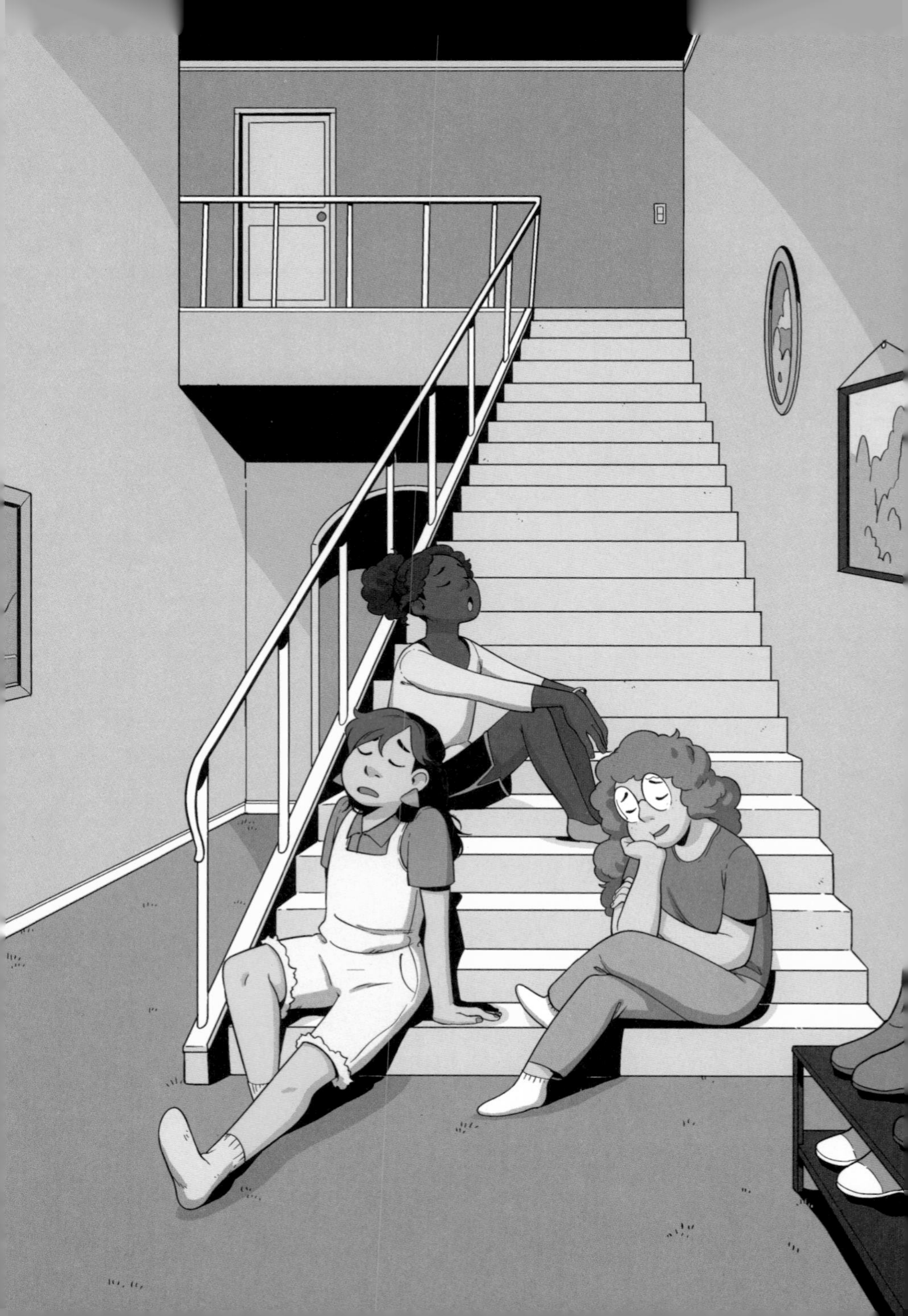

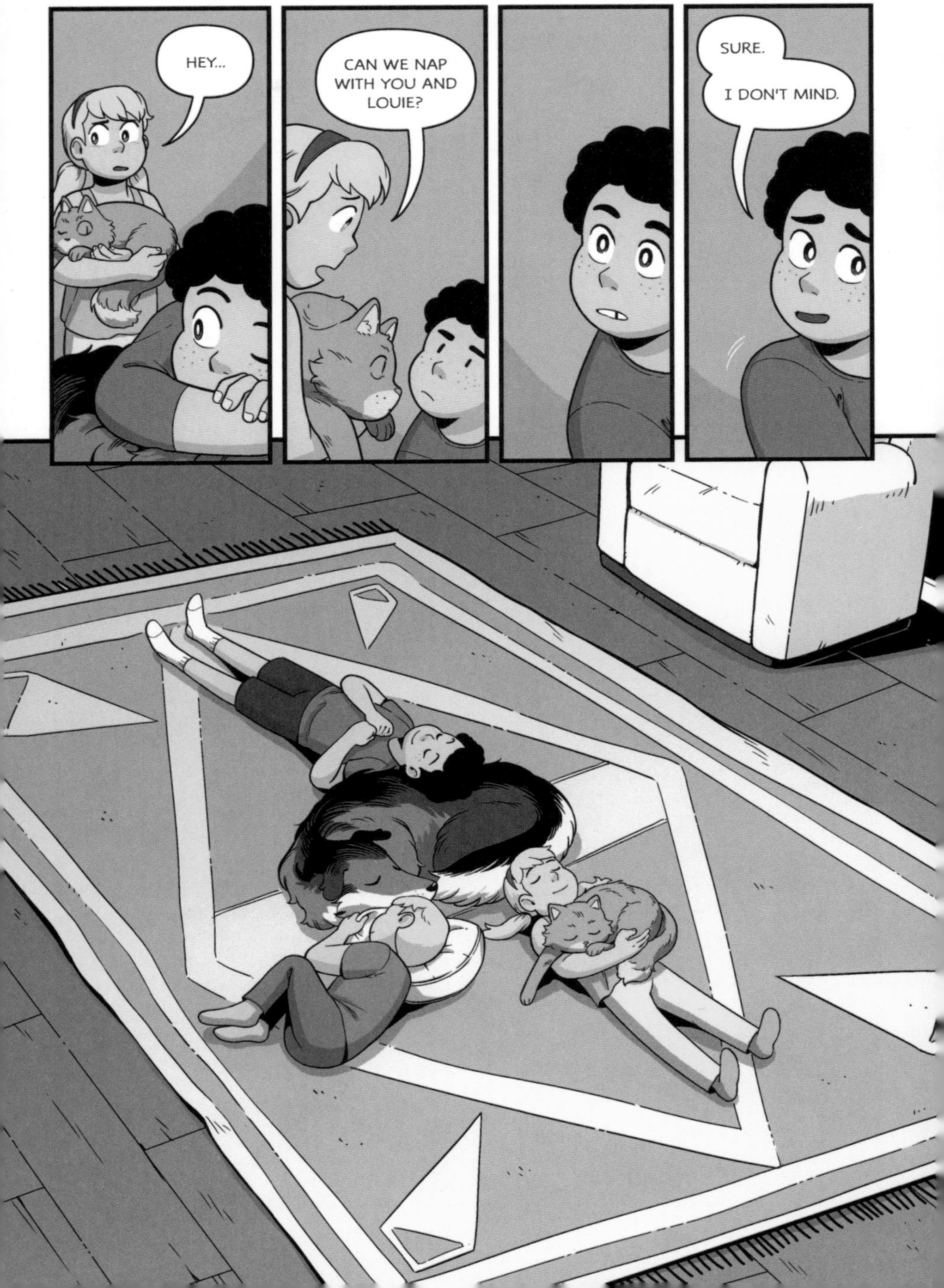
HEY...
CAN WE NAP WITH YOU AND LOUIE?
SURE.
I DON'T MIND.

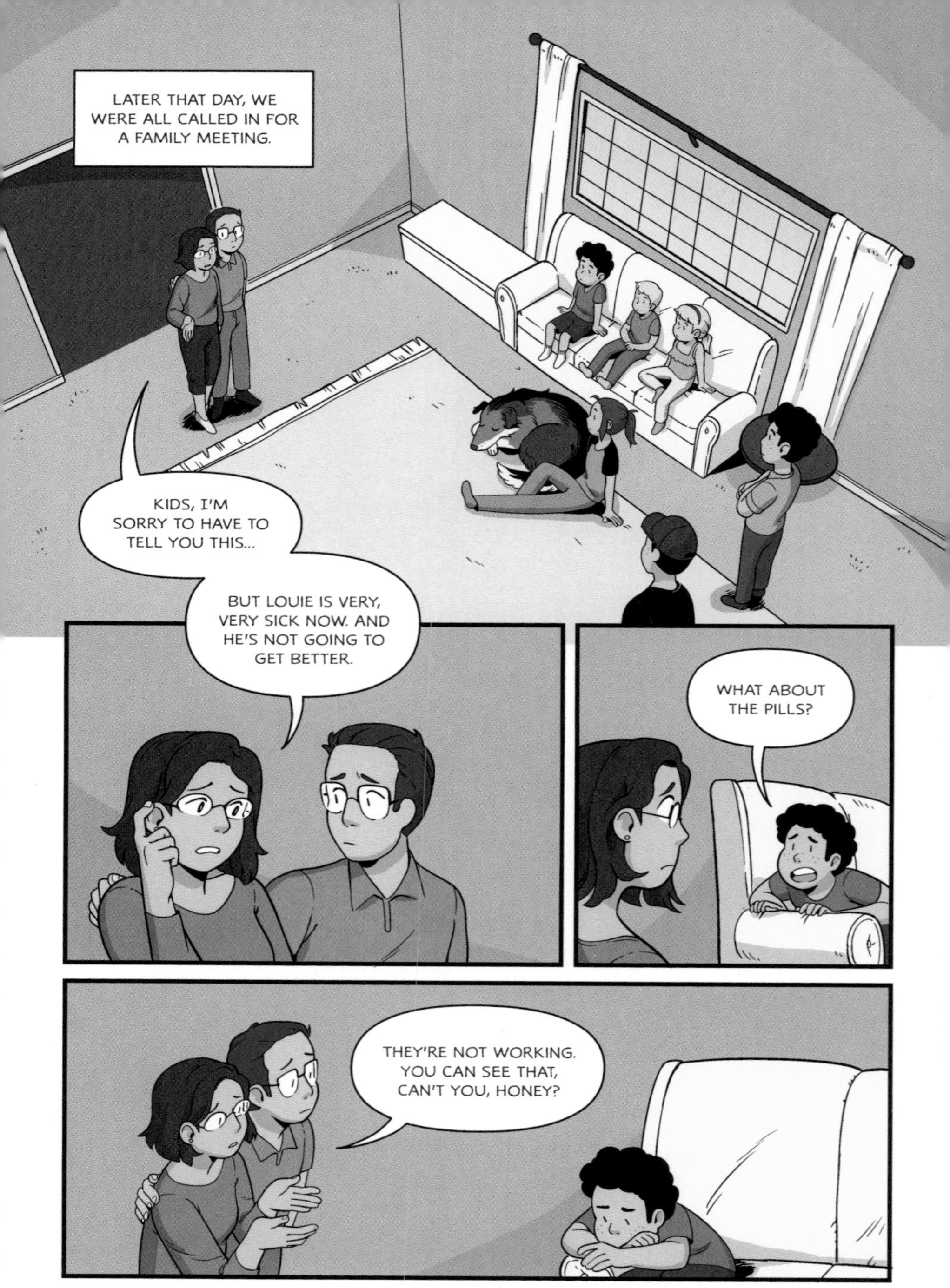
LATER THAT DAY, WE WERE ALL CALLED IN FOR A FAMILY MEETING.
KIDS, I'M SORRY TO HAVE TO TELL YOU THIS...
BUT LOUIE IS VERY, VERY SICK NOW. AND HE'S NOT GOING TO GET BETTER.
WHAT ABOUT THE PILLS?
THEY'RE NOT WORKING. YOU CAN SEE THAT, CAN'T YOU, HONEY?

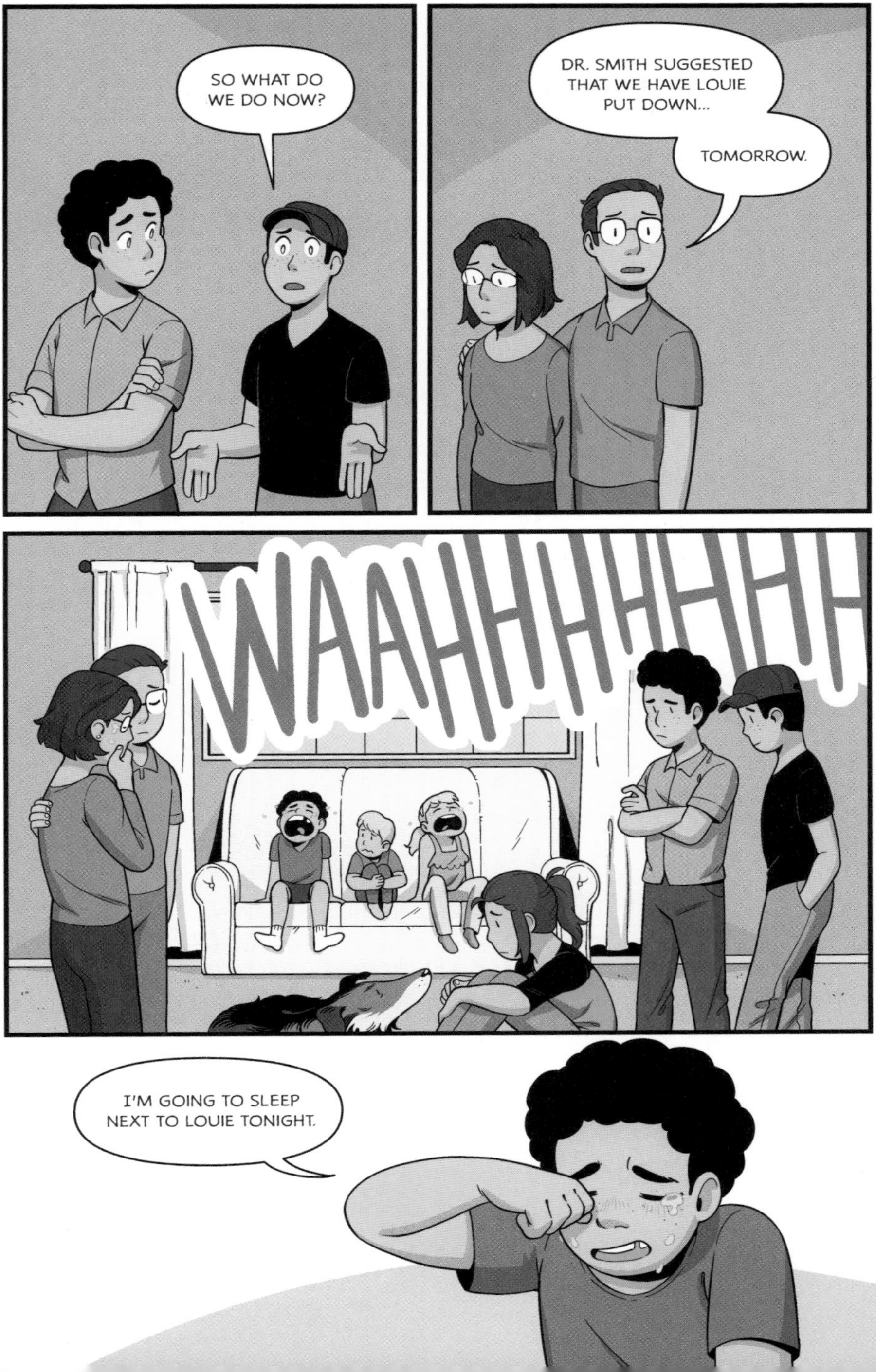
SO WHAT DO WE DO NOW?
DR. SMITH SUGGESTED THAT WE HAVE LOUIE PUT DOWN...
TOMORROW.
WAAHHHHHHHH
I'M GOING TO SLEEP NEXT TO LOUIE TONIGHT.

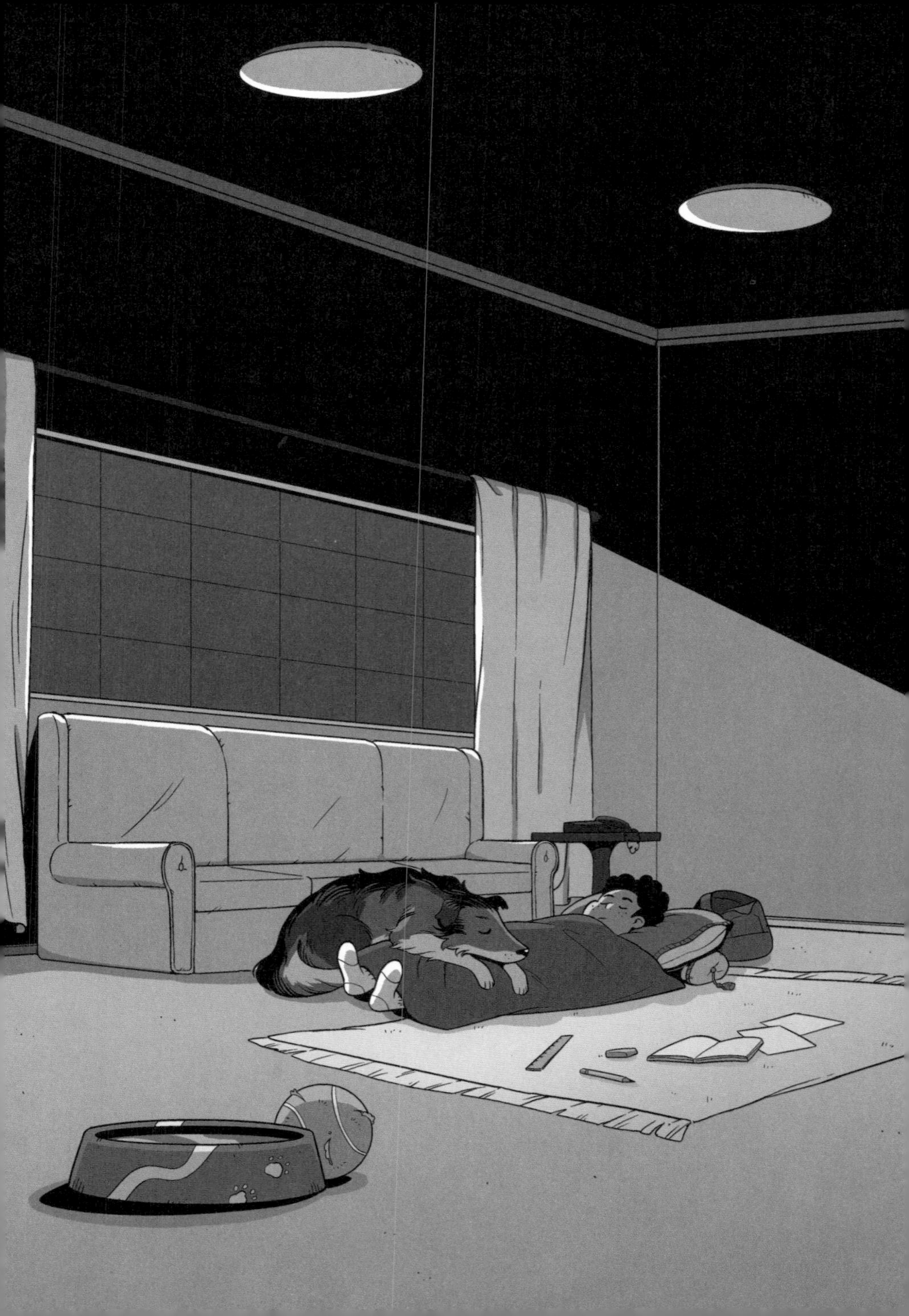

CHAPTER 12

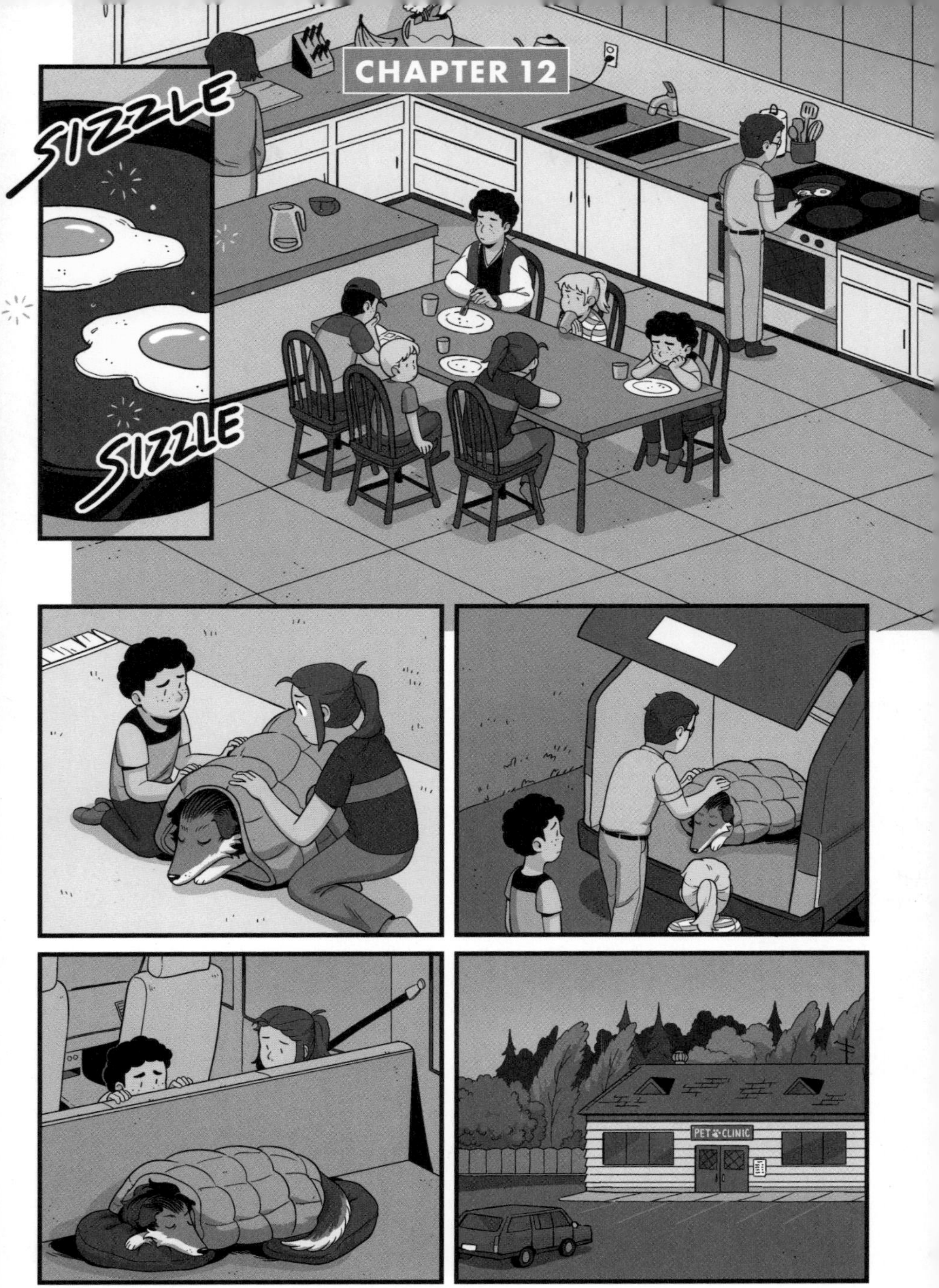
SIZZLE
SIZZLE
PET CLINIC

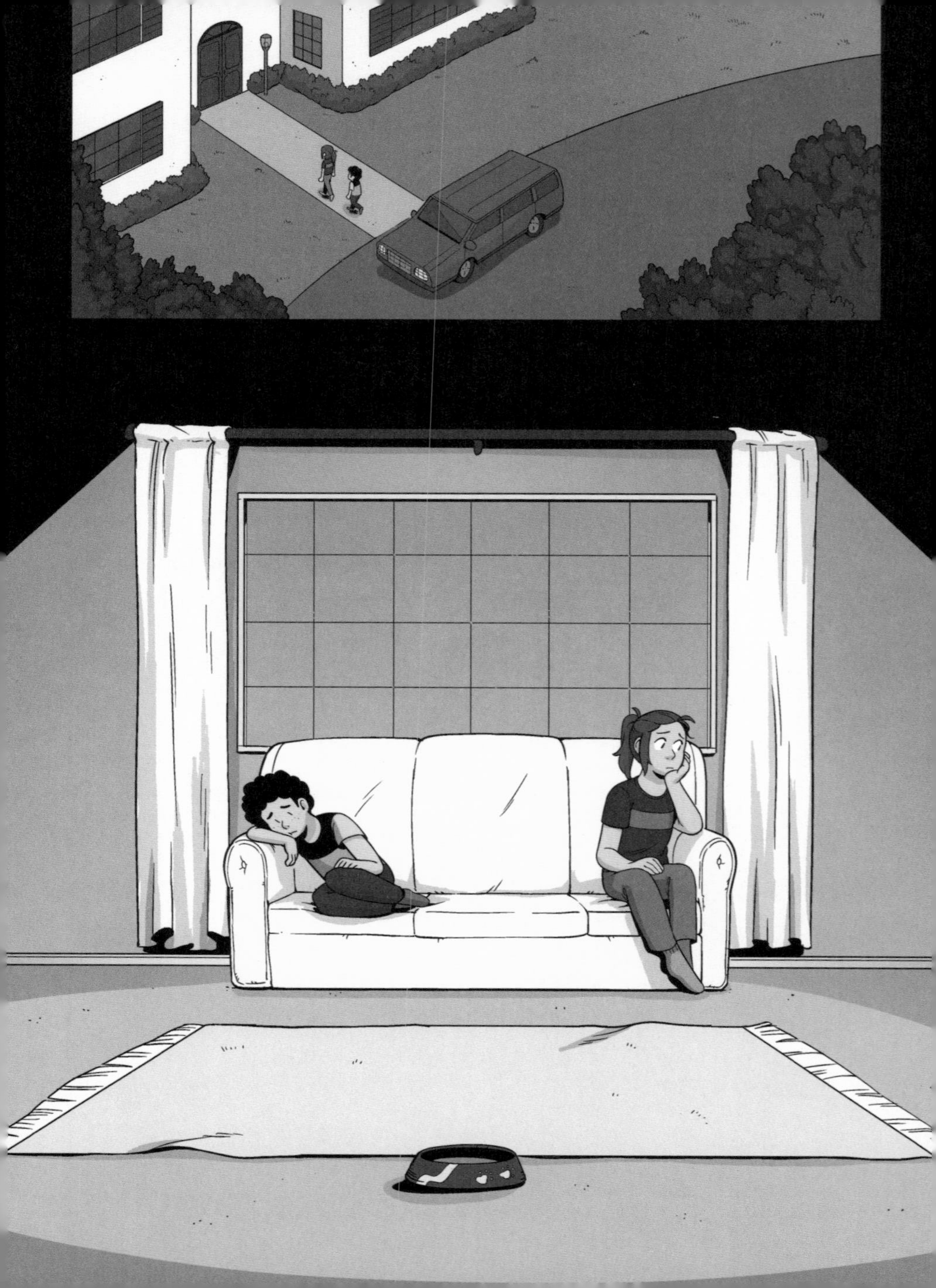

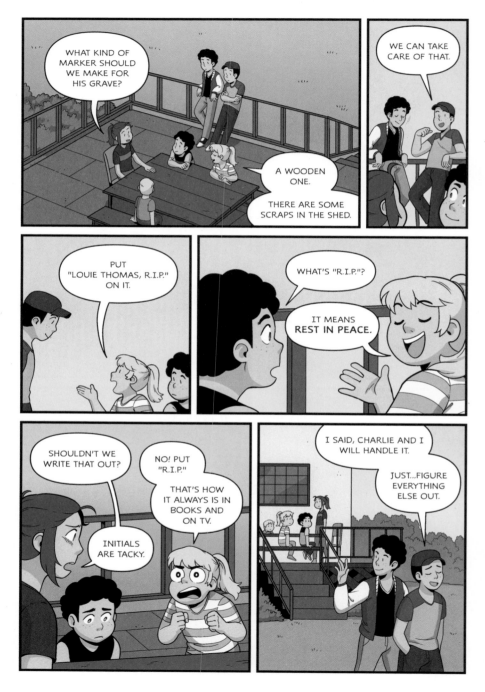

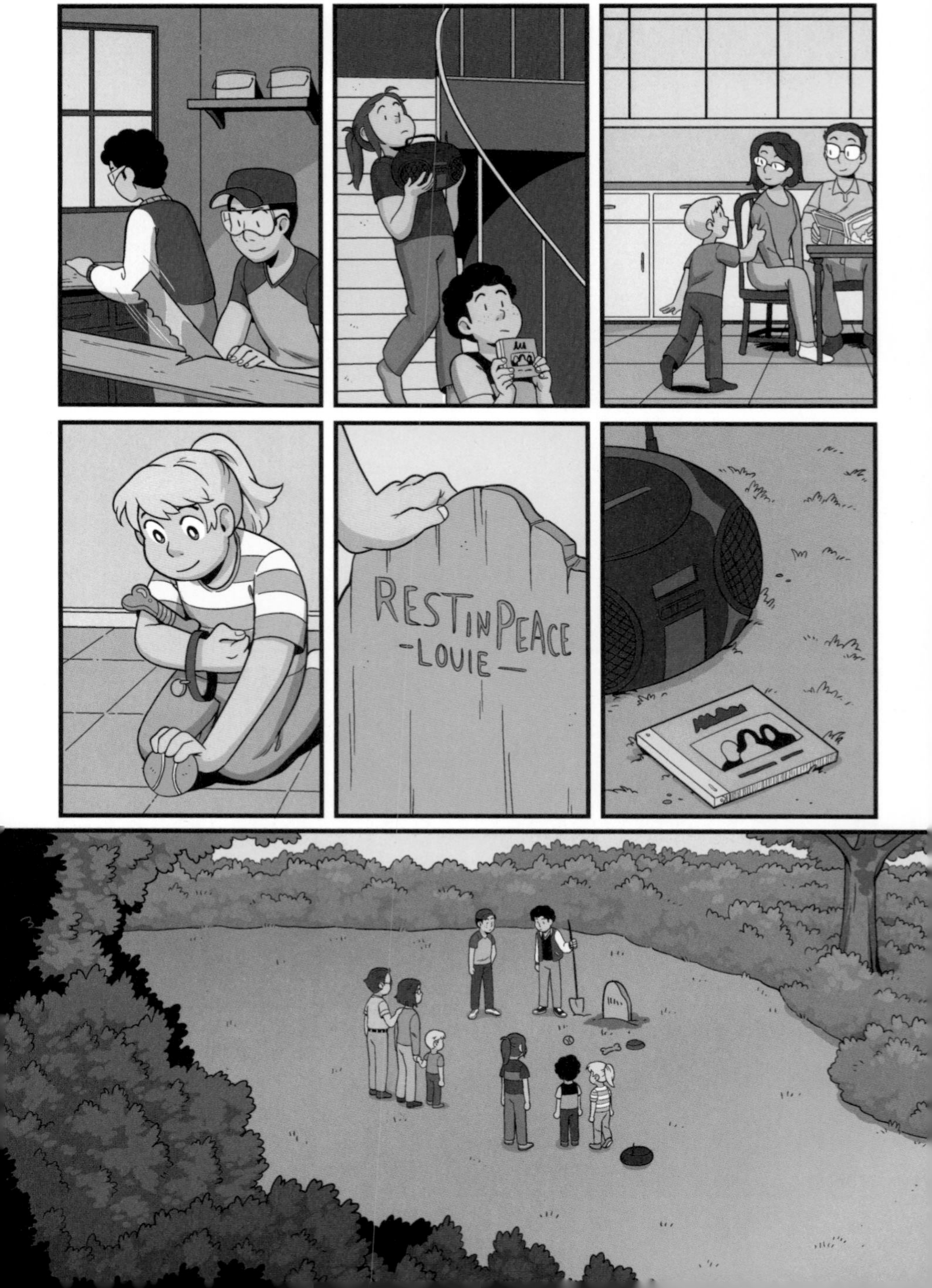
REST IN PEACE
-LOUIE-

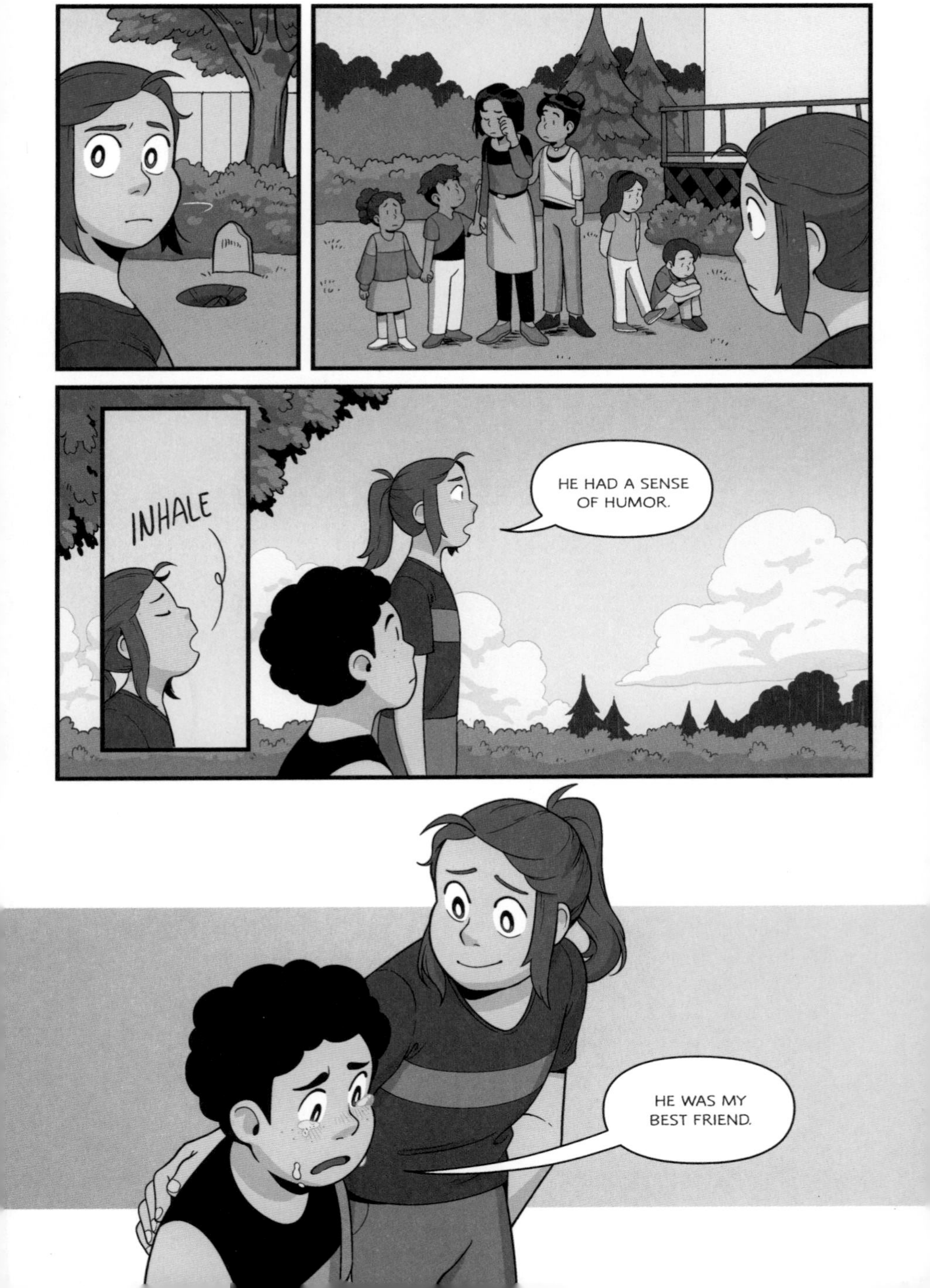
INHALE
HE HAD A SENSE OF HUMOR.
HE WAS MY BEST FRIEND.

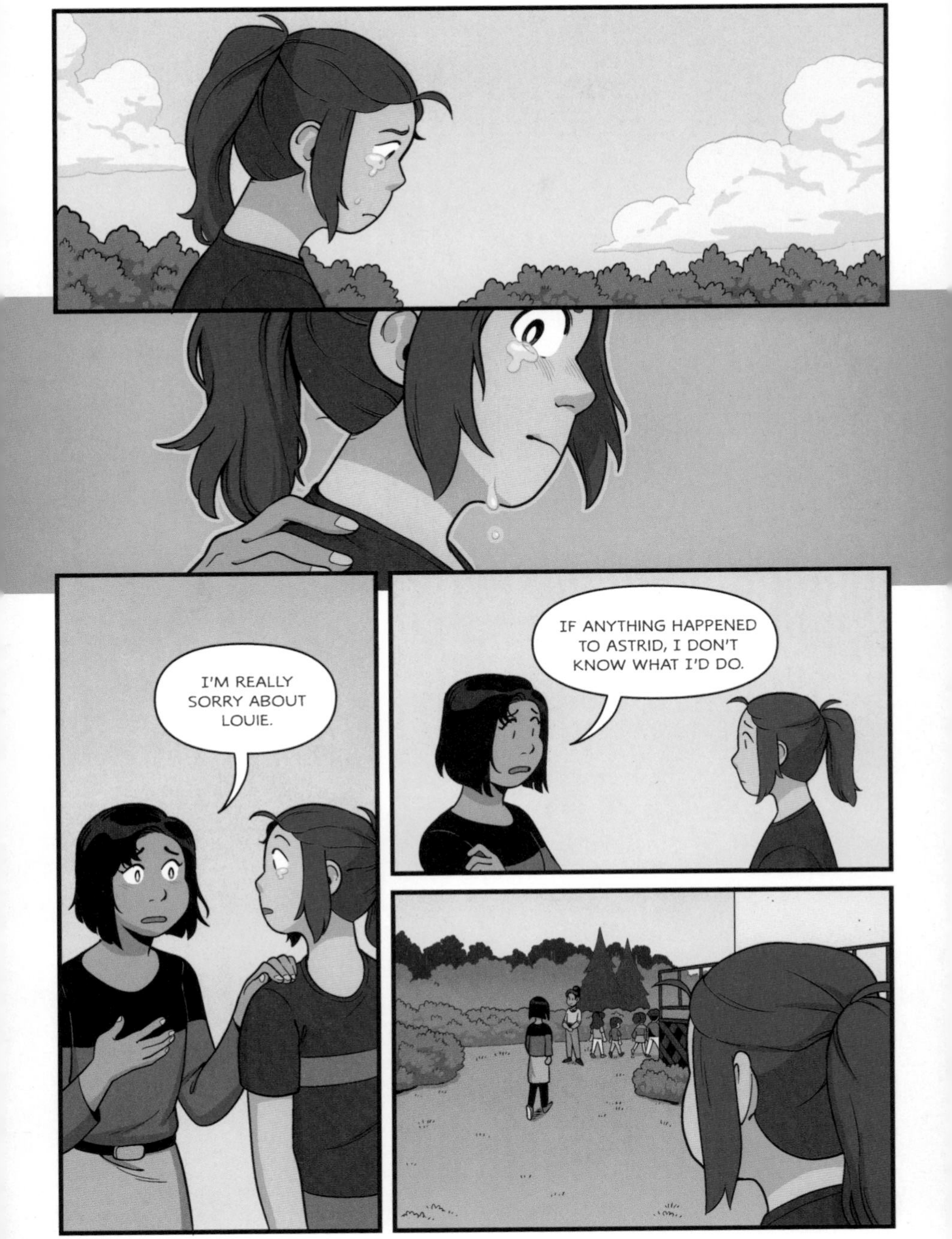
I'M REALLY SORRY ABOUT LOUIE.
IF ANYTHING HAPPENED TO ASTRID, I DON'T KNOW WHAT I'D DO.

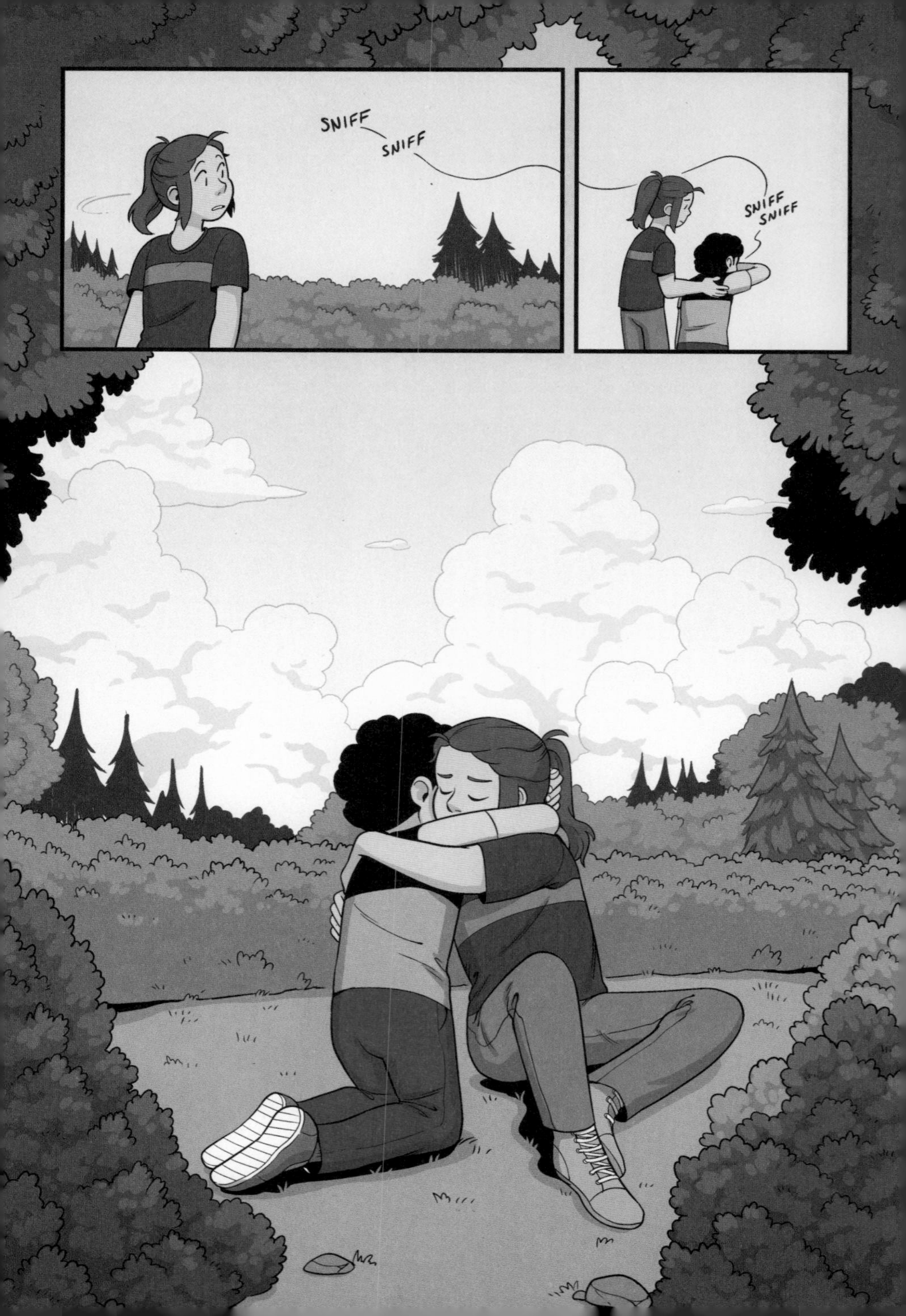
SNIFF
SNIFF
SNIFF
SNIFF

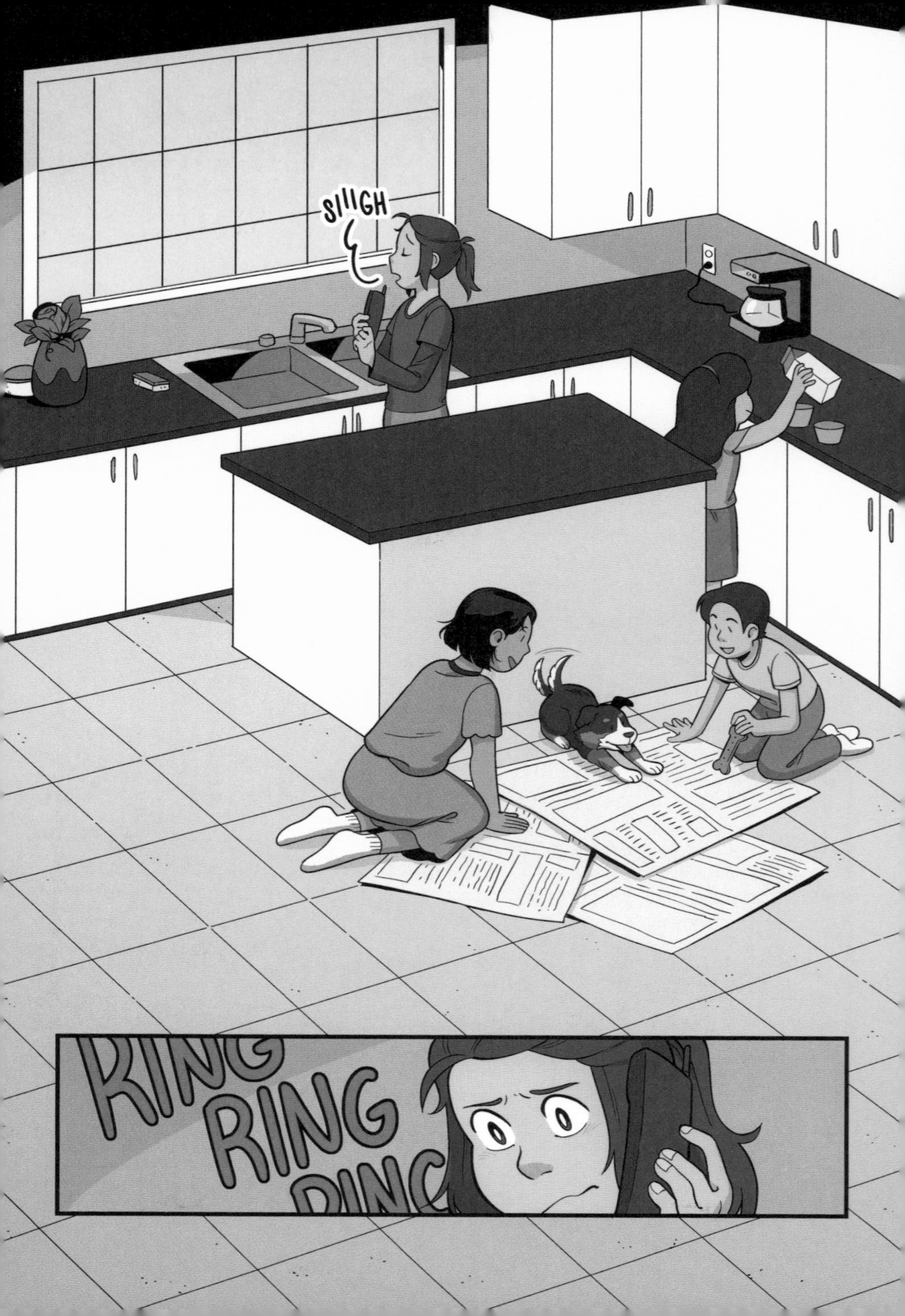

SIIIGH
RING
RING

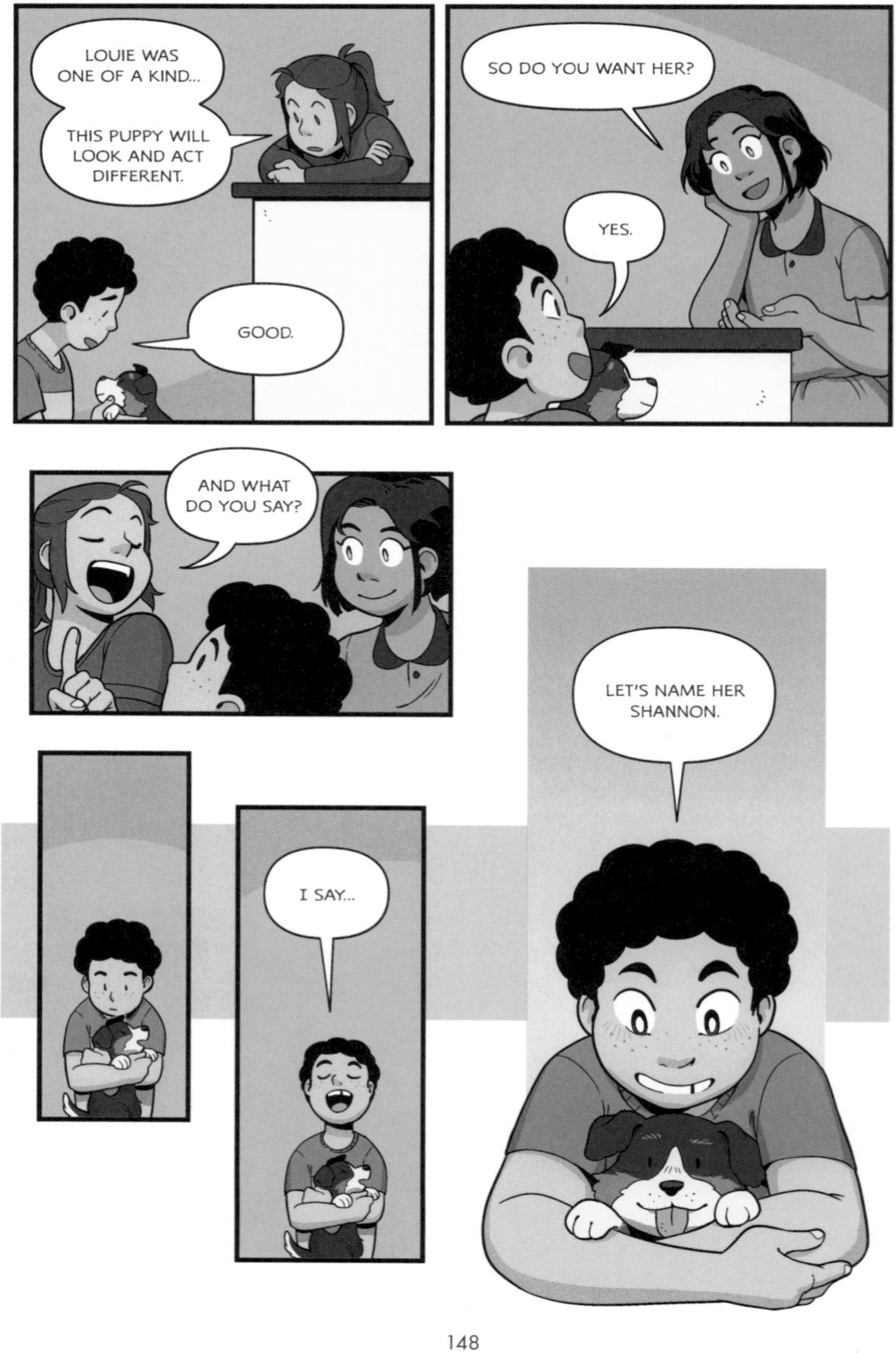
LOUIE WAS ONE OF A KIND...
THIS PUPPY WILL LOOK AND ACT DIFFERENT.
GOOD.
SO DO YOU WANT HER?
YES.
AND WHAT DO YOU SAY?
I SAY...
LET'S NAME HER SHANNON.

150

152

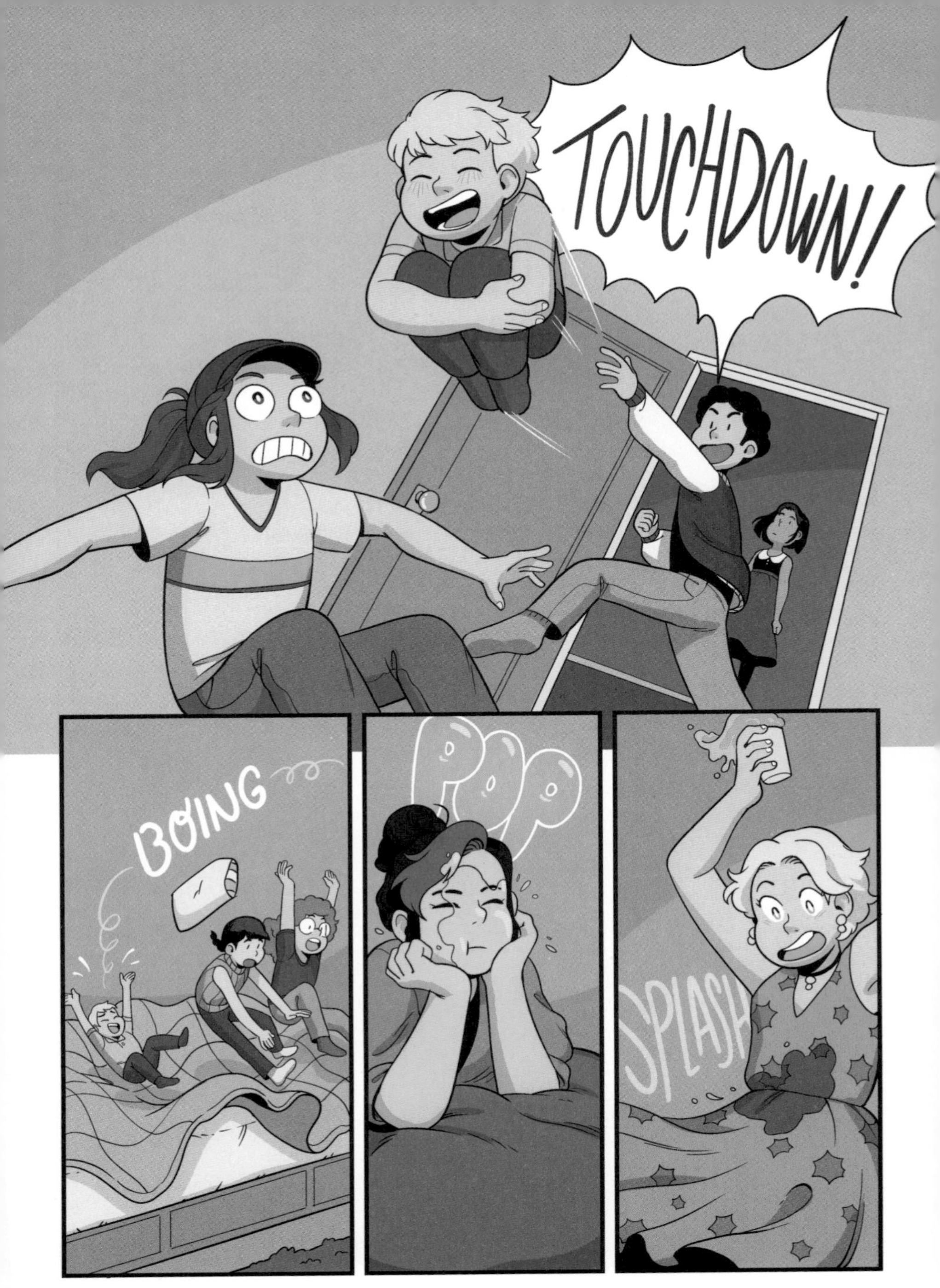
TOUCHDOWN!
BOING
POP
SPLASH